On the Wheel by Ellen Mae Cherche

© 2014 by Aramis Press. All rights reserved.

No part of this book may be reproduced in any written, electronic, recording, or photocopying without written permission by the publisher or author. The exception would be in the case of brief quotations embodied in the critical articles or reviews and pages where permission is specifically granted by the publisher or author.

Physical copies of this novel may be purchased by contacting the publisher at: Aramis Press, aramispress@gmail.com.

ISBN 978-0-578-13549-6

1. Fiction 2. Thriller 3. Romance

First Edition

The history of human culture can be viewed as the progressive development of new energy sources and their associated conversion technologies. These developments have increased the comfort, longevity and affluence of humans, as well as their numbers.

Charles Hall, *et al.*, *Hydrocarbons and the evolution of human culture*

When you are in love with someone, you do indeed see them as a divine being. Now, suppose that is what they truly are and that your eyes have by your beloved been opened. Through a tremendous outpouring of psychic energy in total devotion and worship for this other person, who is respectively god or goddess, you realize, by total fusion and contact, the divine center in them. At once it bounces back to you and you discover your own.

Alan Watts, *Play to Live*

Prologue

Dargan's blood was everywhere. Jill kneeled beside him as he lay on his back in the sand in the dim, mottled light. "Oh my god, oh my god! Dargan, you're going to be all right!" *This couldn't be happening!* She didn't know where to begin, blood seemed to be oozing from his nose, his mouth, his eyes, his chest, dripping down his shirt and congealing in the cold sand.

She needed to get a hold of herself. She was a take-charge kind of person! But that part of her seemed to have oozed away with Dargan's blood.

"Jill. Listen to me. Listen." Jill, with great difficulty, focused her attention on his words. Her hands had been patting and probing his torso, his face, but stopped their frantic motion as she strained to listen to his halting speech.

"What is it, Dargan? I'm listening." She could barely see his face in the dim light.

"Jill, you know what you need to know. Just remember what we talked about. Prometheus' gift, my gift… Remember how important it is. Remember what a revolution this could be… For everyone." Dargan stopped as he coughed blood and phlegm.

"That's not important right now! What's important is that we get you help."

"Jill, this is much more important than you or me. If… If, something happens to me, you must remember what we talked about."

"I will, Dargan, I swear. I will."

"Don't forget, Jill. Zippy. Zippy is my fire. Our fire. Humankind's fire…"

Jill saw a light a few hundred feet away and heard muffled voices. She didn't have much time. The IN men would be there any minute.

BOOK I: JILL IN L.A.

Oil is the world's biggest and most pervasive
business, the greatest of the great industries that
arose in the last decades of the nineteenth century.
Standard Oil, which thoroughly dominated the
American petroleum industry by the end of that
century, was among the world's very first and
largest multinational enterprises… Of the top
twenty companies in the Fortune 500, seven are oil
companies. Until some alternative source of energy
is found, oil will still have far-reaching effects on
the global economy.

Daniel Yergin, *The Prize: The Epic Quest for Oil,
Money & Power*

<u>Chapter 1</u>

Jill needed a donut. Badly. The Krispy Kreme guys were shrewd, wafting donut odor or possibly some canned substitute that smelled better than the real thing into the street. It smelled like a cross between Play-Doh and Lucky Charms cereal. Whatever they used, it was effective.

Jill had stopped in Oxnard on her way to Santa Barbara to get gas. She and a friend had decided to take a day trip north from the less than pristine Los Angeles to remind themselves of what clean air smelled like. Los Angeles, for all its pregnant possibilities, could be a soul-sucking place for those who truly enjoyed natural beauty. Consequently, Jill found her urge to leave L.A. crept up on her slowly until, eventually, her need for a nature fix became all-consuming.

For now, however, a donut fix seemed more important – after Jill had spotted the donut shop from the gas station. Jill angled toward the door of the Rose Avenue Krispy Kreme, anticipating the first bite of a lemon kreme donut. She entered the store, immediately spotting her uncle, Jonas, sitting in a booth. He was facing away from her, but his position revealed enough of his face so that she recognized him before he saw her. Jill sucked in a deep breath and turned on a dime. Holding her breath, she headed back toward the door, hoping to escape undetected. No luck: "Jill! Hey, Jill!"

Turning again, she put on her best smile and said: "Oh - hi, Jonas, what's up?"

"Not much, drinking coffee, reading the paper, getting edjamacated. What are you doing here?" Jonas' mustache bobbed as he talked. It was stained yellowish-brown at the ends, either from drinking too much coffee or smoking too many cigarettes – or both, judging by his breath. He talked with a slight drawl, which was strange considering he was born and raised in Southern California. His hair was lank and greasy, but parted neatly to one side. He wore a navy blue button-down shirt tucked into his slacks. Jill could see donut crumbs on his thumb and fingers. He looked like a cop from hell.

"Just going to Santa Barbara for the day with a friend. Going to check out the Mission. Maybe go for a hike."

"Why don't you join me for a minute? It's been a while since we've caught up."

"Actually, my friend is waiting for me," she gestured toward her car, where her buddy Rahul was waiting at the gas station a hundred feet away.

"C'mon, I haven't seen you in ages. Just a minute?" Jonas had always made her uncomfortable; but particularly since she became an attractive woman a decade earlier. About the same time she had noticed the opposite sex noticing her, she became aware of Jonas paying more attention to her. His actions had never been overtly inappropriate, but his inappropriate attention always made their interactions awkward. She had generally tried to avoid him since her early teens.

Even so, she hesitantly slipped into his booth. "So you're not in the habit of calling family when you're in town anymore, huh?," he said with a slight smile, as if to apologize for his lack of subtlety. When she didn't immediately say anything, he moved his head forward and renewed the query with a rise in his eyebrows.

"I'm kind of on a tight schedule, you know. Sorry. If it makes you feel better, I didn't call Mom either. And didn't we see each other, what was it, a month ago?"

"It *was* about a month ago." They had both attended Jill's aunt's funeral. Jill's aunt was Jonas' sister. It was the first time Jill had seen Jonas in more than two years. Even so, she had talked with him for no more than a minute or two at the funeral. Jill hadn't been terribly close to her aunt, but close enough that she was genuinely upset about her untimely death from breast cancer. Jonas wasn't particularly close to her either, apparently, and Jill really couldn't tell at the funeral whether he had felt much bereaved. It was hard to get any sense of the generally recognized human emotions running their course through Jonas. He was a bit *off*, is how she had always thought of him.

He was also a felon, having recently completed two years in jail for breaking and entering during his apparently overzealous efforts to succeed as a private investigator. Or maybe he just wasn't bright enough to not get caught.

"Your aunt was too young to die, that's for sure," Jonas trailed off.

"She sure was."

After another pause, Jonas said: "How old are you now? Twenty-seven?"

"Twenty-six actually. Don't you know you're always supposed to underestimate a woman's age?" A little attempt at humor by Jill, which she kicked herself for mentally a moment later.

"Yeah, right. I was always bad about that kind of thing." *Could be why you're still single*, Jill thought to herself. "You've done so well, though, Jill, I hope you know that."

"Thanks, I guess." Jill assumed he was talking about her career, but didn't care to seek clarification.

"I like the way you're doing your hair nowadays."

This is not a good conversational direction. "I guess." Jill was proud of her thick, dark hair, but didn't want to encourage Jonas. His comment was even stranger considering she was wearing it in a ponytail, as she usually did.

"You always had great hair." She didn't respond as she pondered how to end the conversation gracefully. "You know, I really didn't get a chance to talk to you much at the funeral," Jonas continued.

"Oh?"

"I was pretty upset – still am in fact – that you wouldn't sit as an alibi for me."

Jill paused. As she feared, he had brought up the unfortunate events that led to Jonas' stay in jail. "Do we really have to talk about this? We've been through this."

Jonas replied: "I'm kind of still bitter about that whole thing."

Jill cut him off: "I'm sorry I wouldn't lie for you. I just couldn't do it. You know I would have made a horrible witness. The jury would have seen right through me."

Also as feared, Jonas became agitated at Jill's words: "We're family Jill, you should have tried! Blood is thicker than water!"

"Look, I really don't want to go through this again. We spent hours arguing about this two years ago. I am sorry. And I'm sorry you had to spend two years in jail. But you know…."

"What?"

"You know… If you did it …" She trailed off.

"Whatever! People do shit all the time and don't do time for it. Blood is thicker than water! Maybe your Chink side diluted your blood a bit too much!" He hit the table with his fist, making his coffee-encrusted cup move slightly, spilling a few drops of black coffee, and glared at her.

"What the…? Are you kidding me? This conversation is over." She stood, shaking her head, and pulled the door to her violently. But the door hit the door frame because it only opened outwards. She pushed the door violently and walked outside, fighting back tears. She half expected to hear Jonas come after her, but he didn't.

Fuck him! How dare Jonas hold her Chinese heritage against her by suggesting that somehow it made her less loyal! Apparently Jonas really was the ass she had always suspected him of being.

Jill quickly covered the hundred or so feet to her aging, but reliable, Corolla where her friend, Rahul, was waiting for her. She sat in the driver's seat as the tears started to come down in full force. Rahul asked: "What happened? What's wrong?"

"I'll tell you in a minute, I just want to get out of here." She pulled out of the gas station and heard a sharp popping noise. Fearing the worst, Jill stopped the car on the side of the road next to the gas station. Exiting the car, Jill's suspicion came true as she watched her front left tire sag and heard a hissing noise. "Shit! This is just not my day!"

"What happened?," Rahul asked again as he exited the car.

"Flat tire. This really sucks. Luckily I've got a jack and a donut in my trunk."

"Donut? I didn't see any donuts when you came back."

"Donut tire! That's what they call the little bitty spare tire you use until you can get your regular tire fixed."

"Oh." Rahul replied.

"It's okay, I don't expect a lawyer to know such arcane information," Jill tried to laugh, despite the situation.

"That's right, baby! I don't do tires." Rahul was apparently serious about this comment, as he watched Jill replace the flat tire, deigning to help only to lift the flat tire into Jill's trunk.

As she finished replacing the tire, Jill said: "I'm sorry Rahul, I'm soooo not up for going to Santa Barbara now. Would you hate me if we just went home?" Promising he would never hate her, Rahul offered to drive back home. Jill gladly accepted and lay back in the passenger seat and closed her eyes.

* * *

As they left the gas station, another car, containing two men, pulled out of the rear parking area of the gas station across the street from where Jill had been. They had been there since shortly after Jill had first pulled into the gas station an hour before.

Chapter 2

Jill awoke, as was her habit, to National Public Radio on her alarm clock. She found NPR strangely effective at luring her out of deep sleep with its interesting programs. The NPR "alarm clock" was far more effective than the overtly obnoxious brawww brawww of the traditional alarm clock radio that inspired nothing in Jill but repeated groggy slaps in the general direction of the snooze button.

When the nasally voice of the NPR contributor announcer came over the radio, Jill finally killed it, dragged herself out of bed, and stumbled to the bathroom. The Saturday incident with Jonas came back to her as she gazed at her own image in the mirror. Jill had suffered much when she was younger because of her Chinese genes. The frustrating aspect of the teasing was that much of it was directed at her alleged Asian features. The truth, she confirmed later in life, was that she really didn't have any obviously Asian features.

She had epicanthic folds. That was the key feature that Chinese people lacked – when compared to Caucasians. And, as with many Caucasian/Asian mongrels like herself, the epicanthic fold reappeared. Most people were surprised when they learned that she was half Chinese.

Jill's mother was first generation Chinese and had given Jill much of her outlook on life despite Jill's less than wholehearted embrace of her heritage, particularly in her early years. Her mother had also given Jill, when combined with her Caucasian father's not-insignificant genetic contribution, a feeling of never quite fitting in with whatever social group she found herself in. Growing up, she had learned that this was a common feeling among biracial people. But knowing this didn't exactly cure the malady of alienation. Despite Jill's full social life and success in her career, there stubbornly persisted a sense that she never quite clicked with people. The easy explanation – but probably wrong, she acknowledged when she was being completely honest with herself – was to blame this feeling on her confused heritage and upbringing.

Jill lived alone in a one-bedroom apartment between the Third Street Promenade in Santa Monica and the more upscale Montana neighborhood. Her apartment was nothing fancy, but was relatively close to the beach and was even closer to her work, allowing her to "commute" via her feet alone. Her ten minute walk took her to the headquarters of Global Green USA, the US affiliate of Green Cross, an international environmental group, started by Mikhail Gorbachev, that focused on various environmental and nuclear weapons issues.

Jill began working at Global Green about a year earlier, as their Energy and Climate Change Program Director. She had felt so adult with a title like that. She enjoyed her work a great deal, feeling satisfied that she was part of the solution and not part of the problem. What she lacked in salary, she made up for in quality of life and genuine job satisfaction.

It was a Monday. She arrived at work at 8:30. She chatted for a few minutes with her neighbors before retiring to her office with the excuse that she had a lot to get done that morning. Jill didn't do mornings very well. Could if she had to. Preferred not to. She generally made an effort at work to be friendly and make sure no one felt neglected. She knew how important good office relations were at every level. But without caffeine, mornings were simply something she preferred not to do in any full-fledged fashion. She sometimes contemplated getting back on the coffee roller coaster. But after having put the kibosh on caffeinated coffee a few years ago, she was wary of giving in to the need for a boost when energy was low. She preferred her constancy at this stage in her life.

Jill's office was relatively magnificent for a young environmental non-profit professional. Being in Santa Monica was wonderful in itself (despite being surrounded by the behemoth Los Angeles). She opened her windows to let in the pristine – it's all relative! – salt-laden air, as she normally did when temperatures permitted, which was most of the time. She took a moment to appreciate the small ocean views as she did so. It was very important, she frequently reminded herself, to enjoy the small things on a regular basis.

As Jill prepared to sit, she noticed an article on the seat of her chair. She picked it up and scanned the title: MAXXON, WORLD'S LARGEST PRIVATELY OWNED OIL COMPANY, NOW THE ONLY GIANT OIL CO. FAILING TO ACT ON GLOBAL WARMING RISKS. She scanned the first paragraph, describing how shareholders had overwhelmingly rejected environmental resolutions supporting reporting of greenhouse gas emissions and urging that Maxxon more actively develop renewable energy technologies. Senator Mary Raley Huberson, a Republican from Texas and a reliable friend of the oil industry, was quoted as saying: "Maxxon is a business. And like any business, it exists to generate profits for shareholders and to create jobs. These decisions are perfectly in line with these goals. The shareholders have spoken and I respect their views."

Depressing, but par for the course, Jill thought to herself. Maxxon was consistently behind the curve on just about every environmental issue implicated in their business. She placed the news release in a stack of similar documents and added a post-it note directing her future self to place the document in her Maxxon file, one of many files she was working on as part of her energy policy work.

After browsing her daily horoscope online and checking her email, Jill got to work. She was in the process of writing a report on White House renewable energy policy, hoping to analyze in considerable detail the main forces driving renewable energy policy and legislation coming from President Colt's White House.

She'd obtained a master's degree in public policy from UC Berkeley and had put her knowledge to good use thus far at Global Green. She was expected to be a policy wonk – writing research papers and critiquing other parties' reports and statements on various energy and climate change issues. But she was also expected to be a public face for the organization on the issues she was tasked with following. This meant that she frequently went to fund-raisers, awards ceremonies and other events. Jill also was expected to make presentations and speeches, at times. She enjoyed all aspects of her job but, like almost everyone, was practically terrified of public speaking. Somehow, she hadn't embarrassed herself or her organization in a significant way – yet.

This morning, Jill had to review a number of documents, both paper and electronic, she'd received from the Department of Energy in response to a Freedom of Information Act request she'd submitted a few months ago. She'd requested documents relating to discussions held by Vice President Twainey's Energy Task Force, concerning support for wind, solar, and other renewable energy technologies. Her goal was to piece together what information and input was used in drafting the White House energy policy with respect to renewable energy. This information would allow Global Green, and other groups like it, to more effectively influence the policymaking process in the future.

Jill began flipping through the numerous documents she'd received when her cell phone began ringing. Her door opened as she went to answer the call. Her boss, Jerry, poked his head in and greeted her with a question: "Jill, can we talk about that white paper real quick?"

"Uh sure," she replied as her cell phone continued ringing.

"Great, can you meet me in my office in five? Oh, also, did you see that news release on your chair?" Jill nodded as her boss continued: "I'm thinking of beginning a campaign against Maxxon." Jerry, a kindly but socially oblivious man of sixty, closed the door behind him with a clunk that flirted with being a slam.

By the time Jill dug her phone out of her purse, it was beeping at her, indicating that she had a voicemail. Calling her voicemail, she was greeted with the soul-less female robot voice: "You have one message marked for deletion. You have one new message and four saved messages." A message was automatically marked for deletion when it had been saved for more than 21 days. The message marked for deletion played first and was, as she already knew, a message she had saved from her ex-boyfriend Dargan: "Hey sweetness, just calling to say hi. I know it's been a while since we talked, but, you know, I kind of miss your voice. Call me when you get a chance." Listening to the message brought back bittersweet memories, as it always did. She had saved the message for almost a year now, renewing the save every 21 days as it expired. But she was letting go gradually. She'd had a number of other messages from Dargan that she had saved since they went their separate ways. One by one, she'd let the messages go as the poignancy of his voice and his mood wore off. She was *almost* over him – a year after the fact.

* * *

Jill met Dargan while she was a fellow at the Natural Resources Defense Council in Washington, D.C. While she was finishing her degree program at Berkeley, she had been pleasantly surprised to win the one-year fellowship at the prestigious non-profit environmental law firm. She wasn't a lawyer, of course, but NRDC tried to influence events in some fairly technical areas of environmental policy and, for this purpose, retained a number of non-lawyers on its staff.

Jill arrived in D.C. early in the summer and had immediately dived into the exciting world of policy and politics as it is practiced only in D.C. But she also made an attempt, as she always did, to get plugged in socially early on. A couple of weeks after moving to D.C., she was invited on a rock climbing trip with some friends of hers, who she had met during her years at UC Berkeley. These friends had conveniently moved to D.C. a year before she moved there. Her friends, John and Autumn, had arranged the climbing trip. And it just so happened that, included in the rock climbing adventure, there had been an exciting prize in the form of a man named Dargan.

The meeting was still fresh in Jill's mind. She had been hanging out with John and Autumn at their new home in D.C., waiting for their fourth member to arrive. John and Autumn were wonderful to be around and she wished they had more time for her, since she was new in town. As the three of them chatted and finished last minute preparations for their climbing trip, a knock had come at the door and in walked a wiry, slightly gangly, man a couple inches over six feet tall. He had a big, somewhat goofy, grin as he said hello to John and Autumn and introduced himself to Jill.

Saying "nice to meet you, Jill" after Jill told him her name, he shook her hand vigorously. His hand was far more callused than she would have expected for a D.C. non-profit type. He looked away quickly after shaking her hand, but looked back and gave her another quick crooked smile. She liked his very dark shock of hair and bright green eyes and found him pleasant to look at, even though he was by no means a conventionally attractive man: features a bit too asymmetrical; ears a bit too far from his head; nose a bit too big; a certain awkwardness about him.

But she also suspected almost immediately that she was going to fall for him very hard, based on what she already knew about him from talking with John and Autumn, as well as the intangibles that had quickly been communicated through a few seconds of contact.

Jill and Dargan didn't have much time to chat as Autumn quickly rounded them up, along with their copious amounts of equipment, out the door to the car. Dargan and Jill shared the back seat of John's SUV.

"So Autumn tells me you're new to D.C?" Dargan said as they drove.

"Yep, just got here a couple of weeks ago actually. Lovin' it so far, despite the heat shock I experience every time I step out of the AC."

"You'll get used to it. D.C. summers are definitely an acquired taste. Hate to tell you, but it's been relatively cool so far this summer."

"Yikes. I'm going to have buy one of those hats that come with the built in beer cans or something." She laughed and he obligingly followed suit, seeming to be genuinely amused by her little joke. He had a great laugh, she caught herself thinking, as she internally tallied all his positive and negative qualities thus far.

They arrived at Great Falls Park after a half hour's drive, thankfully before the rush, and made their way to a climbing face a scant few feet from the Potomac River. It was a beautiful day. John and Autumn had agreed this would be the best place for the experienced climbers (John and Dargan) to get some good routes in while allowing the relative rookies (Jill and Autumn) the chance to gain confidence on easier routes. They picked a face on the Virginia side of the river, which meant they would stay cooler longer. John and Dargan set up the anchor at the top of the face.

Autumn asked Jill, with a pixie smile, once they were out of earshot at the bottom of the face: "Isn't he adorable?" Jill smiled back with what she thought was probably her own version of a goofy grin and said: "I'll get back to you on that one." She didn't want to jinx anything before it had a chance. "You're no fun," was Autumn's grinned reply.

It wasn't Jill's first time rock climbing, so she had a basic familiarity with the notion of climbing high on a sheer rock face with nothing but a skinny rope and the diligence of a friend to keep death away. The guys had been gentlemen and had let Autumn have the first attempt at scaling what seemed, from below and looking up, to be a quite daunting slab of granite. Autumn did very well and talked trash with her boyfriend and Dargan as she made her way quickly up the 5.8 rated face.

Once Autumn arrived at the top, she let out a yell and sat back in the classic "L" rappelling position and walked gently down the face as her belayer, John, slowly let the rope out. At the bottom, Jill hugged her and gave her high fives and low fives and behind the back fives, congratulating Autumn on her great climb and descent.

John tied himself into the rope next and quickly and very competently scaled a 5.11 route next to the route Autumn had climbed. He talked less trash than Autumn. He was typically the more subdued half of their very effective partnership.

Then it was Jill's turn and she surprised herself at getting the tie-in knot correct on the first try. Autumn had volunteered to belay Jill and, once Autumn was hooked in on her end, Jill yelled out the traditional belay commands before beginning her climb. "On belay?" "Belay on!" "Climbing." "Climb on!" Cheesy, but effective.

Jill struggled a little as she attempted to follow Autumn's route up the 5.8 face. Dargan offered, once Jill hesitated shortly after beginning: "Try the foothold about a foot above your left foot and to the left a bit." She appreciated Dargan's quick recognition that she was fairly new to climbing and that she didn't mind some coaching at times. Just not too much!

Without any falls, Jill made it to the top well after the sweat had begun to flow liberally. She regretted now wearing the spandex pants she had chosen, even if they did show off her curves! Shorts would have made her sweat less. *But whatever*, she thought to herself. She wasn't exactly a girly girl anyway.

She yelled to Autumn: "Ok, I'm coming down." She started shuffling her feet down the rock as she felt Autumn steadily give her slack. Jill was about halfway down and feeling a little more comfortable when she felt the slack stop coming for about a half second. As she turned her head around to look down and ask what was going on, she dropped precipitously. *Oh shit!* was the only thought that had time to form fully as she tried at first to keep up with her fall by quickly moving her feet down the face. As her body began to become more vertical and lose its "L" shape, she felt the rope snap tight again – at the same time as she felt arms around her lower back and thighs.

"Oh my God, what the hell happened?" Jill asked as Autumn, Dargan and John asked in unison: "Are you all right?" She found herself back at ground level a half second after she had been at the top of the face.

"I'm fine," she replied, realizing she was unscathed. "What the hell happened?"

"I'm so sorry, Jill. I got distracted and lost my grip on the rope for a second. Then it took me a second to catch it again. Are you okay?" Autumn was crying in shock or relief or both.

Jill realized that Dargan had caught her at the same instant that Autumn had regained control of the belay, which caused Jill to bounce back to a relaxed "L" position as Dargan had attempted to literally catch her! Then she realized that he was still supporting her even though her feet were now on the ground. She couldn't help notice his smell, an indescribable mélange of pleasant odors, reminiscent of candy and fresh sweat.

"You want a hand unhooking, Jill?" Dargan asked. "Sure," she was still dazed from what she felt at that moment had been a narrow escape from death's clammy grip. Dargan untied her rope and took off her helmet in an assured but gentle manner. Jill sat down and contemplated whether rock climbing was really a sport she wanted to focus on.

Later that morning, Jill understood why Dargan's hands were so callused as he demonstrated that he was an expert climber, with a natural grace on the rock face that he didn't always demonstrate on the ground. His forearms looked like they were built literally of intertwined ropes as he ascended steadily up a number of difficult routes. His calves were equally gnarled and she was surprised to see that his body made perfect sense on the side of a rock face, if not on the relatively passé flat earth most normal people inhabited.

After the shock of the fall wore off, the shock of meeting Dargan came over her. It was definitely on.

Chapter 3

The year she spent in D.C. was one of Jill's best. She found her fellowship tremendously rewarding in terms of hands-on experience with Washington politics and policy. And she also enjoyed the company of her fellow fellows at NRDC, and other D.C. non-profit types.

But what really made her year satisfying was the time she spent with Dargan. Though their relationship had its ups and downs – no surprise there – it was easily the most rewarding relationship she had been in. Dargan's personality was a rare combination of passion, knowledge, confidence and gentle humor. Somehow, she didn't feel totally swallowed up by him, largely because she was the type of person who always relished a challenge to her limitations, seeking to grow through contact with others who obviously had a lot to offer.

Dargan worked at another D.C. non-profit, the Energy Coalition, which focused exclusively on energy and climate change policy. He was a few years older than her, in his mid-thirties, when she met him. Dargan had worked in D.C. for a number of years after earning his doctorate in energy and natural resources policy from Harvard.

Their year together was punctuated by a cross-country trip at the end of Jill's fellowship.

Dargan had suggested they take his car and drive back to Santa Monica, where Jill was set to begin her job at Global Green. Driving would save her money and would allow them to have some quality time together. It would be a test run to see if they could make their relationship work beyond the fantasy year in D.C. Dargan had agreed to spend some time in Los Angeles to see if it was a place he could consider making home.

Toward the end of their cross-country romp, Dargan suggested they stop by one of the many wind farms in southern California; he was the energy policy guru after all. Jill agreed and they took a southern detour along the I-10 to San Gorgonio, one of the three major wind farm sites in California. As they drove through the desert heat toward San Gorgonio, they watched as the wind machines grew large. Some were spinning, some not. Some were a respectable size, others monstrous, with blade diameters of almost three hundred feet. The behemoths spun slowly in the warm air like latter day megaliths. Some complained about the "blight" they caused on the landscape. But to Jill they were beautiful because they were clean and elegant. Their stately rotations provided relatively cheap, practically pollution-free, power to millions of Californians.

Apparently, Dargan had done a little research before leaving D.C., or perhaps at one of the many Internet cafes they had stopped at during the drive, as he seemed to know exactly where to go. "I think this is it," he muttered as they pulled off a secondary road onto a dirt road marked "No Trespassing."

"Uh, don't you reada de English very a-well? Typically, that means we shouldn't enter," Jill asked.

"Come on, be a little adventurous," he smiled at her. The sun was about to set and the ambient light glowed with an orange hue that felt more like a movie than reality. "Did you know Terrence Malick created a whole movie, *Days of Heaven*, back in the Seventies using only this kind of lighting, golden hour? He could film only about fifteen minutes each day, but he felt it was worth it because of the cinematic qualities this kind of light gave his movie."

"Good to know," Jill muttered as she appreciated the surroundings.

Dargan pulled the car up to the fence on the right side of the road. Jill asked "how about that one?" She pointed to a graceful giant on top of an otherwise barren hill about half a mile away.

"Sounds great."

"All right, beat ya," she yelled as she jumped the fence and began racing up the hill to the windmill.

Dargan quickly caught up to her. He had the legs. They ran side by side the rest of the way to the base of the tower, breathing heavily as the sweat started flowing. "You sandbagged," she said. He just grinned at her as he assessed how best to get up the tower.

There were no ladder rungs for the first ten feet, requiring that those seeking to ascend the tower bring their own ladder – or be resourceful in finding other ways of scaling the first ten feet. The tower was approximately twelve feet wide at its base and, unfortunately, was silky smooth. There was, however, a seam about six feet off the ground. "I bet we can jam something into this to get up to the first rung," he said.

"Hey Jill dear, you wanna run back to the car and get my knife?" As she spluttered: "I ain't your servant, homeboy" he said: "I'm just kidding. I'll be right back." Dargan loped back to the car, retrieved the knife and was back at the base of the tower in about five minutes.

The knife was a high-end skinning blade of one-quarter inch carbon steel. Plenty strong to hold a person's weight. Dargan jabbed it into the seam, opening it up enough to fit the whole blade. He tested his weight on the handle and it seemed fine. Jill was yet again surprised at his strength and dexterity as he raised himself up so that his waist was at knife's height. Then he pushed off abruptly, replacing his hands on the handle with his left foot and angling his body into the tower. Dargan's hands could easily reach the first rung from this vantage point and he swung up onto it. "All right, your turn."

"You're such a show off. There's no way I can do that and you know it."

"I *don't* know that. Why don't you give it a shot at least."

"I've got a better idea. Why don't you hang off the rung by your legs and reach down to pull me up." She was half joking, but it seemed somewhat plausible.

"The trapeze was never my strong suit, but what the hell." He fumbled around for a minute and then secured his legs through the first rung, let loose a whoop and lowered himself backwards so that his hands dangled down past the knife. Now she had two handholds – his hands and the knife handle. She was able to scramble past the knife handle and place a foot on it. From that point, once Dargan had moved out of the way, she easily moved up to the rungs. They climbed the rest of the way as the sun was setting, Dargan in the lead. "Your ass looks nice from this angle," she said teasingly. "Quit looking at my ass!," he said in mock exasperation.

The climb took about two minutes and Jill was pleased to find that their rate of ascent apparently matched the rate of the sun's descent: the sun's position remained constant on the horizon as they climbed. "This is the nacelle," Dargan said as they reached the top of the ladder. "The nacelle is where the turbine and all the guts are." There was a small platform attached to the nacelle, allowing them to look due west at the setting sun.

"This is unbelievable," Jill said as they stared through squinting eyes at the setting sun, windmill blades majestically slicing the air in front of them and a gentle hum as the turbines generated electricity. "Oh my god, yes," Dargan agreed. He looked at her with ineffable affection and they shared a long kiss as they held each other. "You know what I feel when I look at you?," Dargan asked.

"All gooey inside?"

"Hah! That too. But the strongest emotion I feel is *relief.* I can't tell you how relieved I am to have found you. I can stop looking. When I walk into a party or a bar or a meeting, or wherever, I don't have to immediately look around for my soulmate, or whatever you want to call it. I've found her. And she's standing in front of me."

"Dargan, you can't know how good it feels to hear you say that because it's exactly how I feel. I'm so tired of looking!" Tears. They held each other as the sun's last rays lit up the clouds high above them. "The one nice thing about southern California," Jill said, "is that all the air pollution makes for killer sunsets."

***

That was the sweet of their relationship. The bitter was when Dargan decided he couldn't tolerate southern California and returned to D.C. after only a few weeks in L.A. They had talked for a while after he left, but their conversations had petered off gradually. The last she heard of him, he had taken a job at the Department of Energy, which surprised her somewhat because it seemed like Dargan would normally consider such a move selling out. So much for "soulmates."

Chapter 4

On Tuesday of the week following Jill's ill-fated trip to Oxnard, she received a call from Rahul, her companion on that trip and one of her better friends. "Jill-dawg, let's go for a hike tonight, eh? It's staying light real late these days and I figured it would be nice to make up for our lost nature fix on Saturday."

"All right," Jill replied. They arranged to meet for a hike after work, with their frequent third partner in crime Joe. It was June and it was a much-appreciated luxury, beginning at that time of year, to be able to enjoy the outdoors late into the evening.

Jill picked up Rahul at his home in the Montana neighborhood, the ritzy part of Santa Monica. "How's the lawyer life?" Jill asked as he got into her car.

"You know, the partners are still cracking the whip on the slaves they like to refer to as 'associates' and the bloodthirsty corporations are still despoiling the world, with our help of course."

"You're really too nice to be a corporate lawyer," Jill replied. It was not the first time she had told him this.

Rahul laughed and said: "Are you trying to get me in bed? You know flattery will get you everywhere."

"Yeah right. You're on to me."

Rahul worked in natural resources law – for the corporate side generally. Jill prided herself on the fact that she was friends with someone on the "dark side," knowing full well from her discussions with Rahul and others that most resource environmental issues were not black and white. As Rahul liked to say – generally accompanied by a wince from Jill if she was within earshot – "even polluters deserve their day in court." Jill, if in a puckish mood, would reply: "Yeah, well so did Jeffrey Dahmer." Rahul would just laugh.

If confronted, however, Jill readily admitted she had benefited greatly from the perspective Rahul provided regarding environmental issues. She hoped to be more than a mere gadfly to corporate America and she had actually learned a lot from Rahul and other corporate types in terms of presenting arguments and proposals to corporations or law firms when she hoped to influence outcomes without litigation.

But she and Rahul didn't often discuss environmental issues, preferring to avoid this generally contentious difference in their lives. The bottomline with Rahul, Jill had learned after knowing him for more than a year now, was that he had a superlative personal ethic but didn't care to extend his personal ethic to the realm of environmental issues, politics or policy. He was that rare breed who was very intelligent but not particularly interested in devoting more time than he already spent at work on thinking about complex issues. Jill often wondered why Rahul hung out with her because they didn't have much in common.

"Are we picking up Joe too?" Rahul asked Jill.

"No, he's meeting us. Normally I would, but because we're kind of tight on time, he agreed to just meet us there."

"What's up with you and Joe anyway? I can't figure you guys out."

"There's nothing 'up' with us. We're just friends."

"Does he know that?"

"What? You think he wants ... more than friendship?"

"Uh, yeah. It seems pretty obvious to me. And didn't he tell you that one time?"

Jill realized he was right. Joe had told her quite clearly on one occasion that he was interested in "getting to know her better." "He did actually. Good memory Rahul. I'd kind of forgotten about that."

"Funny how women have such selective memories."

"Hey! It was kind of a drunken night, you know that. And he hasn't mentioned it again since that time. And I really don't think of him that way anyway."

"Did you tell him that?"

"Well, not explicitly. I figured he would get the message if I didn't do anything to follow up."

"Kind of through the ether? Like telepathy or something?"

Jill cast her best withering glance at Rahul and said: "All right, I get your point. If it comes up again, I'll tell him directly. But I just really like hanging out with him and don't want to hurt his feelings, you know?"

"Why aren't you attracted to him?"

"Well, doctor... I'm not sure really. I mean, there are a lot of things I could point to that are small hurdles. He's just not my type really."

"What are the 'small hurdles?'"

Jill paused for a second. "First, you can't tell him any of this, all right?"

"Of course!"

"Well, I like hanging out with him and I think he's got a great sense of humor. But he has such a hard edge sometimes. Real cynical. And on the physical side, you're going to think I'm really superficial, but he's just not in very good shape. You know me – I'm not all about looks by any means, but I do like a guy to take care of himself."

"Actually, I don't know your type at all because you haven't dated anyone since I've known you."

"Touché. Well, put it this way, I've dated some guys who weren't exactly Ken doll types. Anyway, enough about me. What about you? Any hot girls in your life?"

Rahul didn't have time to answer as Jill pulled into the parking lot in the upper Pacific Palisades at one of the many entry points to the Santa Monica Mountains. Jill hadn't seen either Rahul or Joe since the ill-fated trip to Santa Barbara the previous Saturday, so it was nice to be reunited with her buddies, her "support group" as she thought of them.

They began walking through the small stream, the first dose of nature hikers receive on the Palisades Canyon Trail. She'd been on this hike many times before, but couldn't help remarking after noticing once more the concrete circular stepping stones through the channelized portion of the creek: "That's so LA – artificial stepping stones over an artificial channel. I wonder if the water is artificial?" Joe and Rahul responded with grunts only. They'd heard the same theme from Jill many times over. Jill certainly appreciated the fact that there was an abundance of trails through the Santa Monica Mountains and that the mountains were so close to Santa Monica and the Los Angeles region, but she was – admittedly – snooty in her nature appreciation. The bottom-line for Jill was simply that the Santa Monica Mountains, while better than nothing, were not exactly the height of Nature's glories.

Joe was a long-time friend of Jill's and they had a sibling-like relationship. At least that was how she viewed it. He apparently didn't see it the same way.

They quickly reached the top of the hike they'd agreed to previously – a brisk four-mile hike up and back. The trio sat on the already brown grass and silently appreciated the sunset that they'd been lucky enough to time precisely right.

Rahul spoke up: "So there's this guy. He runs into a friend of his one day at the mall. The friend tells him, 'Jim, you look terrible, anything wrong?'" Jill and Joe looked at Rahul with bemusement. Jill realized, after initial confusion, that Rahul was telling a joke. Or maybe a parable. Rahul continued: "So Jim told his friend 'that's funny, I feel great.' But his good friend told him again, 'I don't know Jim, you look really bad, you should go see a doctor.' Jim relents and goes to see his doctor. He tells the doctor 'Doc, I feel great, but my friends tell me I look terrible. What's wrong with me?' The doctor examines Jim briefly and says, 'I don't know, Jim, I can't find anything wrong with you. But you do look bad. Why don't you just sleep it off?' So Jim goes home, has a good night's sleep, and gets up again. He goes to work and the first person he sees asks him what's wrong? Jim says – again – nothing's wrong, he feels great."

Jill interjected: "This is a really long Joke, Rahul. Is there a punchline or what?"

"Hold your horses! I'm getting there. Jim's colleague convinces him he should go back to his doctor to find out what's wrong. So Jim goes back to his doctor. He says 'Doc, I'm back again. Same thing. I feel great, but people are telling me I look like hell. What's wrong with me?' The doctor examines Joe again, in more detail this time. He's initially stumped and tells Jim that he can't find anything wrong with him. Then he asks Jim to redefine the problem. Jim tells him, 'like I told you, Doc, I feel great, but everyone's telling me I look bad.' A light bulb flashes above the doctor's head and he tells Jim, 'I've got it. You're a vagina.' 'What?,' Jim asks. 'You're a vagina. Looks bad, feels great.'"

Jill cried out: "Oh, that's terrible. That's so bad!" Joe lay back in the grass and guffawed as Rahul watched with a smile. Jill laughed despite herself, despite her protest. After the laughter subsided, Joe brought up a favorite topic of his: "Speaking of vaginas, any new prospects, Jill?"

Is this all these guys want to talk about? "Hey! You guys are pushing it today! If you mean guys in my life, no, no one new."

"Ay yi yi, when are you going to stop moping girl? It's time to move on."

"Come on, I'm tired of talking about this. When I'm ready, I'm ready. And it's not like I've met anyone that I've been that excited about anyway." Joe was silent as he absorbed this comment. What Jill hadn't told Rahul was that Dargan still occupied Jill's thoughts and emotions much of the time. Jill would never tell anyone this, but she still imagined him lying next to her in her bed when she went to sleep. She would even face toward the empty place in her bed, rather than to the edge of the bed, in order to make her imagining more authentic. She knew it would seem pathetic to her friends, but she gained some comfort from her imaginary bedmate. And abstinence was the safest sex, after all.

After the sun had finished its slow wink below the horizon, they began the easy part of the hike back to the trailhead. A few minutes after they began the downward hike, Jill spotted two men coming up the trail in front of them. As the two men approached, they smiled and said hello. The man in front on the trail, wearing a tank top, long baggy shorts, backwards baseball hat and tennis shoes, asked Jill, who happened to be in front of her small hiking party: "So how much further to the top?"

"Not much longer at all, just a few minutes. You should be able to make it out before it's dark."

"Yeah, if we hurry. Too bad we missed the sunset from the top," he smiled, showing off a great set of teeth and highlighting his stubble-covered cheeks. He had a classically handsome face and, judging by his obvious confidence, seemed aware of his hunk status. He surprised Jill by saying: "What's your name? I'm Adrian" and held out his hand for her to shake.

"Nice to meet you, I'm Jill." Adrian's companion also thrust his hand forward, saying only: "Ben." To Adrian and Ben's credit, they also introduced themselves to Joe and Rahul. Jill wasn't too comfortable with the newcomers' friendliness – it seemed to her it could be based on one thing only – and she said that they had to get back to their cars quickly. Joe and Rahul, obliging as always, followed her. After moving out of earshot, Rahul said: "Someone's got the hots for Jill."

"Oh come on, they were just being friendly."

"Give me a break," Rahul shot back. "They wanted you. You know you're a hottie."

"Whatever. You guys, all you think about is sex. You think everything's about sex."

"Isn't it?" Rahul asked, apparently serious, though it was hard to tell with him sometimes because of his deadpan delivery.

"Well, no," Jill responded after a pause, while she contemplated answering the question or letting it stand as a rhetorical question, acting as its own response. "Under that logic, the only reason you guys hang out with me is because you want to have sex with me, and vice versa."

"If the shoe fits..." Joe responded playfully.

Rahul said: "Or maybe we hope to get sex through hanging out with you, but not necessarily from you. Your friends perhaps. Wait, you don't have any female friends."

"Hey!" Jill responded, even though she knew he was joking for the most part. But there was a kernel of truth to what he said. She didn't have many female friends. Jill felt more comfortable with guys. Male friendships involved a lot less drama typically and she was by no means a girl's girl.

Jill considered this a serious flaw in herself. Not that she wanted to be a girl's girl exactly; rather, she wanted to be the kind of girl who could attract and keep female friends more easily than she did. The underlying suspicion remained, when considering her many male friendships, that they were interested in her largely because of her looks, not because of who she really was as a person.

Joe chimed in during this moment of self-reflection: "Yeah, Jill, we could care less about your brain or your ideals or even the fact that you're pretty fun generally. We just like you because you're hot."

"Obviously I don't need any more friends when I have such good friends like you guys," Jill said with her best effort to sound icy.

They quickly reached the trailhead and their cars. As they said their goodbyes, Rahul said: "Hey, it's a Tuesday, why don't we head out on the town for a bit tonight? We could clearly all use a good time."

Joe and Jill agreed this was a good idea.

* * *

A few hours later, Jill found herself at a bar enjoying a pleasantly strong buzz. She felt a twinge of guilt – it was a "school night," after all. But she had the luxury to punish her body as she pleased, being an adult now… In the year since she moved to Santa Monica, she had, by necessity, perfected her own special hangover recovery recipe. It involved lots of water, painkillers, and a fair amount of practice drinking copious amounts on regular occasions. She was also blessed in not suffering from the "Asian glow" – a strong blush from only a couple drinks.

Jill and her group of friends had settled on the West Side for their evening of mild debauchery. Rene's Courtyard Café, a couple of blocks from the Third Street Promenade, was the current favorite among her little clique. The almost maze layout had a certain appeal, as did the Old Europe feel obviously intended by the owner.

Jill perched at the bar, waiting for a drink from the bartender. A drunk guy next to her offered her a shot. In her already boozy state she thought, *why not?*, and did a shot of Patron tequila with the guy.

"Jill! Where've you been?" Jill turned to see Rahul at her elbow. "I've been right here, genius," she said as she pushed his arm. "Where've *you* been?"

"I was hanging with the rest of the gang in the lounge area, waiting for you to get back with the drinks."

"Oh. I guess I got sidetracked." Jill was apparently a little more inebriated than she had thought. "Too many damn rooms in this place," she muttered to no one in particular. She felt her cell phone vibrating against her leg. She pulled it out of her cargo pocket and saw the 805 area code, recognizing her uncle's phone number. She pushed the button to turn the buzzing off. *Why the hell is he calling me late at night on a Tuesday?*

"Jill, we missed you so!" Joe yelled out as Jill and Rahul returned. They were joined that night by a few others from Jill's "posse." They could be a fun group at times, often with the help of liquor. One of Joe's favorite statements, repeated to the point of irritation to those around him: "Don't knock the lickah too much. No one would get laid without it."

As Joe loudly announced Jill's return to the group, he moved to the side of the bench that a number of their party was sharing, making room for Jill. Sitting down next to Joe, Jill appreciated the warmth of his body against hers and was happy to let him chatter on about nothing. The atmosphere was just right at that moment. Good music was playing, but not too loud. The soft lighting made everyone look their best. And she was very happy to be in the company of her pseudo-family in pleasant surroundings.

Joe's hand was gently caressing her thigh. He kept his hand on the top of her thigh, not too dangerous. She noticed it with a certain detachment, thinking how interesting it was that Joe's hand was where it was. She was vaguely aware of her friends glancing over at this new development and looking away, giggling to each other. His touch felt good, but she knew she should make him move it. But, in her buzz, she didn't.

Jill surprised herself when she noticed that the small glass of tequila was entirely gone. The man at the bar was so right about quality tequila. She was more surprised when she found Joe's lips on hers. For the briefest moment, she returned the soft pressure of his lips with her own. But then, even in her besotted state, she knew better and pushed Joe away – gently. "Joe, you know it's not like that between us."

She was aware that everyone knew exactly what had just happened, even though they were doing their best to pretend not to notice. Seeing Joe's hurt look, she tried to defuse the situation. "Did someone slip some ecstasy in your drink or something? I thought that stuff made you rub yourself, not other people." Joe smiled a little and said: "Just feeling good Jillypoo. I've got to go drain the main... you know." He got up to go the restroom to relieve himself and, in the process, relieved the tension so painfully apparent to everyone at the table.

Shortly after Joe came back from the restroom, they all said their goodbyes and departed for their respective homes. Luckily, Jill was close enough to walk home. Rahul volunteered to walk her home after Joe left fairly abruptly. On the walk home, Jill's cell phone vibrated gently against her leg as a reminder that she had a voice message. She remembered that Jonas had called and she retrieved his message: "Jill, it's your uncle. I just wanted to call and tell you that I'm really sorry for what I said the other day. You know I didn't mean it. Please don't take it personally. Call me sometime if you get the chance. We still haven't really had the chance to catch up since … well, since a long time." Jill appreciated the apology, but it didn't do much to change her opinion of her awful uncle. She also resented the syrupy sweet tone of the message, as if he thought that one phone call in his fake nice voice could actually make things right between them again. As if things had ever been right between them.

Chapter 5

"Now that is a very Buddha-esque Buddha, if I ever saw one," Jill said to the store clerk at Indochine, the southeast Asian knickknack store on the Third Street Promenade in Santa Monica. She was eyeing a large stone statute of the Buddha at his chubbiest.

"He is truly enlightened, no?" the clerk responded.

"Enlightened, maybe, but definitely not light. He must weigh a couple of hundred pounds." Jill had taken her lunch break that Friday to shop for a gift for her mother's upcoming birthday. Her mother would have been a hippy if she had been white, but was considered merely eccentric as a first generation Chinese woman in the United States. Jill would most definitely not tell her mother she had bought her birthday gift at a store named Indochine, if she did in fact buy a gift for her there. Jill didn't want to suffer through a lecture about the hypocrisy and indecency of naming a store of Buddhist and other religious statuary and paraphernalia after the French colonial name for southeast Asia. Jill agreed, in principle, of course, but was a bit more forgiving of other people's ignorance than was her mother. Jill suspected the store's owners merely thought the name had a nice sound to it and were perhaps unaware of the lengthy and quite harmful history of French, not to mention American, involvement in southeast Asia.

* * *

Jill's mother, Sue-Mei, was a nurse who had raised her daughter with some respect for her Chinese traditions. But she had never held Jill back from anything Jill had been interested in merely because it wasn't Chinese. In high school, Jill had been quite the all-American girl. She had played soccer and ran track all four years and had done well at these sports. She excelled in school, of course – her mother would never have let her play any sports if her grades had not been excellent. Jill was class president her senior year, but had never become homecoming queen, even though she had waged a half-hearted campaign to win this coveted honor. She had also been a cheerleader her sophomore year, as she would admit only in hushed tones when the topic arose in her adult life. She realized toward the end of her high school years that she had been trying very hard to fit in to widely held notions of what it meant to be successful and liked. It was her Chinese heritage that was responsible for much of the teasing she had to put up with as a young girl and, therefore, was also responsible for her efforts to "just be normal."

Luckily, as Jill grew and developed a stronger sense of self, less dependent on the opinions of her peers, she had become comfortable enough to re-embrace her Chinese heritage and to do things or express opinions that were not necessarily "normal." In other words, she had become an adult.

It was in her early college years at Berkeley that she began this trend – unsurprisingly, considering the steaming racial cauldron that is Berkeley – and made a genuine effort to reconnect with her Chinese heritage and with her mother.

Jill's mother was an interesting mix of fire and ice. Jill recalled a conversation she had had with her mother while Jill was home during winter vacation during her first year at college. "Mom" – as she called her mother despite her mother's dislike for this very American appellation – "why don't you date? You know, try and get yourself out there a little and meet someone."

"Don't be silly, you know I'm perfectly happy by myself."

"But are you? Don't you get lonely? I know I'd be lonely if I were you."

"Well, you are not me are you? I did not grow up in this culture, with its loose dating culture and the idea that you have to have a man in order to be fulfilled. Besides, I have a man: your father."

"But Mom, he's been dead for ten years! And I don't think you need a man to define you exactly. I just think you might have some fun or something. I mean, don't you get lonely?"

"I do not have time to be lonely. I work and I have to take care of you and I volunteer at the sangha, as you know." Sue-Mei's Buddhist faith was very important to her and it had rubbed off on Jill a little. But at eighteen, Jill was not that interested in defining herself by any faith, let alone a man.

"Newsflash, Mom: I've moved out. You don't have to take care of me anymore. Well, I do have some laundry for you to do if you want," Jill laughed, receiving in return a tight-lipped smile from her mother. "I just worry about you sometimes, you know?" Jill added.

"Jill, it is not your place to worry about me. It is my job to worry about you. I am very proud that you are at an excellent college – and hopefully doing well, of course – but you do not need to worry about me." This was the ice.

Despite Jill's feeling that she knew her mother inside and out, her mother would never share her innermost feelings with her daughter. And it was quite frustrating for Jill, who was essentially her mother's best friend – and vice versa for many years of Jill's life – that her mother would not reveal her true emotions or insights into her hopes and insecurities. As Jill grew, she realized that she was expecting her mother to be like a girlfriend to her, and she simply wasn't like her girlfriends in this regard.

The fire came out more often than the ice, as Sue-Mei frequently lectured and tutored her intelligent and curious daughter on topics from political philosophy to Chinese medicine, with a passion that at times seemed misplaced.

"What you do not understand," Sue-Mei had told Jill during another conversation early in Jill's college years, in which Jill had wanted to share some of her new understanding of American politics, "is that in America, selfishness is worshipped as a god. It doesn't have to be this way. In other nations, including our homeland, people actually care about others and are willing to make sacrifices for the greater good. In America, people sacrifice nothing if it is not for immediate personal gain." Jill let the "our homeland" reference slide. She didn't feel like China was her homeland in any way. She hadn't been there and, at this point in her life, she was only just beginning to do anything other than run from her "Chineseness."

"Are you kidding me, Mom? In China, people are killed just for expressing their disagreement with the leaders."

"This is not true! At least I never saw it. Yes, it is good to be able to express yourself and to express disagreement with leaders. But it is more important to have food in one's belly and to have a roof over one's head. In China, it would not be possible to maintain any type of society if people were granted the same freedoms people in America enjoy."

"But aren't you contradicting yourself? I mean, what about Tiananmen Square? You saw that on TV, right? And why can't Chinese enjoy freedom and economic opportunities?"

"Tiananmen Square was an exception, a regrettable exception. In general, people can express their concerns at the appropriate level, and if those concerns are valid, they will be addressed. Yes, Americans enjoy more freedoms, but this is a luxury that China cannot afford now. With China's population of 1.3 billion people, can you not see what would happen if suddenly everyone was allowed to be an individualist and criticize everyone else, drive their own cars, access whatever information they wanted? China would collapse immediately. No, the path China must walk is one of gradual change. And this is the path China's leaders are walking. Too much change will destroy China." Her mother delivered this monologue in a fast-paced, overly-enunciated harangue, as she always did when she was speaking on topics she was passionate about. This was the fire and it came out frequently. Too frequently for Jill's taste, who was not as interested in such heady topics as her mother was.

"I don't know, Mom. I just don't think it has to be that way." But Jill couldn't do much more than express her general unease concerning her mother's point of view on this topic. At eighteen, she wasn't exactly a political philosopher. "If China is so great, why didn't you go back after your studies?" Sue-Mei had come to America to obtain her graduate degree in nursing.

"You know why, dear. I met your father. He was finishing his doctoral program while I was doing my master's degree. I was in love and stayed. Once you were born and began learning to be an American, it didn't seem like going back to China would be good for either of us, even after the divorce."

"I don't know, Mom ...," Jill repeated.

* * *

Jill left the statuary area of the store and continued down the aisle, looking for something a lot more portable and a little more affordable than the large Buddha statues she had been examining. She felt a hand on her arm and a voice saying: "What do you think of this as a gift for a girl I've

had one date with?" Jill turned to see the face of a
good-looking man with short dark hair and a great
smile – with perfect teeth. She recognized the teeth
as belonging to the man who had introduced
himself to her and her friends on the hike in the
Santa Monica Mountains. He was holding a copy
of the *Kama Sutra* in his hand and apparently was
waiting for her response to his question. "I hope
you're kidding. Because if you're not, you're not
going to get a third date, that's for sure."

"Hah! Definitely kidding. You're Jill, right?
We met last Tuesday in the mountains."

"That's right, what's your name again?"

"Adrian," he held out his hand.

Jill shook the proffered hand again and
said: "Nice to meet you, again."

"Small world for sure. Even in a city the
size of LA. What brings you here," he inquired
pleasantly.

"Shopping for a gift for my mom. She's
turning fifty."

"Oh, you've got to get something nice to
soften the blow, for sure."

"Actually, she's strange. She seems to
really like aging. She's one of those rare people
who seems born to have been an old person."
Adrian chuckled at this thought, as did Jill as she
realized the truth of what she had just said. Her
mother really didn't mind growing old and in fact

did seem to relish it. Turning fifty was, for her mother, another progress point on the road to true wisdom. She could imagine her mother at eighty, still the same ultra-opinionated, ultra-sharp-tongued little Chinese woman with a strong accent but otherwise perfect English. At eighty, her mother would just be a little smaller and a little skinnier.

"In that case, I take it back. Get her something to emphasize her age."

"Like what?"

"I don't know. Maybe a . . . maybe a . . . Damn, I don't know. What kind of gifts celebrate aging in our culture? Not much that I can think of. Prune juice?"

Jill laughed at this suggestion and said: "Yeah, that will be appreciated: a bottle of prune juice and a gift certificate for some dentures. She's not that old, for crying out loud." As Jill spoke, she moved back from Adrian to rest her elbow on a display case. The case was not too steady and it began to fall as Jill rested her elbow on it. Luckily, she was able to halt its fall before it got very far and before any items resting on it fell off.

"Don't knock that over – you wouldn't want to break the doodad." Adrian was referring to a "perpetual motion machine" that rested on top of the case Jill had knocked.

"I've never heard it called that. We always called it a perpetual motion machine." The device was like many sold for years in knickknack stores. It consisted of two rails with a dip in the middle. A three-pronged star-shaped device, with heavy weights at the end of each prong, rolled back and forth on the rails for a long time -- but not perpetually. For those with short attention spans, it might seem like forever.

"Same thing, right? Same idea. Something for nothing. Too bad it ain't true."

"I guess. I used to think they were real when I was younger. Till I learned a thing or two about energy and physics."

"A thing or two?"

"Well, I guess more than a thing or two. It's actually my field now."

"What? Physics?"

"No, energy. Renewable energy."

"Interesting."

"I think so." Jill looked away.

"Jill, I shouldn't keep you any longer, I'm sure you're busy. But… Well, I'm not normally this forward. Do you think I could call you sometime?"

Jill was surprised by his boldness. It wasn't very often, even in LA, that relatively random guys asked her out. She didn't give off the "ask me out because I'm single" vibe, even though she had been single for a long time now. It was a simple trick, really. All she had to do was not make eye contact. Very few men will approach a woman who doesn't first at least acknowledge the man with a glance. Jill was certainly flattered that Adrian had asked her out even though he wasn't really her type. He seemed far too whitebread American for her. Too mainstream. Too good-looking. But he was at a store like Indochine, which wasn't exactly Ma and Apple Pie fare, and he did seem like a nice guy with a pretty good sense of humor. And he had a disarming manner about him despite his obvious confidence. "I guess so, sure," Jill replied after a small pause. She gave him her phone number, realizing it was the first time she'd given out her phone number to anyone with obvious romantic intentions toward her since she and Dargan had ended their relationship.

"I'll definitely give you a call, Jill. Good luck finding the right, uh, age-celebrating gift for your mother."

* * *

Jill didn't find anything that felt right for her mother's fiftieth birthday at Indochine. Walking back the few blocks to Global Green, she wondered if she really was ready to let go of the idea of Dargan and her being together again.

Meeting Adrian reminded her of the initial stage of her relationship with Dargan. He had been quite slow to let her know of his intentions, as had she. Neither of them were the type to dive in to a relationship without testing the waters with the toes.

After their first rock climbing "date," they had exchanged email addresses. He hadn't even asked her for her phone number, which she thought was kind of strange. Dargan certainly wasn't a "normal" type of guy in any way, however, so it fit with his personality.

Even his body was unusual. Jill spent the night at Dargan's for the first time about two weeks after she met him. They had had dinner and shared amazing conversation, mostly about areas of shared intellectual interest. Jill enjoyed learning and was happy to be with a person who knew enough about any topic to be able to talk as an expert on that topic. But she had her limit for this kind of talk. Dargan had a tendency to lapse into intellectual discussions far too easily for Jill's taste. "For crying out loud, I know how smart you are. Can we talk about something a bit less … cerebral?" Jill had cried out in exasperation toward the end of their date after Dargan had been expounding on the importance of the fair trade movement versus free trade theory, for what had seemed like an eternity to her. Dargan had surprised her by doing a spot on impression of Jerry Seinfeld, googly eyes and all, doing an impression of a working class New Yorker: "What? You want I should start talking about the Yankees and who's getting voted off next on Survivor? You want it? You got it!" He made the last point with a sharp upward gesture of his left arm, index finger pointed straight up. Jill laughed, half in astonishment at this extreme change in character and half in genuine amusement at his impeccable impression.

Jill had gone home with him, protesting: "You know you're not going to get me in bed, right?"

"Right," he replied.

An hour later, they were in his bed, undressing each other slowly, tenderly, cautiously. She liked his strong hands on her skin as he removed her shirt over her head. They kneeled on his futon bed. With her shirt no longer in the way, he ran his hands up her arms and along her neck, cupping her face and kissing her in long, relaxed, repetition. She reciprocated by unbuttoning his shirt and pulling it over his shoulders and down his lean, hard, arms.

Dargan's body was as unconventional as his facial features. Not classically handsome, by any means, but somehow tremendously attractive to her. His shoulders were hard balls of muscle and sinew and his trapezius muscles stood out in sharp relief against his neck and shoulders. His chest was flat and smooth, but dipped strangely at his solar plexus. As he pulled her down on the bed, she placed her fist in the hole formed by his dipping chest and prominent abdominal muscles. Her fist disappeared almost halfway as Jill said: "What's this about?"

"That's my chest cup. You've never seen that?"

"Your cup! Hmmm. Coffee in bed in the morning – without dirtying a cup." They laughed and Dargan replied: "Presumptuous aren't you – assuming you'll be here in the morning."

Jill's presumption turned out to be accurate. But Jill ensured that Dargan's presumption about his hopes of getting her into bed – in the metaphorical sense – was not accurate. She admitted to him later in a friendly argument, however, that he had indeed gotten her into bed in the literal sense.

A week or so after this incident, Jill had pulled back emotionally, fearing that her growing feelings for Dargan were not entirely mutual. It wasn't that she was trying to play any type of game with him. It was merely that she was very afraid of being hurt and was naturally wary when it came to relationships. She had canceled a couple of dates because she was genuinely not in the mood to hang out with him after she had expressed what her intentions were toward him in terms which, to her at least, seemed pretty clear. She hadn't received much in the way of confirmation from him that he was feeling the same way.

They were lying in bed one morning about three weeks in to their budding partnership and Jill found herself feeling well-rested for the first time in weeks. She always lost sleep after first meeting someone who pushed all her right buttons, waking up ridiculously early and fully alert for some time after the first meeting. But this apparently biological phenomenon took its toll and she found herself exhausted at inopportune times throughout the day as her body let her know that the hormones of infatuation could only kick start her body for so long before what went up had to come down. This morning, however, she had slept well until seven and laid in bed until she felt Dargan shading into consciousness beside her.

As he woke, Jill slipped her arms around him, moved her body as close as possible to his, and said: "This feels so good, I think I could do this forever." She hadn't meant to say this. It just came out. And Dargan's reaction was not what she would have hoped: "Mmmmm, yes, glad you like it. You feel good too." *Typical Dargan*, she thought, even though she had only known him for three weeks.

There were other incidents as Jill had tried to express to Dargan the very strong emotions she was feeling, seeking some confirmation that he was feeling the same thing. It hadn't happened, so Jill began to pull back. As wonderful as Dargan was, in so many ways, she wasn't about to let herself fall completely for someone who was not on the same sheet of cheesy music as she was. After the pull back, Dargan had not abandoned her and had, instead, stepped up his courtship, as she hoped he would. After a pointed email exchange in which he was clearly getting frustrated with her for not agreeing to any definite plans after she had canceled their last planned date, he sent her a poem, which she read with great pleasure on her bright Macintosh screen. She recited it to herself as she walked down the Promenade, dodging lunchgoers on the busy open air mall. She relished its nonsensical lines and its obvious emotion:

Brave Motorola Mother

Lend me your eyes for a few bytes of electronic jabber,
And we'll see how many toes you can count on your sheep.
In the midst of anger and oblivion, a balance is found
With the rising of the sun and the downing of the waters;
In that moment, peace of a kind can be known.

You, you with your eyes glued to the new boob tube,
What do you know of intimacy and embodied warmth?
Is all you know the yielding keys and enfolding chair,
And perhaps the keyboard-forsaken hand as it
Slips between your thighs for guilty gratitude?

In the glorious days of the fin-de-siecle
The chips with their bits reign supreme.

You surf, you say? On those metaphorical waves,
Riding the net crest, catching info-spume in your
mouth.
How do they taste, those noospheric bubbles?
Aren't they a little flimsy, a little lank in meat?
How about some real substance, some animal heat?

Let's wander through the knotted interface skeins,
Finding ourselves and each other in those wire-portraits,
With their elephant dregs and zebra pegs, scouting out
New frontiers of fun and fresh adventures in solitude.
Why not be lonely together?

In the glorious days of the fin-de-siecle,
The chips with their bits reign supreme.

This mortal coil with all its extensions into x-dimensions
Can't find the same sanctuary that you know in
prudence.
Let our bauds pray and our disparate parities
intermingle,

And, perhaps, in the harsh squeal of the connecting
lines,
Our bends will be straightened and our hands joined.

She had been tempted to let Dargan know –
after she looked it up – that "fin-de-siecle" didn't
seem the appropriate term in light of the fact that
they had met in 2002, a little after the "end of the
century." But poetic license was poetic license. She
also resented his implication that she had been
pleasuring herself during their email exchanges.
Who the hell does he think he is? Nevertheless,
shortly after, Jill and Dargan had become "Jargan"
to their D.C. friends, as they became inseparable
after work hours. Jill protested when she first
heard herself and Dargan referred to as Jargan:
"That's so sexist: I only get one letter?" "Would
you rather people called us Dill?" "Good point,"
Jill conceded.

Chapter Six

"Well, well, well, I thought I might run into you around here." Jill looked up as she recognized the voice as her uncle's. She had been reading the paper at an outside table at Elsie's, a coffee shop in Santa Monica. It was one of her favorite morning haunts because it was so close to Global Green. And it was independently owned, which was important to her, even though the coffee really wasn't that good.

"Hi Jonas, what brings you here?" A twinge of guilt passed through her as she remembered that she hadn't called Jonas back after his call from the previous Thursday. She simply hadn't gotten around to deciding yet whether or not she would bother to return his call.

"I'm just down for the day on some business and thought I'd take a stroll down the Promenade. That's what you do on promenades right?"

"Yes ... I guess so. Though we're not quite on the Promenade right now, you know."

"Well, close enough, right? Do you mind if I join you for a little?"

It would have been very hard to deny him this request without being completely rude, so she acquiesced.

"Did you get my message, Jill?"

"Yep, I got it. Apology accepted, I guess." She was way too nice. It had always been her biggest flaw.

"Jill, I really am sorry about the way I behaved. I was under a lot of stress that day and just, well, I obviously let my mouth get way ahead of where it should have been going. You know I didn't mean anything by it, right? You know I have the utmost respect for your mother?"

"Look, I accept your apology and I don't really feel like talking about it. Just do me a favor and don't ever go there again."

"Absolutely." A pause. "So how's work, Jill? Save the world yet?" Making fun of Jill's work and idealism was a constant theme of Jonas' attempts at humor.

"Not yet, couple more years and it will be saved." Jill replied.

"You never told me what you do exactly at that outfit you've been working at here in town. Some kind of energy thing, right?"

"Right, I'm the climate change and energy program director. I coordinate Global Green's campaign to educate people about the problems of climate change and the relationship between energy generation and use and its effects on climate change."

"Well, that's definitely sexy. What does that mean you do on a daily basis?"

Jill was surprised he was taking such an interest in her work. He never had before except in the most general way. Was he really interested or just trying to make up for his outrageous behavior last time she saw him? She was content to talk about her work, as opposed to any other topic. She didn't really want him knowing much about her personal life. They chatted a few minutes more about her work, until Jill felt it would not be completely rude to excuse herself to go to work.

"You've got to go? Must be rough being a nine to fiver," he grinned.

"Somebody's got to earn an honest living," she said, hoping he didn't take her comment too literally as she realized he could interpret it to be a criticism of his earlier work-related misdeeds.

"Jill, do you mind if I check out your workplace? I've heard it's a great example of, what do they call it? Energy efficient building?"

"Wow, I'm impressed. Yes, Global Green's building has won a bunch of awards for its design. But you know, it's not much to look at. I mean, it's not like the design features it's won awards for are that evident or glamorous."

"I've got time. I'd like to check it out if you don't mind. And I'd like to see your office, you know. I want to see where the magic happens. Call me sentimental."

"All right, I guess. You can't stay long, for real. I've actually got a lot to do." She lied. Jill did appreciate his newfound interest in her work even though she was suspicious of his motives. Maybe there was a green gene in him somewhere after all, despite strong evidence of its absence since she'd known him.

They walked the two blocks to her office, chatting about family issues for the most part. Jill introduced Jonas to her colleagues and showed him the more obvious features of the generally modest building in which she worked. Global Green's headquarters was not particularly large or by any means luxurious. It was largely utilitarian with some very tasteful ornamental touches added for enhanced livability. However, the building had indeed won a number of awards for its efficient design, which incorporated many passive and active energy saving features, such as south facing double pane windows, compact fluorescent lights, daylighting through strategic placement of skylights, and many other features. During the tour, Jonas made the right appreciative noises, sufficient to convince Jill that he was at least paying attention.

Jill ended the brief tour at her office, saying: "And there you have it, Uncle, the grand tour of Global Green USA's headquarters. It was cool seeing you. I hate to rush you out, but I do have to get some work done."

"Thanks a bunch, Jill, I'm definitely impressed. Real nice digs you've got. We're all very proud of you." Jill did not attempt to take issue with his presumption that he spoke for her whole family – his intentions appeared, at least, to be good.

"No problem. Can you find your way out, or should I walk you out?"

"I'm good, as you younguns say. I'll find my way myself." Jill's cell phone rang as she said goodbye to Jonas. She didn't recognize the number, but answered it anyway.

"Hi Jill, it's Adrian. How are ya?" Jill hadn't spent much time thinking about Adrian since she ran into him at Indochine earlier in the week. She hadn't even decided if she would go out with him if he asked her out on a date. She punted: "I'm good, Adrian. Actually, right now's not a good time to talk, can I call you back later?"

"Sure, you've got my number now, right?"

"Yes, it showed up on my cell. I'll call you back."

"Cool, talk to ya."

Jill's morning was consumed with meetings with her boss and colleagues. By the time she thought about Adrian again, she decided she would call him back and see what he had to say.

Not surprisingly, Adrian invited her to dinner. He suggested Saturday night. It was Friday. Chuckling internally, Jill thought about the "Rules girls'" prohibition on accepting a weekend date after Wednesday. She had never considered herself a "Rules girl" anyway, so she was betraying no faith. Jill was still a little surprised, however, when she decided to accept his proposal. They arranged to meet for dinner at Saka Sushi, on Beverly Avenue. It was approximately halfway between their respective homes, so seemed a good choice.

* * *

A week after Dargan and Jill arrived in Santa Monica after their cross-country trek, they had taken a walk along Venice Beach. The beach was known worldwide for its incredibly colorful assortment of street performers, vendors, and visitors from every country around the globe. They had no agenda as they strolled down the boardwalk on a Sunday morning, but Jill saw a Tarot reader to her right and tugged on Dargan's arm: "Hey. Let's get a Tarot reading! They're kind of fun."

Dargan looked skeptical. "I don't know. You go ahead."

"Oh come on! It can't hurt you can it?"

"Why don't you get one and I'll decide after yours if I'm going to get a reading."

"Jesus, you're a stick in the mud sometimes. All right." Jill approached the woman with the Tarot booth. She had a small table in front of her, covered in a pretty woven cloth that looked Indian in origin. On the table was a single large deck of cards, face down. The woman smiled as Jill approached. She had been watching Jill and Dargan's exchange with evident interest.
"Hi there. I'd like to get a reading."

"Great. Have a seat. Are you familiar with the Tarot?" The woman smiled at them both. She had a European accent of some kind. She was in her forties or fifties and wore a colorful hat and a long robe that hid most of her body.

"A little. But I don't think my boyfriend is. Why don't you explain it to refresh my memory and give him some insight?"

"Sure. What is your name?"

"Jill." Jill held out her hand. The Tarot woman took it with a look of mild distaste on her face. Jill hoped the distaste was not directed at her, but rather at the very Western greeting Jill had offered.

"Gretchen," the woman said as she lightly shook Jill's outstretched hand. "And your friend?"

"Dargan," Dargan said as he offered his hand. She shook his hand with an equally flaccid grip.

"Well, nice to meet you both," Gretchen smiled. "The Tarot is a method of divination that has its origins in medieval Europe. It probably evolved from dice, after playing cards were introduced from the East. The cards act as a guide through their interaction with our inner world. The cards bridge the gap between the physical world and the psychic world. This bridge is made possible through the archetypes we all share deep in our collective unconscious. The most basic archetypes are numbers, which form the basis for physics and biology. And as biological beings, we are embodied numbers. By concentration of psychic energy on the cards, the cards can help you resolve important issues in your lives. That is, we are *creating* a synchronistic event – a meaningful coincidence through merging the physical and mental words." Dargan shot Jill a quick glance after listening. Jill liked the reader's rap and thought it sounded quite plausible. She hoped Dargan would at least give it a chance.

"As for the cards, there are many kinds of Tarot decks. This particular deck is the Pythagorean Tarot, a deck based on the mathematical and esoteric insights of Pythagoras, the ancient Greek philosopher and mystic who predated Socrates, Plato and Aristotle."

Jill looked at Dargan with a smile as Gretchen paused in her monologue. He rolled his eyes subtly at her this time. "Now, Jill," Gretchen continued, "what is it you are most concerned about right now? What's going on in your life?"

Jill glanced at Dargan again. "Despite the fact that he's here," Jill gestured toward Dargan with her eyes, "why don't you tell me what my love life holds?"

"All right, then." Gretchen placed part of the deck in the middle of the table and asked Jill to cut it. Once she did so, Gretchen placed the cut deck in front of Jill in a fan. "Go ahead and pick one of the Major Arcana, Jill." Jill picked a card to the left of center and handed it to Gretchen face down. Gretchen turned it over and laid it on the table above the fanned cards. "You have picked the Empress. This is good. The Empress is the mother figure, the compassionate one. She nurtures at the same time as she rules." Jill looked again at Dargan. He smiled back at her.

"Pick another card." Jill chose one to the right of center this time and handed it to Gretchen. Gretchen placed it face up on the table. "You have picked the fool, Jill. But it's not as bad as it sounds." Gretchen smiled. "The fool represents innocence, hope, and a can-do attitude. The fool doesn't let pessimists keep him down. He strives to accomplish his goals no matter what the naysayers say he can't do. This means, in your love life, that you will keep on trying no matter how hard things get." Jill wasn't sure she liked the sound of this one.

"Pick another card." Jill searched the remaining cards with her eyes.

"Let's take that hidden one, right here," she said as she picked a card that was almost entirely obscured by another card. Gretchen laid it on the table. Jill read the title as Gretchen said it: "This card is Setback." Jill definitely didn't like the sound of that one. "Setback means that you might not immediately find your happiness." Gretchen glanced at Dargan as she spoke. "But it does not mean all is lost. It just means that in love, as in life, the road is not always a straight one." Jill was more upset by this card than she displayed externally. She wasn't sure how much faith she placed in the Tarot. But she sure as hell didn't want to be hearing bad news like this. "I like to say when setbacks occur, we need to just *sit back* and work on ourselves. This is often the best response we can have to a world that does not always match our expectations. As our internal world improves, the external world will often follow."

"That's comforting," Jill said sarcastically.

"Now pick an ally from the Minor Arcana," Gretchen said as she fanned out the larger deck she had kept back. Jill anxiously picked a card and handed it to Gretchen. Jill gasped quietly as she saw the title. "This card is Fear. This is your ally. It may sound bad, but fear can be a great motivator. Without fear, much would go undone in this world. And we of course all have fear in our lives, particularly in matters of the heart. Keep in mind, Jill, that you are the Empress, the great mother, and the fool. You will nurture and overcome, despite setbacks and despite fear. And fear may in fact be your ally."

Jill sat silently for a moment. Fear was too prevalent in her life. Fear of rejection. Fear of failure. Fear of death. She didn't see how fear could be an ally. The card just seemed to reinforce her worst fears about herself! She looked up at Dargan, who attempted a look of reassurance. She didn't feel reassured, but Dargan surprised her by saying. "Let me try a reading. But I want to keep it short. Don't you have a one card reading? I've heard about that somewhere."

"Yes, I can do that. But I warn you it may not be pleasant for a first-time reading." Jill stood and allowed Dargan to sit.

"I can handle it. I'm just curious to see what will pop up."

"All right then. What is your major concern in your life right now?"

"Since Jill focused on love, why don't I focus on the other big one: career?" *Typical*, Jill thought. *I care about love and he cares about career.*

"Okay. Career. Since we're only going to draw one card. Why don't you tell me more about what you're looking to find out. This will focus your mental energy more, allowing the deck to better bridge the gap between the physical and mental worlds. Cut the deck while you think."

"Well… I'm up in the air now. I just moved out with Jill to be with her here. I'm officially on sabbatical from my job in D.C., but I'm thinking about making a clean break and making a go of it out here on the West Coast."

"All right. Concentrate. And when you're ready, pick a card." Gretchen fanned the Major Arcana in front of Dargan. Dargan hesitated for half a second and then picked the nearest card to him. Gretchen turned it over. "This is the Hanged Man." Jill examined the card with dread interest as Gretchen spoke. It depicted a naked man hanging upside down from a tree. He was suspended by his left ankle, a sash tied around it. His right leg was bent at the knee behind his left leg, forming a figure four out of his legs. His arms were crossed behind him. His penis hung down as though he had an erection. His side was gashed by a large wound and from his head emanated what appeared to be a halo. He had a smile on his face. A snake crawled among the branches of the tree.

"The Hanged Man is an enigmatic figure. He is known also as the Trickster or the Traitor. Even though he is hanged, he doesn't appear to be in great pain. He is smiling, as you can see. And we hope it's not merely gravity pulling his cheeks up." Gretchen emitted a chuckle. Dargan didn't respond as he gazed at the card.

"He is the Trickster because he is thought to be akin to Prometheus, the Titan who tricked Zeus into accepting the lesser part of animal sacrifices, reserving the best parts for Man. He is the Traitor because he challenged power and lost. He suffers. But he suffers gladly. You will notice that if you turn the card upside down, he appears to be dancing a jig." She turned the card upside down quickly as she spoke. She returned it to its original orientation and continued. "Now. This means for you that you care passionately about your work. Your cause. For you, your work and your cause are probably one and the same. You will sacrifice much for your passion." Jill looked at Dargan. He didn't meet her eyes, but, instead, continued to stare at the card. "You are not afraid to challenge power when it disagrees with you. And you may pay the price for that hubris. At the same time, you relish the chance to be a martyr, to be an example to others. The Hanged Man may be redeemed, but the outcome is always uncertain." Gretchen stopped speaking. No one spoke for an uncomfortable length of time.

Dargan finally looked up and said. "Interesting. Thanks very much. What do we owe you?" Dargan paid and they continued their walk, neither of them speaking further about their respective readings.

Chapter 7

"Wow, you look great," Adrian greeted her as she entered the restaurant.

"Thanks. You look all right yourself." Jill had, for the first time since Dargan, made an effort to look good for a man. She was wearing a skirt that rode just above her knees, a blouse that was not too tight, and two-inch high pumps that matched her skirt. Not too prudish. Not too slutty. At least she hoped this was the message. She had even worn some eyeliner, which was quite removed from her "natural girl" character.

Adrian gave her a hug, which Jill returned brusquely, turning her body to prevent her breasts from pressing against his chest. It had always seemed to Jill a bit fake to literally embrace someone that you had just met. But it was social convention. Adrian had wisely made reservations and, as they were seated, Adrian pulled out Jill's chair for her.

"I'm really glad you agreed to have dinner with me, Jill," he smiled.

"Has a girl ever refused your dinner invitation?" She smiled back mischievously.

His grin broadened: "If you only knew. I'd say an acceptance is the exception to the rule for me. This town is strange for singles, as I'm sure you know." She appreciated his modesty, even though she suspected it was false modesty. "You might be surprised to know how many times I've got a girl's number, called her, and never received a callback."

"So you get a lot of girl's numbers, then?"

"Well, uh, not that many," he backtracked. "Here and there, you know, when I meet someone very cool."

"So you're not a player?"

"Exactly." He grinned again as he realized she was playing with him. But she wasn't entirely playing with him. She was, of course, concerned about any prospective match for her not being a player type. In a town the size of Los Angeles, it was very easy to become anonymous and do all sorts of things without getting "caught." Not that Jill actually had experience dating in Los Angeles. But she had girlfriends who did and all large cities were alike in that respect. She'd heard too many nightmare stories from her friends and colleagues about relationships gone awfully bad. Dating in Los Angeles seemed to be very different from her experience in Berkeley, which had its own rather strange dating environment.

"So I don't know a thing about you, Adrian. In five hundred words or less, please tell me about yourself."

He smiled. "The SAT approach, I see. All right, I see how you operate. But you know that's not as interesting. What do you want to know about me? I don't want to just regurgitate my resume to you."

"Well, I hate to ask this because it's generally the first thing people ask of strangers and it's so uncreative. But I guess I'll give in to the uncreative trend and ask what you do."

"It didn't take long did it? I'm a lawyer, actually." He said this with a slight dip in the volume of his voice.

"Lawyers are everywhere nowadays! You needn't be ashamed. At least you're not in the movie biz," she teased.

"I'm not ashamed, believe me. I'm happy with what I do generally."

"What type of law? I've got a good friend who's an environmental lawyer at Arnold & Packer in Century City."

"Securities law. Helping rich guys get richer."

"Great, sounds like you're a real do-gooder."

"That's me. But please let's not talk about my work anymore, it's deathly boring for the most part."

"Ok, I guess. But I would like to know more at some point, if we end up hanging out more. A lot of my work revolves around corporate environmental responsibility and stuff like that, so I'd be curious to get your perspective and your impressions of your clients' views on certain things."

"Well, sure. But enough about me, what about you?"

"One more question on you: who do you work for? Oh, I guess two more questions: are you an associate or a partner?"

"I work for Jones Davis downtown. And I am a partner. Just got hired there a couple of months ago."

"Wow, impressive. You seem pretty young to be a partner at a major law firm."

"I'm not as young as you might think I am."

"Really, what are you? Thirty?"

"I'm actually a well-preserved thirty-five."

"Hmmm. You realize you're robbing the cradle, don't you?"

"Why, how old are you? I'm afraid to guess because I might offend…"

"You're not going to get off the hook that easy! How old do you think I am?"

"Well, you look pretty young, but your manner and bearing and overall demeanor projects a maturity that your looks belie."

"Oh you're good. Please go on."

"All right, you're still not letting me off the hook, clearly. I'd say you're twenty-five."

"Wrong! I'm twenty-six. You were way off," she joked.

"That's a great age. Nine years difference. Is that robbing the cradle? Does it matter that I'm emotionally very immature?"

"Great sales pitch, mister. You actually make emotional immaturity a positive feature. But, no, I guess nine years isn't that bad. And I am very mature for my age," she laughed at her own immodesty. The waiter arrived and Adrian asked if Jill would like to share some sake and edamame. The food was great, as she knew it would be from her previous experience dining at Saka Sushi. As the sake was consumed, the conversation continued to be interesting. Jill found herself quite attracted to Adrian – despite his good looks and overall charm. He continued to be self-deprecating in talking about himself, which lulled her suspicions about him. He also was a great listener as she went on at length about her work and experiences in Los Angeles. Jill did enjoy talking about her work because, for her, work was not just something that she resigned herself to for eight hours a day. She had a genuine passion for what she did and loved the people she worked with. Despite the fact that she'd only been with Global Green for a year, she felt that she had been quite effective thus far.

Fortunately, Adrian seemed genuinely interested in listening to her talk about her work, despite his self-professed lack of overt idealism.

He seemed particularly interested in hearing about her work on energy policy. "How do you get information about energy policy, then? I know it's pretty hard for non-profits to work with this administration."

"We have various means available. We have some pretty good contacts at the EPA and the DoE – the Department of Energy. I can call a couple of different people with basic questions. For more serious information requests, we typically use a FOIA – Freedom of Information Act – request." *This is strange*, she thought. Typically, people got glazy-eyed the moment she began talking about energy policy and the intricacies of her work.

After dinner, feeling very good and flushed with the warmth of good sushi and heated sake, Jill suggested they get some drinks at Mazie's, a local bar. Adrian agreed this was a good idea and they walked to the bar, continuing the enjoyable conversation. After two mixed drinks and much laughter, Jill agreed to go to Adrian's apartment after he offered a somewhat plausible reason for her to go: he wanted to burn a CD for her. They had been discussing music and he had offered to make a copy of an album she had previously listened to but did not own. It was highly out of character for Jill to agree to go the apartment of a guy she had just met, after a first date. Her friends would give her shit, that was certain, when they found out. *But whatever.*

Promising to pay for her cab back to her car, Jill agreed to share a cab to Adrian's apartment in the new Soho development downtown. On the cab ride, Adrian, during a pause in their conversation, leaned toward Jill and kissed her. Feeling a twinge of guilt in remembering Joe's recent rejected kiss, she responded, after a moment of surprise, by warmly kissing him back. She wasn't surprised to find that he was a very good kisser and told him so. Adrian didn't attempt anything further after the single kiss and they returned to casual conversation for the rest of the cab ride. When they arrived at Adrian's apartment, to his credit, he did at least have the CD he'd promised to copy for her. He quickly copied it and joined Jill on the couch where she was sipping a glass of Coke that Adrian had provided for her – she had to sober up at some point to drive home because she wanted to avoid paying for a cab back to Santa Monica from Beverly Drive.

"So where were we?" Adrian asked.

"I think we were about right here," Jill replied as she leaned in his direction and kissed him. After kissing for several minutes, Jill felt Adrian's hands on the outside of her thigh. She liked it. She felt his other hand on her side just below her right breast. As their kissing became more passionate, Adrian slid his hand upward to cup her breast from the outside of her blouse. Jill also liked this. Their kissing heated up. But, to Jill's surprise, Adrian pulled back a second later and held her in his arms as he looked at her from about a foot away. Jill was definitely turned off when he said: "So do you ever get involved in anything juicy at work? You know, drama, intrigue?"

"What?" She took a moment to shift mental gears. "Oh, sometimes, I guess. Nothing *that* juicy though." *Why the hell is everyone so interested in my work all of a sudden?* His question had killed the mood. Or maybe her buzz was simply wearing off. But, regardless of the cause, Jill suddenly felt uncomfortable and told Adrian: "You know, I'm getting pretty tired. Can you call a cab for me?"

"That's too bad." He seemed surprised at her sudden change of heart. "But, sure, I'll call one now." The cab arrived a few minutes later and they talked awkwardly during the interim. She realized Adrian was not quite as polished as she thought he was, considering his apparent incomprehension at to why she would feel uncomfortable all of a sudden. There was something not quite right about him, despite his obvious charm and intelligence. It was too bad, though, because she really had enjoyed his company for most of the night. On her journey back to Santa Monica, she felt quite relieved that she hadn't done anything more than kiss Adrian. She begrudgingly paid the cab driver when she got home, consoling herself that at least she could get a ride back to her car with Rahul or another friend.

* * *

"If I were to ever, for even a second, contemplate not devoting my life to making the world more livable for all people, I'd have to commit suicide at that very moment," Dargan had said to her on their first "official" date a week after their first meeting. *Just a small contrast to Adrian.* Yet again, Jill was comparing Adrian to Dargan. They were about as different as two men could be and still be attractive to her.

Jill and Dargan were enjoying a meal at Kramer's Bookstore on Dupont Circle in D.C. Dargan had suggested they go there. He was the native, after all. He reminded her, trying to be funny, that this was the bookstore where Monica Lewinsky had bought books for Bill Clinton, which later became the subject of a subpoena request by the Starr investigation. He added: "I wonder if she bought him a copy of Cigar Aficionado too." She responded only with a courtesy laugh – she wasn't about to encourage weak attempts at humor like that one. *Not to mention tasteless.*

Dargan's comment about the need for instant suicide should he ever consider a life not devoted to service to others, had required Jill to take a second or two to recover. It was definitely a strange thing for someone to say on a first date, or any date. But, in his defense, she thought, she had asked him why he had decided to go the non-profit career route. And she had always been highly attracted to men who were motivated by more than the desire for a high salary. She had no idea what Dargan made in terms of income, but she knew that non-profits in general didn't pay that well.

And that, in itself, was a shame, she had learned in her short time in the non-profit sector, because it showed quite starkly that trying to change things for the perceived good of all was not considered worthy of high salaries. Looked at another way, it showed that the work must itself be highly rewarding because most non-profit types were generally highly intelligent and motivated people who could have found positions in more lucrative fields.

"Well, you certainly are committed," Jill finally responded.

"I am, Jill. But I'm guessing you are too. You're at NRDC, right?"

"Well, yes. But I still haven't decided what I'll do for my permanent career. Don't get me wrong, I definitely want to be part of the solution too. But I'm not sure yet where that will take me necessarily. I certainly don't hate money."

"I do sometimes," he said. Jill wrinkled her brow at this comment. Seeing her response, Dargan said: "But don't get me wrong either. I understand we've got to make a living in this world. But I'm just really sickened by people's willingness to sacrifice their principles and their better ethics for money. It's seriously what is at the heart of all the problems we face today."

"Yeah, I guess. But do we have to be so bloody serious?" She smiled.

"You asked the question! But damn it, you're right! Would you care to dance?" Dargan was joking, Jill realized, as he put up a hand to keep her in her seat at the same time as she realized there was no music playing. *Thank God, that would have been way too cheesy.*

Chapter 8

After a less than restful night's sleep in her Santa Monica apartment, Jill decided to get around to what she had been too busy to do during the previous week. Feeling very industrious, Jill arrived at her office on Sunday morning at about eight and began reviewing the stack of documents she had received in response to her FOIA request regarding the formation of White House renewable energy policy. She took a few hours to read through the physical documents, finding some interesting items from the Department of Energy and other federal agencies relating to renewable energy and energy policy more generally. Jill was encouraged to find that staffers at the DoE and other federal agencies seemed to support what she considered progressive energy policy for the most part. There was a noticeable change in tone and emphasis, however, between the lower level staff reports and the more senior policy statements and memoranda.

Where, for example, a lower level staff report, entitled "Examination of Potential for Large Scale Reliance on Renewable Energy Sources in the 21st Century," stated: "It is imperative for reasons of energy security and sound environmental policy that the United States obtain a substantial portion of its energy from renewable sources during this century," the higher level report, now entitled

"Traditional Energy Generation and Renewable Energy Generation: Finding the Right Balance," changed the statement to read: "While a substantial shift from fossil fuel energy generation to renewable energy generation over the course of this century would likely enhance energy security and further environmental protection, such a shift should be made prudently and with full consideration of existing economic needs and interests." This shift was perhaps cause for concern, but, even though she noticed a few examples of this kind of thing, it was not exactly a federal case in the making.

Moving on to the CDROM that accompanied the paper documents, Jill found that the vast majority of documents on the CDROM were duplicates of the paper documents she had already reviewed. However, there were some additional files, with minimally descriptive and innocuous sounding names. She clicked on a file entitled "Meeting1-30-01." Immediately upon opening the document, the bold letters of one word screamed out to Jill: "CLASSIFIED." Jill leaned in closer to her computer screen and scanned the document with growing interest. The document was a transcript of a meeting on January 30, 2001, apparently between the Vice President's office and Saudi Arabian officials from the Saudi government and the Saudi state-owned oil company, Aramco.

Jill knew there was a court case pending to force the Vice President's office to release a list of parties it met with during the creation of the 2001 National Energy Policy report. The Sierra Club, an organization with a similar but much broader mandate than Jill's Global Green, was one of the plaintiffs seeking to compel the Vice President to release the list of parties. It was quite a high profile case and had received a great deal of media attention. The outcome remained uncertain as it – and at least two other similar cases she knew of – worked its way through the federal court system. After reading through the transcript, Jill understood perhaps why the Vice President was reluctant to release even the list of parties, let alone transcripts of meetings such as the one she was viewing.

The meeting was conducted by an unnamed representative of the Vice President. Saudi Arabia's Minister of Petroleum and Mineral Resources, Ali bin Ibrahim Al-Naimi, was present, as was Abdallah S. Jum'ah, President and CEO of Aramco, the world's largest oil company. A few other people were present on both the US side and the Saudi side. As evidenced by the transcript, the meeting began with the understanding that the Saudis were meeting with the Vice President's office to discuss formation of the Vice President's energy policy recommendation for the President.

The January meeting was apparently not the first time the parties had met, as the discussion quickly came to a head:

VPOTUS: Gentlemen, I would like to state again our appreciation for your generous help throughout the history of our nations' mutually satisfying relationship. I hope you feel that we have been equally generous. Today, of course, we are here to discuss more specific matters than general goodwill between our two great nations.

Jum'ah: Mr. ████████, we do, of course, reciprocate your feelings of appreciation stemming from events during the course of our shared history. And we understand why we are meeting today. We would like to stress, however, what you already know, if only to ensure that our primary concerns are not overlooked in any fashion.

She tried to see beneath the large black blot that covered the name of the representative for the Vice President. No luck. Jill found the somewhat flowery language used by the diplomats in keeping with her limited experience in this area, if somewhat distracting. It had often seemed to her that diplomatic language was designed to confuse issues rather than to actually convey information in a clear fashion. *Is this why so many wars have occurred after attempts at diplomacy?* The transcript continued:

VPOTUS: Of course, *Saydat* Jum'ah, we are aware of your primary concerns. You and your colleagues may rest assured that our product will reflect a wise reliance on a continuation of our strong relationship and a continuation of support for your company's products. We understand the importance of good relations and wise energy policy to both our nations. As we discussed previously, we are still not entirely clear, however, on how you and your colleagues plan to help us help you.

Al-Naimi: Mr. ████████████, let me please interject here. Again, we do fully appreciate your generosity in committing to continuing the strong relationship between our nations. We will not leave such generosity unrewarded. You and your colleagues may rely on our commitment to ensure that President Colt will receive our utmost support – throughout both terms of his presidency. Is this clear enough for you?

VPOTUS: *Saydat* Ibrahim, *Saydat* Jum'ah, your statements are quite clear and I thank you again for your generosity. Now that this is resolved, are there any other issues you'd like to discuss?

Jill was taken aback by what she had read, but unsure of what it actually meant. Was this discussion simply *de rigeur* diplomatic posturing? Or was there a *quid pro quo*? There was definitely some kind of *quid pro quo* – just not terribly clear to her somewhat inexperienced mind. If there was a *quid pro quo* agreement, what exactly was being agreed upon? Jill re-read the transcript in its entirety. Then she read it a third time. It dawned on her that the best interpretation of the artful language was that the VP's Office had made a commitment to the Saudis to support the continuing close relationship between Saudi Arabia and the United States and, more incriminatingly, had committed to pursuing an oil-friendly energy policy in return for unspecified favors from the Saudis.

It seemed to Jill the most reasonable interpretation of the transcript was that the Saudis were concerned that the United States may seek to limit reliance on the increasing amount of oil imported from Saudi Arabia, which, Jill knew, supplied about twenty percent of America's oil imports. It wasn't quite clear what the Saudis had promised in return for a renewed commitment to an oil-friendly energy policy, but the reference to "both terms of his presidency" certainly suggested a Saudi commitment to helping to ensure a second term for President Colt.

Jill had had enough for the time being and, as a means of having the documents to examine at home at her leisure, saved the most important documents to the Internet by sending them as attachments to her own email address. Also, as a backup measure in case her Internet was temporarily disrupted at her home, as it often was, she saved the electronic documents to her keychain USB thumbdrive.

As Jill left her office, she received a call from her old friend Jamie, one of her few good female friends. "Hey Jamie, long time no talk! How are you?"

"I've been really good. Just thought I'd give you a jingle and see what's been going on in your exciting life. We really need to catch up."

"I know! We really do, what has it been now? Three months? You got married and fell of the face of the earth, it seems."

"Oh come on, it's not that bad, I've tried to get in touch with you, but you're not the easiest person to get a hold of, Jill dear."

"All right, just giving you a hard time. I guess I might have forgotten to call you back the last time. Are you free tonight? I would really like to see you and I have some things I'd like to bounce off you, if you're free."

"I am free, in fact. When and where?" They arranged to meet at Q's, a local bar and billiard hall, which was a relaxed place to hang out and have a drink or two. As long as they didn't stay too late, they wouldn't have any problems with obnoxious guys, Jill hoped.

As she walked home, her cell phone rang again. Checking to see who was calling, she saw Adrian's number displayed. She didn't answer, waiting for the voicemail chime to ring. A few seconds later, the chime did indeed ring. Checking her voicemail, Jill heard Adrian's strong and mellifluous voice: "Jill, hey there. I just wanted to call and let you know I really enjoyed our date last night. I hope we're still cool after... well, it seemed like you left in a bit of a rush last night. I hope things are all right. Give me a call sometime." Jill saved the message, still unsure of how she thought about Adrian.

* * *

The patio at Q's was always comfortable despite the abundant traffic on Wilshire Boulevard, even on a Sunday. Q's was a pool parlor and bar that appealed to attractive Angelenos looking for a decent beer in an unpretentious environment.

Jill and Jamie had arranged to meet at five that evening to enjoy a happy hour beer or two. As Jill had hoped, the bar was pretty slow at that hour. Even in Los Angeles, a city that never slept, it was a good bet that Sunday afternoon was not a busy hour for bargoers.

Jamie was a friend from Jill's college years. Jamie was from Los Angeles originally and had returned to the city after she had graduated from Oregon State University in Eugene. Though Jill and Jamie had little in common other than their college years, they had kept in touch off and on. Jamie, married just a year before, seemed like a "real adult" to Jill because of this large difference in their lives. Jill knew it probably wasn't a valid judgment, but she found herself respecting Jamie's opinions on various topics more now that Jamie was married. And Jamie was, in her own right, a very intelligent and capable professional who shared a physical therapy practice with her husband in West Los Angeles.

After catching up with Jamie's married life existence, which seemed so foreign to Jill's quite single life, Jamie asked what was on Jill's mind. "I need a reality check, Jamie. Some strange things have been happening lately and I want to make sure I'm not going off my rocker."

"Interesting. What's up?"

"First, let me just tell you about this new guy I met."

"You met a new guy? About time!" Jamie interrupted.

"Well, yes, but I'm not sure he's on the up and up. I mean, it sounds really silly even when I think it to myself."

"What do you mean?"

"Let me start at the beginning and then I'll tell you what I mean." Jill told Jamie the details of how she had met Adrian and about their first date. Talking about it left Jill feeling astonished that it was only the previous evening that the events she was talking about had occurred. Somehow, the events seemed much longer ago.

Jill continued: "But get this. As we're kissing at his apartment and getting a little hot and heavy, he suddenly stops, leans back and asks me a lame question about my work! I mean, you can't do that to a girl."

"Hah! That is strange. Maybe he was just shy?"

"I don't think so. He comes across as a super-confident guy in every other way. He's a young partner at a major law firm, very good-looking, funny. I mean, this guy is the all-American attractive male if there ever was one."

"Yeah, I see your point. But guys are weird nowadays. There's so much confusion about what's appropriate and what's not. Not that I'd really know, of course, now that I'm an old married broad..."

"You may be right, but it just seemed so strange that he would be so interested in my work in that way. And to stop what we were doing and ask such a pointed question. I just don't know. But here's the kicker. Because I was a little suspicious – of what, I'm not exactly sure – from Adrian's questions and from some other stuff that's happened lately, I went in to work this morning and reviewed some documents I've had sitting in my office for about a week now."

"What kind of documents?"

"I made a Freedom of Information Act request a few weeks ago seeking documents from the White House regarding renewable energy policy."

"Interesting stuff," Jamie said sarcastically.

"Right! That's usually the response I get. But Adrian seemed so interested in it and it's not even remotely his field. But anyway, I was reviewing these documents this morning and came across a classified document that was, for some reason, included in my request response."

"Now that is interesting. This is getting juicy."

"Right. So this document was a transcript of a meeting between the Vice President's office and some Saudi officials and the Saudi oil company, Aramco. The discussion isn't entirely clear because there's a lot of fluff and convoluted language. But for the life of me, I couldn't avoid getting the strong impression that the VP and the Saudis made a deal where the White House would ensure a strongly oil-friendly energy policy and good Saudi-US relations in return for some kind of help in getting Colt re-elected."

"Wow, that's pretty serious stuff."

"I know. And let me just bore you a bit more real quick." Jamie rolled her eyes at Jill. But Jill continued, feeling like it was necessary that Jamie learn more about this area in order to give Jill her best opinion. "Look. The 2001 National Energy Policy, the document ultimately produced by the Vice President's Office, was widely criticized by environmentalists – including us at Global Green – as continuing business as usual in its prescriptions for America's energy future. The National Energy Policy contained a bit of discussion about renewable energy sources, but the bulk was, unsurprisingly perhaps, committed to continuing the policies of the last century in terms of reliance on coal, oil and nuclear energy."

Jill thought she detected a slight tightening of Jamie's jaw muscles and a suggestion of moisture welling in her eyes. Was Jamie suppressing a yawn? "I'm losing you Jamie. But bear with me please." Jill smiled and Jamie shook her head slightly to sharpen her focus.

"This is where I need the reality check. Could Adrian somehow be interested in my work because of this document? The meeting transcript? I mean, it just seems so egotistical to think that he would be interested in me merely because of my work. Not to mention disappointing. But I have a real hard time believing anyone, government or whatever, would go to such lengths to find out about my possession of some classified document. Am I losing my mind?"

"I don't know, Jill. It does seem pretty far out. And you said you weren't entirely sure what the document really meant, right?"

"Yes, it's sort of ambiguous. But what else could it mean? You don't have the document in front of you, but I'm pretty sure the interpretation I told you is the best one in light of what I know about President Colt's policies and the Saudi-US relationship. But, believe me, I realize it's a big jump to suggest that the VP would cut an explicit deal with the Saudis on this issue. There would be hell to pay for the President if this became widely known, that's for sure."

"Definitely. But can it really be that bad? It was included in your FOIA response after all."

Jill paused. "That's a really good point. I hadn't really thought about how it came to be in my FOIA response."

"Yeah, don't they declassify documents after a while?"

"Yes, they do sometimes, but typically it's done on a set timetable about thirty years later. This document was only two years old."

"Could it be because it wasn't in fact about anything that incriminating and that's why it was declassified?"

"Well, it would normally say 'declassified' in big bold letters if that was the case. And even though I'll admit it's not entirely clear as to what the *quid pro quo* was exactly, I'm very sure that if this document was received by the media, there would be a huge hoopla. But maybe they made a mistake in not putting a 'declassified' stamp on the document or something. I don't know, it's just so weird. I hate drama like this. Why me?"

Jill let the matter rest at this point and turned the conversation back to Jamie and her married life. It felt good to discuss what had been happening to her, but Jill didn't feel like anything had been resolved. She was still as confused as she was before.

BOOK II: DARGAN IN D.C.

Promethean ecstasy strikes like a divine lightning that destroys all the limitations and obstructions and provides entirely unexpected solutions. The individual is flooded by light of supernatural beauty and experiences a state of divine epiphany. He or she has a deep sense of emotional, intellectual and spiritual liberation and gains access to breathtaking realms of cosmic inspiration and insight.

Stanislav Grof, *Beyond the Brain*

Chapter 9

My God, this is painful. No – my Buddha, this is painful. But I really shouldn't be thinking at all. Now I'm thinking about not thinking. And now I'm thinking about thinking about not thinking! Flowing stream, flowing stream, leaf on a flowing stream...

Dargan had joined the Lotus Petal Buddhist sangha approximately three months earlier and – evidently – had not yet become adept at even the simplest meditation practices. But he was patient and would endure considerable discomfort if the goal was worth reaching.

"Okay, open your eyes." The meditation leader's words were truly welcome as Dargan came back fully to the reality of his embodied self and was allowed to remedy the incredible pain in his limbs by stretching out his long legs and relaxing his back's rigid posture. He couldn't believe it had only been one hour.

The meditation leader continued: "I'd like to close with a reading from Tai's latest book, The Heart of the Buddha's Teaching." Tai was devotee shorthand for Thich Nhat Hanh, the Vietnamese Buddhist monk who had written over thirty books and was a spiritual leader for thousands throughout the world. The leader read:

Buddha was not a god. He was a human being like you and me, and he suffered just like we do. If we go to the Buddha with our hearts open, he will look at us, his eyes filled with compassion, and say, "Because there is suffering in your heart, it is possible for you to enter my heart."

The layman Vimalakirti said, "Because the world is sick, I am sick. Because people suffer, I have to suffer. This statement was also made by the Buddha. Please don't think that because you are unhappy, because there is pain in your heart, that you cannot go to the Buddha. It is exactly because there is pain in your heart that communication is possible. Your suffering and my suffering are the basic condition for us to enter the Buddha's heart, and for the Buddha to enter our hearts.

The leader closed the book, smiled at everyone in the room, and announced the end of the session: "Be a buddha in every aspect of your life." Dargan stayed after the other attendees began filtering out. He approached the meditation leader: "Joan, great session today. I really liked your reading selection."

"Thanks, Dargan. How are you doing in the hour-long?"

"Not bad. Still painful as hell, er, heck." Joan smiled. Was she smiling at his perception that he needed to be non-offensive?

"Are you getting from it what you had hoped?"

"Well, here's my plan. I decided a month ago to make a strong effort for a year. If, after a year, I'm not seeing significant benefits, I'll return to my 'in the closet' Buddhist status."

Joan smiled again. "I sincerely hope you find what you're looking for in just a year. But let me add that one year is a very short time considering the eternity of life on the wheel of samsara that may await you."

Dargan wasn't sure he liked the tone of this statement, but he appreciated Joan's point of view. It had a hint of coercion behind it. And no one was about to coerce Dargan into any religious or philosophical practice. "I'll give it my best, definitely." Dargan excused himself and left the meditation center on M Street a few minutes later. He had a dinner engagement with a friend.

* * *

"What the hell? You never told me you were involved in martial arts when you were younger!" Jill exclaimed as she and Dargan were flipping through Dargan's meager photo album.

"Oh, yeah, I did it for a while."

"It must have been quite a while, isn't that a black belt you were wearing?"

"Uh, yes, I guess."

"And what are those little white things at the end of your belt?" She squinted to better examine the blurry picture of Dargan in a karate pose, wearing a white *gi* and a large smile. His feet were wider than shoulder width apart and his hands were held in front of him and away from his sides. If he hadn't been wearing a *gi*, Dargan thought as he looked at the photo again, he would have been indistinguishable from "professional" wrestlers posing for the latest Smackdown.

"Those are *dan* marks. I was a third degree black belt."

"That's pretty bad ass, right? How old were you in this picture?"

"Seventeen. But, you know, I really don't like to talk about that part of my life. It's really old news. It's just kind of boring to me now."

"Well, damn, third degree black belt at seventeen? Isn't that some kind of record?"

"In my tradition, yes, I was the youngest Westerner to achieve that level. But, come on, Jill, I'd really rather not talk about it."

"All right! Sheesh, don't get your knickers in a twist." But Jill wouldn't let it rest, as Dargan suspected she wouldn't. He had forgotten that picture was in his album. Dargan hadn't looked at the album himself in at least five years. When Jill had insisted on looking at it, he hadn't thought to check it first.

That night, as they were lying in bed, with one of Dargan's arms under Jill's head, his other arm under his own, Jill had gently probed: "So what's the big deal about the karate thing? I can tell it's not just that you're being modest." Jill was right, of course, and Dargan again regretted his oversight in not removing that one photo.

Dargan paused for a considerable time, before answering. Jill turned her head and looked at him as he stared at the shadows on the ceiling. "If I tell you, will you promise not to bring it up ever again?"

Sensing the importance of what he was about to tell her, Jill replied: "Of course."

"I dropped karate shortly after that photo was taken. I had been involved in Shotokan karate since I was seven years old. I did very well and found it tremendously satisfying. I actually won a lot of trophies for *kumite* and *kata*."

"Excuse you?" Jill asked.

"*Kumite* is sparring, where you wear protective gear and fight each other, basically. You stop after a point is scored by successfully striking your opponent. It's pretty much a semi-ritualized kind of fighting. *Katas* are kind of like dances in which certain moves are followed, demonstrating the various offensive and defensive moves we were taught. Much more ritualized than *kumite*"

"Sounds cool."

"It was. It was the focus of my life for those ten years. Well, other than school."

"So what happened?"

"I…" He stopped. "I, well, let me back up a bit more. I always had a serious temper growing up. And, obviously, I was attracted to certain forms of violence. I never got in fights, even though I would have destroyed anyone who chose to take me on. I was also very attracted to the weapons of martial artists and used to perform *katas* with *sai*, those dagger-like weapons with metal handles that you've probably seen, and also *kama*, which you may not have seen. *Kama* are like short scythes. You use two and can do some really beautiful moves with them. And I had a whole collection of throwing knives and stars. I guess in some ways I was like many young boys, obsessed with violence or at least the potential of violence. But, like I said, I kept it under wraps and didn't get in fights despite my temper. Until…"

"What happened?"

"I mentioned that I won a lot of trophies for *kumite*. While I was very good at *katas*, I really enjoyed the *kumite* the most because it was the closest to real life combat, which did appeal to me when I was younger. I used to imagine I was a samurai fighting to protect all things good and noble while I was practicing and improving. But… It got a bit too real on one occasion during a tournament. There's a thriving sub-culture in the karate world, which follows the tournament circuit all around the East Coast and sometimes across the country too. I had been matched up in the final round of many tournaments with one kid in particular, who I really came to despise. His name was John Bowles." Dargan paused for a few seconds and Jill thought it better not to interrupt.

Dargan eventually resumed: "He was a couple of years older than me. I beat John in the last five or so matchups we had. But until I was about fifteen, he beat me on many occasions. As I grew taller, stronger, and more skilled, I started changing the record. He didn't like that too much. And he really started to get angry when he realized he couldn't beat me anymore, ever."

"Were you friends?"

"We became friends at one point, at least in terms of being cordial when we saw each other at tournaments. He was always kind of an asshole to me when I was younger, when he would beat me more than he would lose to me. As the record began to change, he started to treat me better. But as the record began to switch clearly to my side, he became an asshole again, but with a new intensity. So shortly after that picture was taken, we were at a tournament in Richmond, Virginia. As had happened in the past four or five previous *kumite* finals, John and I were matched up. My whole team was there – from the *dojo* I'd been with since I was seven. They really got into the rivalry between me and John, partly because John was from another *dojo* in Massachusetts that had this really bad ass reputation. My team would chant 'Dragon! Breathe fire, Dragon!'"

"Hah! Your nickname was Dragon? That's funny I never thought of that. Could definitely have had a worse nickname."

"Yeah, you'll hear one in a second. So in *kumite*, you need to get two full points to win. You can either get a half point or a full point, depending on what type of attack you successfully complete. I ended up creaming John, two points to nothing, which was the first time he'd gotten no points at all against me. He was so upset, it looked like he was about to cry or explode, or both. Once we left the mat, I went to the locker room to shower and change. John found me and told me something like 'you think you're good, Dorkan' – that was his nickname for me."

Jill laughed and said: "You see, I knew it could be worse!"

"Yes, definitely. So John said, 'you think you're good, but you couldn't do a damn thing in a real fight.' I didn't say anything, thinking he was just there to vent a little. But he wouldn't let it go and he challenged me to a 'real fight,' as he put it, that night. I said no at first, but he just wouldn't let it go. He kept on calling me 'Dorkan' and a pussy and other things until I finally agreed, just to make him go away."

"Very big of you," Jill said. Dargan frowned at her in the dim light, reminding her that this was a very serious topic for him. Chastened, Jill shut up as Dargan continued.

"I really didn't want to go, but couldn't see any way out of it. I showed up alone at the place and time he had designated – a side parking lot at a local shopping center. There was no one around, which wasn't surprising because that area of Richmond was pretty sleepy. John had two friends with him. When I walked up, John said to me: 'You made it. Guess you're not a total pussy after all.' I asked what the format was. He responded by delivering a roundhouse kick to my jaw." Jill winced hearing Dargan say this.

Dargan continued: "He knocked me down and seriously shook me up as his friends laughed. They kept on jeering as I got to my feet and waited for John to make another move. He came in with a feinted punch and tried a quick kick to my side. He had seriously pissed me off with his dirty move in the beginning and I just wanted to end it as quickly as possible. So I grabbed his leg, yanked it upward, at the same time as I swept his other leg out from under him, throwing him to his back. I kept a hold of his leg and kicked him in the solar plexus, hard. He avoided the full force of my kick and tried to get away by twisting, but I kicked him again and again until his two buddies jumped me from behind making me drop John's leg. I fought off the other two, but they got in some good hits, slowing me down quite a bit. John had time to get to his feet, at which point I said: 'This is over. Let it go.' 'You're kidding me,' he replied as he wheezed and tried to get his breath back. 'I'm not finished.' 'It's over, John,' I repeated and started backing away, keeping my eye on John and his buddies. They didn't do anything, so after backing away about another twenty feet, I turned to go back to my car. I had hoped John would let it go at that, but he wouldn't. I heard someone coming up fast behind me and I turned around at the same time as I swung my leg in a roundhouse kick, anticipating where the head of whoever was trying to attack me would be. It was John. I didn't realize how strong my kick was, but, my anger and fear combined to make it a lot stronger than it would have been otherwise. I broke John's neck and he died the next day in the hospital."

Silence.

"Oh my God," was the only thing that escaped Jill's mouth. Dargan was drained after telling this story, which he had not told to anyone since the police and his family had inquired about what happened – fifteen years earlier. "Oh my God, what happened after that? Did you go to jail? Isn't that self-defense? That must have been so hard on you!"

"I didn't go to jail. There was a criminal case brought against me, but I was found not guilty because, you're right, it was self-defense. John's friends actually testified truthfully. But, seriously Jill, can we leave it at that? That's why I gave up karate and that's why I don't like to talk about that part of my life. It's just not productive." To Dargan's appreciation, Jill was able to drop it after that, even though he knew she had a million other questions about the incident. Not to mention, he was sure she was a little fearful of the fact that he had killed a man. But Dargan really couldn't bear to talk about it anymore.

Chapter 10

"Brian, good to see you," Dargan said as he shook his boss's hand. "Likewise," Brian replied.

"And great choice of restaurant," Dargan added. "I haven't been here for a while. Too long." After Dargan had told Brian that he'd like to meet Brian for a talk about "serious stuff," Brian had suggested Grill from Ipanema. The Grill was a moderately priced, but high quality, Brazilian restaurant in the Adams Morgan area of D.C.

Dispensing with small talk, Dargan said, as soon as he sat: "Brian, I'm not going to beat around the bush: I've decided to leave the Energy Coalition."

Brian frowned. "I was afraid you were going to say that, Dargan. But please, can't we enjoy a caipirinha and order our food before we discuss such serious things?"

"Of course, my apologies. I just didn't want to keep you waiting, I guess."

"Well, now that I know, let's forget about it for a moment and enjoy some of the best wine D.C. has to offer – for prices even we can afford."

Dargan and Brian discussed everything but work issues for half an hour, until Brian gradually brought the conversation back to the reason Dargan had suggested they have dinner together.

"So what's your plan, Dargan? I'm disappointed, of course, that you don't think you can pursue your goals with us, but understand things change."

"Brian, normally I would not have thought twice about continuing my work at the Energy Coalition. You know I love this organization and everything we do. But recent events have really made me anxious to take a more active role in preventing what happened in Iraq ever happening again."

"What do you mean?" Brian and Dargan were relatively close, which was understandable as they had worked together for almost four years. However, Brian was a rare breed in D.C. in that he preferred not to discuss policy or politics outside of his chosen field. He focused on energy policy from the environmental point of view rather than the foreign policy point of view.

"I think our work is tremendously important and the general trajectory of progress is positive in terms of real achievements. However, with this president in the White House, and the way our nation's political climate has changed since 9/11, I'm getting impatient with our tactics. Education and lobbying policymakers is an honorable way of changing energy policy. But it's slow. I need to see more concrete progress and I think I can make that kind of progress by working for the Department of Energy."

"What? How the hell are you going to see more progress by working for Colt?"

"I wouldn't be working for Colt, of course. I'd be working with a team at the DoE. I've applied for a position as renewable energy program interagency coordinator. I'll be a mid-level staffer, if I get the job, in charge of coordinating renewable energy policy between all the energy agencies."

"That's just fluff! This administration has no serious intentions regarding renewable energy. You know that. How on Earth will that position be more effective than what you're doing with us?"

"Oh, I'm fully aware that what this administration says about renewable energy policy is mostly just rhetoric. I've read the National Energy Policy. But look, by working for the DoE, I can ascertain the real culture inside that, and other, agencies. Kind of a 'know thy enemy' approach. And I hope to find information about the link between energy policy and foreign policy. It's cliché to say that the Iraq war was fought for oil, but I think it may well be true. I may be able to find out for sure if I work for the DoE."

"I don't know, Dargan. I think you might be taking a step backwards. Do you really think that, as a mid-level staffer, you'll have access to high level policy documents? Most of that kind of stuff isn't even written down anyway. Top level planners are too shrewd to leave an obvious paper trail."

"We'll see, but I also know that sometimes we can be more influential working inside the bureaucracy instead of banging our heads on the walls of the bureaucracy."

"Dargan, Dargan. This really upsets me, but it sounds like you've made your decision."

"I have, Brian, and believe me, I don't want to upset you. And I've only just applied. The job's not guaranteed to fall into my lap exactly. But I'm pretty optimistic as I've got a perfect resume for the job. Well, minus my non-profit background, I've got a perfect resume." Dargan and Brian laughed at this reflection of the pro-business orientation of the Colt Administration. "I would also hope that if I do go to work for the DoE and decide it isn't the place for me, that the doors at the Energy Coalition would remain open to me."

"Of course. You're our superstar, you know that. Our doors will always be open to you as long as I'm director."

The two men finished their meal discussing how Dargan could wrap up the various projects he was working on. In talks with various people in the energy industry and from various FOIA requests of his own, Dargan had a strong suspicion that the Colt White House was so in bed with various oil companies that there was a deep and wide groove left by oil company CEOs on President Colt's bed in the Presidential Residence. This issue was directly related to the possible "real" reasons behind the White House's exuberance for the Iraq war, but was also the bigger "back story" that would have to be understood in order to prevent more wars fought for oil. At least this was Dargan's conceit.

* * *

Dargan could practically hear the tears flowing down Jill's cheeks. He could certainly hear the tears in her voice. "So you're not coming back?"

"No," Dargan replied to his cell phone's microphone. "Not right now at least. Jill, I love you so much, but I just can't abandon everything I've been trying so hard to build here in D.C. for the last five years. I thought maybe I could, but I can't, I know now. You know I gave it a shot. A really good shot."

"What do you mean? You were here for all of two weeks!" Dargan had stayed with Jill for almost three weeks after their road trip cross-country from D.C. to L.A. He had helped her settle in to her new apartment and her new job, which she had started a week after arriving in L.A.

"Jill, sweetness. I never told you that I would stay indefinitely in L.A. I told you I'd check it out and see if I could handle it out there.   I gave it a good shot, I think. But my life is really here in D.C. And the idea of trying to build a whole new life in L.A. is … daunting." He realized as he said this that he could have been more tactful.

"What do you mean 'build a whole new life'? What about us? We've been building a life together for the last year and now you want to just give that up so you can stay in fucking D.C.?"

"No, no! I don't want to give up anything we have. I'm not breaking up with you, Jill. I'm just telling you that I can't move to L.A. right now. I might be able to in the future, but not now. I think we can do it. We've got so much in common and, well, it's not that far from L.A. to D.C." Dargan knew how hollow this sounded the moment he said it.

"So you're going to hop on the plane to see me every other week, then? With all that money you make at your job?" Jill's voice oozed with sarcasm. "Or I'm going to be flying back and forth from L.A. to D.C. on Global Green's Lear jet? Goddammit, Dargan, we're going to see each other twice a year if we're lucky."

"Jill, it will be more often than that, come on. Airfare is cheap nowadays, and my schedule is pretty flexible. I can find ways to get out there. It's not like I'm totally broke."

"What was so bad about L.A that you couldn't possibly imagine being here with me?"

"Jill, L.A.'s just not my kind of town. It's the opposite in so many ways of what I'm used to. I'm used to D.C. and Boston. Small cities, you know. But that's not even it. I like Santa Monica, you know that. But it's really about my work here and the projects and contacts I have here."

"Contacts? You're giving up on us for professional contacts? Oh my god."

"I've just got a lot of things going on here that are really important to me. I love my work and I had hoped to find a place in L.A. where I could continue what I was doing. But – and I knew this before going to L.A. with you – what I've been doing in D.C. would be very hard to duplicate in L.A. National energy policy is just not made in L.A."

"So you're ruining what we have because of your work on fucking energy policy?"

"Jill, I wish you wouldn't put it that way."

"How should I put it then? Are you or are you not telling me that you're staying in D.C. and probably ruining any chance of us being together because of work?"

A long pause. "Jill, I love you, but I just can't abandon everything that I have in D.C. Not yet. I've got too much to do."

Jill just sobbed in response. "Jill. You'll see. It'll be okay." No response. "Look, I'll call you soon, okay. I love you." Dargan hung up.

The situation was intolerable for Dargan. He felt like crap for not being completely up front with Jill. But he thought it was better the way he'd decided to let her know. He had told her that he was going back to D.C. to wrap up some loose ends at the Energy Coalition. This statement had in fact been true when he uttered it because he wasn't quite sure at that point whether he was leaving L.A. permanently or if he was just going back to D.C. to finalize his departure. He had been growing increasingly unhappy in L.A. He wasn't used to spending all his time with one person – Jill. And he wasn't used to not having his own space. And he wasn't used to not having a full social and work schedule. Dargan had been searching for work leads for some time in L.A., even before he left D.C. to drive to L.A. No opportunities remotely as good as his position at the Energy Coalition appeared. Jill's job was the best that he had seen, but even a job similar to Jill's would have been a significant step down in terms of responsibility, pay, and potential to effect change.

L.A. and D.C. had one very large similarity: they were both one-industry towns. But just as actors flocked to L.A. to be near Hollywood, policy wonks flocked to D.C. to be near the Capitol and the White House. Another similarity, people joked, is that D.C. is L.A. for ugly people. In Dargan's case, it was true – he wasn't pretty and he had a keen desire to influence policy at the highest levels. And true love, he realized at the time, wasn't that much different than everyday life.

Chapter 11

"Your place at nine?"

"Perfect, see you then." Dargan ended the call on his cell with a warm feeling of anticipation. The rest of Dargan's Friday passed quickly, but not quickly enough. Annabella was anything but uninteresting. Dargan had met Annabella a few months after he came back to D.C. She was easy to be with, low maintenance, smart, and – he hoped – would help him forget about Jill, who had eventually stopped returning his calls.

"Annabella, I'm here," he told the microphone at the entryway to Annabella's brownstone close to the Capitol. Annabella didn't say anything in response, but Dargan heard the door buzz in indication that he could now open the door from the outside. "Darling, so glad you could make it!" was Annabella's greeting as he entered her unlocked apartment door. Annabella was Spanish, with nearly perfect, but accented English. "Hello Annabella." Dargan playfully stressed the third and fourth syllables of her name, pronouncing the two "l"s as a "y," as Annabella preferred. And his emphasis was not mere flattery: Annabella was quite lovely. They had met through friends at a dinner party a few months previously.

"Buenas noches, guapo." Dargan appreciated the compliment but didn't believe she really found him handsome. *A certain animal magnetism, perhaps, but handsome?*

"Buenas noches, mi bella," he replied as he kissed her, pushing her against the hallway wall. She returned his kiss forcefully, placing her hands against the wall above her head. Dargan caressed her sides, sliding his hands up to her full breasts as she moved her hips toward him. He slid his hand over the soft fabric of her blouse, held together at the top by a thick lace. He slid his hands down to her ass and lifted her so that she straddled him. The two-legged beast they had become waddled to the bedroom. Dargan lowered Annabella to her bed. He lay on top of her, pelting her with kisses and running his hands up and down her body on the outside of her clothes.

"Wait. Wait!" Annabella cried. She reached over to her bedside stand's top drawer, opened it, and removed a small mirror. Dargan said nothing as he watched. Annabella removed a small plastic bag of yellowish granules and expertly chopped the granules into a fine powder on the mirror, using a razor blade she also found in the drawer. She formed four thick lines of the crystal meth and offered the mirror to Dargan. Dargan paused. But when Annabella offered it to him a second time, with a casual "come on, sweetie," he took it. He also took the rolled up twenty dollar bill that Annabella handed him a second later. Dargan felt the high coming on even before he sucked in the first line. *I'm Pavlov's dog on crack!* The first line burned his nostril a little, as it always did. He handed the mirror and bill to Annabella with a smile. She took it and, in one long inhalation, took in the second line. They repeated this ritual with the third and fourth lines and replaced the mirror and bill in the drawer. "Goddamn, I'm flying already," Dargan said as his body was consumed with warm waves of pleasure like a low level full-body orgasm.

"Where were we?" Annabella's accent became even more sensual in Dargan's enhanced state. Her lips, as she kissed him again, were pure heaven. She removed his shirt and kissed his chest and belly, sending shivers up and down the length of his torso. She kissed his neck and his lips again, as she unbuckled his belt. Passive no longer, Dargan pushed Annabella to her back and pulled undone the lace holding her top closed. She smiled as her breasts were bared and Dargan caressed their curves with a sure hand. They enjoyed each others' bodies for timeless hours, finally succumbing to the need for release. Great waves of pleasure rolled through Dargan's body as he came inside Annabella. He collapsed on top of her, eyes closed, breathing hard.

"Oh that was good. Really, really good," Annabella said into his ear an inch from her mouth. Dargan responded with a muffled "mmmm."

Annabella quickly became restless and rolled Dargan off of her. Dargan carefully removed his condom as he pulled out of her. "Look away," he joked as he stood, holding the offending item squeamishly in his hand. He flushed the condom down the toilet and returned to the bed where a satisfied-looking Annabella smiled at him and said: "I love how you fuck me." Dargan frowned. He didn't like this aspect of Annabella: her crudity.

Sensing his disapproval, she changed the subject: "So check out what I've been reading lately, my dear Dragon." Annabella stood and retrieved a hardbound book from one of her many bookshelves. It was one of the Great Books published for many years by Encyclopedia Britannica.

"Oh?"

"This is a volume of Aeschylus, the Greek playwright's, plays. I was just reading through his works and came across *Prometheus Bound*. Do you know it?"

"Of course, at a basic level. It's been years and years since I read it though."

"This is some cool shit!" It sounded like *sheet* when she said it. "Listen to this. On 'A bare and desolate crag in the Caucasus, Enter Might and

Violence, demons, servants of Zeus, and Hephaestus, the smith.' Isn't that a great scene setter? Just one line, and we're so in the moment!"

"Keep on going! You going to read the whole thing to me?"

"Just the juicy parts. Shut up and listen. So Hephaestus – as an aside – is the same as Vulcan in Roman mythology. He's the blacksmith god, in charge of fire and said to have been hideously ugly and to walk with a limp. And Prometheus, as you remember, was punished by Zeus for stealing fire to give to Mankind. Might begins the play by saying:

This is the world's limit that we have come to; this is the Scythian country, an untrodden desolation.
Hephaestus, it is you that must heed the commands the Father laid upon you to nail this malefactor to the high craggy rocks in fetters unbreakable of adamantine chain. For it was your flower, the brightness of fire that devises all, that he stole and gave to mortal men; this is the sin for which he must pay the Gods the penalty – that he may learn to endure and like the sovereignty of Zeus and quit his man-loving disposition.

"So just in case you missed it, Prometheus stole Hephaestus' 'flower' and Prometheus had a 'man-loving disposition.'" Annabella laughed uproariously at her own wit. Dargan laughed along with her, but said: "You're joking right? You know that's not what it means?"

"Of course, silly, I just think it is funny in light of the fact that the early Greeks were known for their homosexuality. I have another version of this play, and they translate the Greek phrase as 'philanthropist' instead of 'man-loving disposition.' I think the Great Books guys were a little awkward with that one. But my point – and yes I did have a point! – is that you've got to read this play. I think it says a lot about you. Prometheus is a lover of humankind and sacrifices much to give fire to humans, inviting the wrath of Zeus, the king of the Gods. Prometheus also gave much else to humans. Listen to this – Prometheus was one bad motherfucker!" Dargan loved listening to Annabella cuss in English. It always made him laugh as she over-pronounced the words.

Annabella continued reading: "So check this part out:

But hear what troubles there were among men, how I found them witless and gave them the use of their wits and made them masters of their minds. I will tell you this, not because I would blame men, but to explain the goodwill of my gift. For men at first had eyes but saw to no purpose; they had ears but did not hear. Like the shapes of dreams they dragged through their long lives and handled all things in bewilderment and confusion. They did not know of building houses with bricks to face the sun; they did not know how to work in wood. They lived like swarming ants in holes in the ground, in the sunless caves of the earth. For them there was no secure token by which to tell winter nor the flowering spring nor the summer with its crops; all their doings were indeed without intelligent calculation until I showed them the rising of the stars, and the settings, hard to observe. And further I discovered to them numbering, pre-eminent among subtle devices, and the combining of letters as a means of remembering all things, the Muses' mother, skilled in craft. It was I who first yoked beasts for them in the yokes and made of those beasts the slaves of trace chain and pack saddle that they might be man's substitute in the hardest tasks; and I harnessed to the carriage, so that they loved the rein, horses, the crowning pride of the rich man's luxury. It was I and none other who discovered ships, the sail-driven wagons that the sea buffets. Such were the contrivances that I discovered for men – alas for me! For I myself am without contrivance to rid myself of my present affliction.

"And he goes on – this guy, god, whatever, claims to have given practically all knowledge to humans. But fire was the first and most important gift because fire was the starting point for ceramics, defense, warmth, cooking, light. Without fire, man was nothing. Prometheus was humankind's great benefactor. Before Prometheus, humans lived in holes in the ground and didn't know a damn thing about the world. You're a bit like Prometheus aren't you Dragon? You're a 'man-lover' aren't you? Your whole life is about man-loving, right?"

"Yes, I am a 'man-lover'! But I'm also a woman lover, in case you aren't convinced yet." Dargan raised and lowered his eyebrows repeatedly in a mockingly playful way. "And I don't know if I like the idea of you comparing me to a Greek Titan. I mean, that's a little arrogant."

"It's all in good fun, darling. But there are many similarities. Prometheus translated literally means "forethought." From what you've told me of your work and ideas, you seem to me to be quite a visionary. What is visionary thinking if not forethought? And Prometheus was known for his cleverness. In other parts of the Prometheus mythology, he tricks Zeus into accepting the inedible parts of animal sacrifices, leaving the good meat for humans. You're pretty wily – don't think I don't know how you get your way. You're very subtle and tricky sometimes, my dear. And Prometheus was arrogant. Here's one more line from the play … if I can find it … yes, here it is: *This is what you pay Prometheus, for that tongue of yours which talked so high and haughty: you are not yet humble, still you do not yield to your misfortunes, and you wish, indeed, to add some more to them… Since your mind is so subtle, don't you know that a vain tongue is subject to correction?*

Despite your claims to modesty, if that isn't you, I don't know what is!"

"Well, thanks for nothing! I don't know whether to be flattered or offended now. But you know what I like to read aloud with friends? Shakespeare's comedies! Come on, you'll love it. We can see who has the worst British accent."

Dargan was vain. He would never admit this to Annabella – or anyone – but he was a bit like Prometheus, in his intentions at least. *Forethought. Prometheus. Energy. Fire.* It kind of made sense. He suspected all do-gooder types had innate megalomaniacal tendencies. There was a fundamental connection between the desire to live for others and the tendency to think of oneself as a savior. And who was the prototypical savior figure if not Prometheus? One could pick a worse role model. As the warm glow of methamphetamine fire coursed through his veins, the idea had a certain seductiveness to it.

Annabella and Dargan talked throughout the night, fueled by their crystal-charged brains and the pleasure of each other's company. Conversation eventually flagged in the early hours of the morning. Dargan left the as the sun was rising – without sleeping a wink. He borrowed Annabella's copy of *Prometheus Bound.*

Chapter 12

Dargan looked up at the façade of the Department of Energy building on Independence Avenue. It was a relatively new building, reflecting the fact that the DoE was a relatively new agency. Jimmy Carter created the DoE in 1977 in response to the oil crisis of 1973. It had survived numerous attempts by Republicans in Congress to eliminate it. Those advocating its abolition claimed that it was a needless bureaucracy, performing duties that could just as well be performed by independent agencies, other departments, or not at all. Much the same arguments had been made for abolishing the Department of Education. All such arguments had been beaten back.

The DoE building's façade was boring utilitarian D.C.: all concrete and windows, but with a twist in this case. The twist is that the Forrestal Building, which houses the DoE most visibly, floats on 35-foot high columns. The architecture had the desired effect on Dargan as he entered the building, despite his many trips there during the last few years: its scale and importance in national and world affairs humbled him a little. This visit was different because he was there to become part of the DoE, in name if not in spirit. As he entered, he felt the ponderousness and power (literally, in this case) of the federal government as it was wielded by the DoE. The impression of *gravitas*, age, and wisdom was reinforced by the artwork and statuary in the lobby. How could one person change this institution?

Dargan signed in and took the elevator to the fourth floor. "Hi. Dargan Brennan to see Mr. Smith, please," Dargan told the receptionist. Shortly after, a portly African-American man appeared and led Dargan to a small conference room. "Dargan, it's good to see you again. It's been some time now."

"Yes, good to see you again, Mr. Smith." Dargan had met Caleb Smith a couple of years earlier, during the course of his work as gadfly to the DoE. Dargan hoped that he had come across in a professional manner during their earlier interactions, even though their philosophies concerning good energy policy were quite different. Dargan assumed the fact that he was there for an interview indicated that he had been sufficiently professional.

"Caleb, please! Caleb. Just because you're interviewing with us now doesn't mean you have to be obsequious." Smith laughed.

Dargan smiled uncomfortably. "Good to see you again, *Caleb*." Smith was an assistant Undersecretary of Energy, which placed him two levels down from the top of the DoE hierarchy. Smith was a jovial man with a quick mind and quick wit. Dargan's dealings with Smith had always been pleasant. But Dargan wasn't sure that he had had much effect on the man whenever he had attempted to influence his decisions. Dargan was interviewing to become one of Smith's staff. In government terms, Dargan was seeking to obtain a GS – Government Service – 13 position. The GS system went up to GS-15 with many grades within each GS rating.

"Likewise, Dargan, likewise. Let's wait a moment or two until Sharon can join us."

They chatted about inconsequentials for a minute or two, at which point a woman entered the room and introduced herself as Sharon Carnie. Carnie was approximately the same government grade as Dargan would become if he were given the job he was seeking. Carnie was relatively new and Dargan had not met her before. She was a slight woman, a few inches shorter than Dargan – tall for a woman. She did not smile when Dargan shook her hand, which he chalked up to a sour disposition, or an eagerness to appear completely professional.

Smith began: "All right, let's get started then. Unless you need some coffee or water first, Dargan?"

"I'm fine, thanks."

"Okay then. Let's get to the meat here. You know we're looking for a renewable energy interagency coordinator. Your background is of course quite well-suited to this position and your resume is quite impressive. Why don't you go ahead and tell us a bit about what you've been doing, though, and why you want to join the dark side." Smith laughed again at his own joke. Dargan obliged with what he hoped was a convincing chuckle.

"Well, I first became interested in energy issues a long time ago when I studied natural resources policy at Cornell. That was my undergraduate area of focus and I piggybacked on that effort to continue my studies at Harvard. My Ph.D work at Harvard focused on wind energy policy in Europe. I analyzed the policies put in place by governments in Germany, Spain, and Denmark regarding wind policy. I tried to ascertain what about those policies worked and what could have been improved."

"Were those policies successful?," Smith asked.

"For the most part, they have been. Denmark obtains a substantial amount of their electricity from wind power – fully twenty percent, last I checked. They have a great wind resource off their coasts, with shallow channels and good steady winds to catch. Germany has a bigger installed amount of wind power at fifteen thousand megawatts – enough for about ten million German homes – but they obtain a lesser portion than

Denmark of their overall electricity from wind power. And Spain is similar to Germany, when considered in relation to its size. Though I didn't study the United Kingdom, they are in fact swiftly catching up and Tony Blair, to his credit, has strongly advocated renewable power, particularly offshore wind."

"So these are government-driven efforts?," Carnie asked.

"Well, it's private enterprise in all three countries, for the most part, that is taking advantage of favorable government policies to build wind projects. All three nations have made it a top priority to reduce their fossil fuel usage and make the transition to renewables."

"Well, they are European after all," Carnie responded. "Socialists, for the most part," Carnie added, for Smith's benefit. Dargan bit his tongue. He wasn't about to get into a debate about fossil fuel subsidies in Europe or in the US. If Carnie knew the degree to which all Western governments subsidized fossil fuels, she might revise her opinion of the "socialist" nature of Europe's support for renewable energy.

Smith continued: "Well, that's good stuff, Dargan. But what I'm really curious about is why you've decided to join us?"

"I've seen some strong signs that this administration is serious about renewables,"

Dargan lied. "The fact that this position is open is good evidence in itself. I've spent almost five years in the non-profit sector now and I'd like to try my hand in the governmental sector and see how much influence I can exert in shaping renewable energy policy. I understand this position is largely a coordinating job, but there will of course be many opportunities to help shape the debate along the way."

"Of course. And I've seen you in action at the Energy Coalition. Though I can't say I've always agreed with your positions, I do respect your organization's professionalism. Yours has been a valuable voice." Dargan wasn't sure if this was just diplomatic tact, but it was nice to hear nonetheless.

"Thank you very much, seriously. I'm glad you hold such a good opinion of the Energy Coalition."

"And on that note, I need to ask you if you could, if you were to work with us, subordinate your personal views when necessary. We're a team, as you know, and our department - and our government more generally – is going to make decisions you may not necessarily agree with."

"I understand. Obviously, you know where I'm coming from on energy issues. But I have to say I'm not a dogmatic person and I'm certainly a team player. I'm open to new ideas and I'm open to compromise in order to achieve long-term goals." What Dargan didn't say was that the "compromise" he was referring to was his own compromise at seeking to work for the DoE.

Carnie spoke up again: "I'm still not clear on why you would decide to leave the Energy Coalition and come here. Weren't you promoting enlightened energy policy enough there?" It was subtle, but Dargan was quite sure Carnie had spoken "enlightened" with a hint of sarcasm. Smith hadn't seemed to notice. Or if he had, he chose to ignore it.

"Well, I'm not exactly getting rich at the Coalition, you know. And I'm not getting younger. I'd like to have a family someday." Dargan was lying again. He didn't give a shit about money, but he knew that bringing up financial concerns would appear to be a convincing motivation to his interviewers.

"We know what you mean, Dargan. It can be difficult to make ends meet being the good guy all the time," Smith laughed again.

Dargan chose to show his initiative by asking a number of questions about his expected duties if he were hired. It was always good for interviewers to visualize the applicant actually performing the available job, Dargan had learned from his research prior to the interview. Once Dargan's questions had been exhausted, Smith and

Carnie wrapped up the interview with further questions concerning his time frame for beginning work and other logistical details. This seemed to be a good sign, which was borne out when Dargan received a congratulatory call two weeks later from Smith, notifying him that the job was his should he want it. "No more interviews?"

"No. We're satisfied you're the best candidate for the job, Dargan."

* * *

"Jill, what about you moving back to D.C.?" It was about two months after Dargan's return to D.C.

"Dargan, we've talked about this. You know I can't leave my family."

"But you wouldn't be leaving them. You'd be a relatively short plane ride away from them."

"I can't afford to fly back and forth all the time. Anyway, I love my job here. And…"

"And what?"

"Nothing. I don't know."

I don't know either, sweetie. We're in a shitty situation. I don't know what to do."

"It is shitty." Awkward silence.

"At least think about it then," Dargan added finally.

"I will."

"All right then."

"Okay."

Another awkward silence.

"I guess I'll talk to you soon then," Dargan said.

"Definitely."

"Ok, bye then."

"Bye."

They had a few stilted conversations after this episode. But the spell was broken. Dargan called a few more times, but Jill didn't call him back.

BOOK III: JILL TAKEN IN
Thus-Gone to Thus-Gone,
I with a Buddha's hand
Offer the unplucked flower,
the frog's soliloquy
Among the lotus leaves,
the milk-smeared mouth
At my full breast and love and,
like the cloudless
Sky that makes possible mountain
and setting moon,
This emptiness that is the womb of love
This poetry of silence.

Aldous Huxley, *Island*

Chapter 13

Damn, I left my running shoes at work. Jill had left Q's just after 8 PM. Conversation with Jamie was getting stale and she had some errands to do at home that night. She wanted to go for a run the next morning because she had skipped her usual Sunday workout to meet Jamie. Unable to find street parking – *typical!* – Jill parked in one of the many parking structures built and maintained by the City of Santa Monica to attract business to the Third Street Promenade. Jill generally avoided these parking structures, finding the frequent smell of urine in the stairwells just a little unattractive. She held her breath and walked briskly to her office just off the Promenade.

Global Green's building was, like most new commercial structures, equipped with an electronic security system. Out of habit, Jill began entering her pass code into the keypad after entering the building through the front door. But after hitting the first two numbers in her five-digit passkey, she noticed that the alarm was not armed. This was not in itself highly unusual. People did occasionally forget to arm the system as they left. Or perhaps someone was working, even though it was past eight on a Sunday evening.

Jill walked warily upstairs to her office. As she entered her office, she noticed immediately that something had changed since she was there earlier that day. In fact, many things had changed, she noticed, as she felt a cold wet sensation envelop her face. Inhaling strongly in alarm, Jill quickly lost consciousness and slumped into the arms of the man who had been standing behind the office door.

* * *

A dull throbbing behind her eyes greeted Jill as she awoke. Slowly opening her eyes in the brightly lit room, Jill's alarm abruptly returned as she realized she was not in her bedroom. The memory of being in her office – and apparently blacking out – returned. She must have been kidnapped. *What's that stuff called? Chloroform? This isn't actually happening to me!?* This was just too strange, too melodramatic to actually happen to someone like Jill. Jill looked around the small room, her stomach churning with anxiety and her head feeling like she'd drank three bottles of tequila the night before. She lay on a single bed against the wall on one side of the room. She looked down at herself. She was wearing a light blue jumpsuit – and apparently nothing else underneath, she discovered as she peered down the front of her suit. There was a pair of plastic slippers on the floor next to the bed.

There were no windows. It was silent except for a low hum, perhaps of electrical lines. A single light hung from the middle of the ceiling. The door was in the middle of the approximately eight by ten foot room. There was no window or peephole in the door. Jill tried to twist the doorknob to open the door, but, as she had feared, the knob did not move. In frustration, she banged on the door and yelled: "Hey! Is anyone out there? What the hell is going on?" No response. There was a steel commode on the left side of the room, with a roll of toilet paper on the floor next to it. There was no flip-up toilet seat. Instead, the toilet seat was fashioned out of stainless steel and was an integral part of the commode. There was nothing in the room other than the single bed and the commode.

"This is ridiculous," Jill muttered to herself. She sat on the bed and tried to clear her mind and assess what had happened to her. Her head still throbbed and she couldn't even begin to figure out who had kidnapped her and imprisoned her in this cell. "This must have something to do with those documents," she again spoke to herself. "This is crazy. I didn't do anything other than make a damn FOIA request!" Confusion started to give in to anger and grief. She felt tears welling, but suppressed them. Crying would most definitely not help the situation.

"Ok, what do I know? I made a FOIA request about renewable energy. Pretty damn innocent. I received some documents in response. One of these documents appears to be potentially very incriminating for the White House. This document isn't even directly responsive to my FOIA request, but somehow it made it in to my documents. Couldn't they just have asked for it back? Or am I way off? Is this totally unrelated?"

Finding this exercise not particularly fruitful, Jill lay back on the bed, massaging her throbbing temples. Shortly after – though how long after Jill had no way of telling – a knock came on the door. Before Jill could even decide whether she should invite the knocker to come in – was there a rule of etiquette for answering doors after one had been kidnapped? – the door opened. Jill gasped as Adrian walked through the door.

He smiled and said: "Hi Jill. I hope you're feeling all right."

Jill stood immediately and shrank against the back wall of her cell. "You motherfucker! What's going on here? Why am I locked up? Why did you knock me out, you creep."

"Whoa, slow down. One question at a time."

"Well, why don't you begin by telling me who the hell you really are? For some reason, I have a feeling kidnapping women isn't what your law firm pays you for."

Adrian smiled a humorless smile at this comment. "First, we haven't kidnapped you. We have a warrant for your detention. Second, I am in fact a lawyer. That's my day job. I also have a night job working for the United States Government. I can't tell you who I'm with, but suffice it to say, what we're doing here has been sanctioned by people at very high levels."

"What do you want with me? I didn't do anything!"

"We haven't accused you of doing anything, Jill. But we are concerned about what you might have learned. You received certain documents from the Department of Energy in response to a FOIA request. We're concerned about the contents of some of those documents you received."

"That's what I thought, but I can assure you I didn't…"

Adrian cut her off: "Jill, we shouldn't discuss this anymore right now. I just wanted to make sure you were all right and to let you know why you're here. We'll come back for you in a little while to question you under polygraph. We need to know you're telling the truth."

"Glad to see you're such a humanitarian. Asshole!"

"Jill, please don't be angry with me. I really did like you. That wasn't an act, believe me. But I have a job to do. And I've done it. I do what I do for the good of the nation." Without giving Jill a chance to respond further, Adrian left, closing the door curtly behind him.

Adrian's involvement was strangely satisfying. It showed, at least, that Jill's intuition was correct about him. She certainly hadn't intuited that he was some kind of secret agent, but she intuited that he was probably shady in some fashion. Also, having a familiar face involved with this wacky affair was perversely comforting. At least he was a real person. And, despite his excellent deception in taking her out for dinner and expressing a romantic interest in her, she felt she knew a fair amount about him. Then she realized that everything he had told her may have been a lie. He had said he really was a lawyer, but maybe that was a lie. Was his name even Adrian? It didn't matter, she realized. Whatever the truth of the situation, she was incarcerated against her will and could do nothing except wait and see what developed.

She didn't have to wait long as she heard a knock again on the door.

Adrian reappeared and, smiling again, he said: "Jill, can you follow me?" Feeling that cooperation was probably the best course of action, Jill nodded. Adrian added: "I hate to do this, but I've got to put the soft cuffs on you, Jill."

"Are you kidding me, what am I going to do, attack you with my bare hands? Aren't you secret agents trained in self-defense?"

Jill's sarcasm was not appreciated: "I don't make the rules, Jill. But I can tell you this. If you cooperate fully, you'll be able to get out of here quickly. The more you resist, the longer you'll be here." Jill gave in and allowed Adrian to place the plastic cuffs around her wrists behind her back. She heard the whir of the plastic teeth clicking quickly through the clasp of the plastic cuffs and her stomach clenched again as nausea welled through her.

Chapter 14

Adrian led Jill down the antiseptic and windowless hallway. There were no other people present. Jill couldn't hear any voices or any other signs that humans actually inhabited the building they were in. They walked in silence. Jill could see that she would obtain no further information from Adrian at this point. Adrian, walking one step behind Jill, looked ahead, stoic duty written all over his face.

"Stop," Adrian said after they had traveled about two hundred feet. He pulled a plastic card out of his shirt pocket and swiped it through a small card reader next to the door handle. The door emitted a small beep and Adrian opened the door. He held the door as Jill, at Adrian's urging, passed through.

The room was approximately fifteen by twenty feet. Again, there were no windows. An innocuous-looking white man with spectacles and a beard was seated at a table in the middle of the room. The man looked up as Jill entered, but did not smile or evince any other sign that he acknowledged Jill's presence. "Jill, this is Mr. Fortney." Upon Adrian's introduction, Mr. Fortney directed a thin-lipped smile at Jill. Out of habit, Jill nodded and said: "Nice to meet you." Then she kicked herself internally for being so damn polite. Adrian pulled out a chair across from Mr. Fortney and, with a hand gesture, urged Jill to sit. Jill sat.

"Jill, Mr. Fortney is a polygraph technician. His only role here today is to ask you a number of questions. He will monitor your answers on the polygraph machine in order to determine if you are telling the truth. We hope you will tell the truth."

"Adrian – whatever your real name is – why don't you start by telling me why I am here? I've broken no laws that I am aware of. And last I checked, this country was one in which Americans could not just be scooped up and kidnapped for no good reason."

"Again, Jill, we have been authorized to detain you and question you. The Patriot Act has, wisely, given the US Government broader powers to protect our security."

"What? I'm not a terrorist, for crying out loud! What the hell have I done?"

"We're not accusing you of terrorism. We're not accusing you of anything. You're here, Jill, because we are concerned about certain documents that came into your possession recently. We need to ask you some questions about those documents."

"This is crazy. I didn't do anything but make a FOIA request."

"Well, that's what we're here to find out. Again, let me remind you that the more you cooperate and answer our questions truthfully and fully, the quicker you'll get out of here. And no more outbursts, please." Jill fumed silently as Adrian went on. "Mr. Fortney is going to hook you up to the polygraph and then ask you a number of what may seem like silly questions in order to calibrate the polygraph. Be patient with this part of the process. It sometimes takes a little while. Mr. Fortney, please begin."

Still without speaking, the technician attached a metal cap to Jill's index finger, a band about her chest, and a heart rate monitor to her chest. He explained each of these devices as he applied them: the finger cap was to measure moisture on her fingertip, which allowed the technician to measure how much Jill was sweating. The band around Jill's chest would measure her breathing rate. And the heart rate monitor measured the speed of Jill's heart beat. These three measurements would allow the technician to judge when Jill was "not being truthful," as Fortney put it.

Adrian stood against the wall ten feet away as Jill underwent this process. Arms folded across his chest, he watched expressionless as Jill cooperated with the technician.

Mr. Fortney sat back down across from Jill. "Okay, first question, Ms. Boyd: what is your full name?"

"Jill Wu Li Boyd." Jill heard the scratching of the polygraph as it inscribed her vital signs on the paper rolling through the machine.

"What is your date of birth?"

"February second nineteen seventy-nine." The technician looked up at Jill's response. "Groundhog Day," Jill added with a twitch of her mouth resembling a smile.

Still evincing no emotion, Mr. Fortney continued asking Jill innocuous questions until he was satisfied he had a good read on her base state. "By calibrating the machine to your current state, I can tell how your body will react if you state anything untruthful." Jill noted the fact that neither Adrian nor Mr. Fortney had yet used the word "lie" in their sentences. She assumed this was because an accusation or even intimation that someone had lied or would possibly lie was generally received badly. "We're now ready to begin the questioning," Mr. Fortney continued. "Please answer my questions only with a 'yes' or 'no' answer. First, some general questions. Are you a communist?"

Jill almost laughed, despite the seriousness of the situation. "Uh, no," she replied.

"Are you a member of Al Qaeda?"

Jill couldn't help herself: "Are you kidding me? No, of course I'm not a member of Al Qaeda."

"Please just answer the questions with a yes or no answer, Ms. Boyd."

"Okay, but are you guys serious, here?"

Adrian broke in: "Jill, this is very serious. And you'd best follow Mr. Fortney's instructions precisely. It's in your own interest that you do so. These are routine questions we have to ask of all detainees." *Maybe you should update them!*, Jill thought to herself.

Mr. Fortney continued: "Are you affiliated with any terrorist group hostile to the United States of America?"

"No."

Fortney paused for a long moment. He resumed just as Jill was about to start asking more questions of her own: "Did you, on or about, March 1, 2004, submit a Freedom of Information Act request to the Department of Energy?"

Jill thought for a second: "Yes."

"Did you receive, on or about, March 14, 2004, documents from the Department of Energy in response to your FOIA request?"

"Yes."

"Have you read these documents?"

"Yes. No. Well, I've read most of them."

Mr. Fortney paused, stood, and walked to where Adrian was standing against the wall. He whispered something to Adrian that Jill couldn't hear. Adrian said to Jill: "We'll be right back." The two men left Jill alone in the oppressively quiet room, the only sound the slight whir of paper moving through the polygraph. A few minutes later, the door opened and Adrian and Mr. Fortney reentered. Mr. Fortney resumed questioning: "Ms. Boyd, have you talked to anyone about the documents you received?"

Jill paused a moment, then said: "Yes."

"Please identify all persons with whom you have discussed the documents you received."

"That's not a yes…"

Fortney cut Jill off: "Please just answer the question, Ms. Boyd."

"I've only discussed the documents with one person, Jamie Herrera, a friend of mine."

"You've discussed the documents with only one person, a Jamie Herrera?"

"Yes."

"Is Jamie Herrera male?"

"No."

"Did you discuss the documents with Jamie Herrera in an oral capacity."

"If you mean did we talk about them, yes."

"Did you discuss the documents in detail?"

"Yes."

"Is it normal that you would discuss your work in detail with Ms. Herrera?"

"No."

"Have you discussed the documents with anyone in a non-oral capacity?"

"I'm not sure what you mean."

"You could have discussed the documents with someone through a face to face conversation, through email, through text messages, over the phone, through letters. Did you discuss the documents with anyone in a non-oral capacity?"

"No."

"Did you send any of the original documents to any other party?"

"No."

"Did you send any copies of the documents to any party?"

"No."

"Did you make any copies of the documents?"

"No. Wait, yes, I did. I sent a copy of some of the electronic documents to myself in an email."

"You made an electronic copy of some of the documents by sending an attached file or files to yourself via email?"

"Yes."

"Did you make any other copies, either electronically or traditionally?"

"No."

"Did you make any notes about the documents you received?"

"No."

"Did you in any other fashion transcribe or transfer information from the documents you received?"

"No." Mr. Fortney stood again and he and Adrian left the room a second time. They returned shortly. Adrian, to Jill's relief, said: "That's all we have for now, Jill. Mr. Fortney is going to analyze your answers with the polygraph record and get back to me. We can go now."

"Great, the sooner I get out of here the better." Jill felt enormous relief as Mr. Fortney removed the various items attached to her body. She felt good about the outcome of the "test" she had just been given. She had been entirely truthful, so hoped that the polygraph machine agreed!

Adrian led Jill back to the room in which she had awoken. "This shouldn't take too long, Jill. And if you did in fact answer truthfully, we may able to release you very soon."

"Great," Jill muttered as Adrian disappeared again behind the closing door. "Wait!," Jill cried out as she realized that Adrian had forgotten to take the soft cuffs off her. "Oh, this is just great," Jill said as she sat on the side of the bed, her hands still locked behind her. Adrian did not reappear. "Shit shit shit. This sucks!" Jill sat for some time on the side of the bed, pondering what to do. The cuffs were too tight to allow her to slide them off. There were no sharp objects in the room that she could use to saw through the plastic. Eventually, Jill resigned herself to awaiting Adrian's return. She slumped down on the bed, on her side, positioning her hands and arms as comfortably as she could behind her. It was tolerable – barely. Tears slowly formed as Jill gave in to her sadness and frustration. She quietly wept as she drifted into sleep.

Chapter 15

"Jill, wake up. Jill, it's Adrian." Jill raised her head and saw Adrian, in the same clothing, looking down at her with a concerned expression. She swung her legs to the ground and attempted to sit up. Without the help of her hands, she began to fall back, but Adrian caught her and helped her to an upright sitting position. As Jill blinked the sleep and dried tears out of her eyes, she said: "Take these damn cuffs off me! I can't believe you left them on."

"I'm really sorry about that Jill." Adrian pulled a small pair of plier snips out of his pocket and cut the plastic cuffs. Jill sighed in relief and stretched out her aching shoulders and arms.

"Did you have to leave them on, damn it?"

"That was my mistake, Jill. Again, I'm very sorry. But, listen, good news. You passed the polygraph with flying colors. We can let you go immediately – as long as you agree to certain conditions."

Jill smiled at hearing this news and said: "That is great! What are your conditions? I'm sure there's no problem with them."

"Let's hope so. First, I want to tell you a bit about why we detained you."

"That would be nice…"

"Yes, I'm sure it would. Jill, we detained you because you came into the possession of some documents of the highest sensitivity. My job, and the job of my agency is to ensure the energy security of our great nation. I was assigned to get close to you in order to determine whether you were hostile to the interests of our national energy security. And to determine what you had gleaned from the documents you received. We knew you had received certain sensitive documents – through a process that I am not at liberty to discuss. These documents, and the information in them, could not be released to the public. Once I determined, through our contact, that you were not hostile to our national interests, I arranged to have the documents you received retrieved. We also had to know who you'd talked to, what you'd talked about, and if you had otherwise disseminated the information in the documents in any way. It is of the utmost importance that you not reveal any of the information you learned. Only if you agree to this condition can we let you go."

"Whoa whoa whoa. This is all too much. Like I said, all I did was make a FOIA request. I got some documents from the DOE in response to my FOIA request and I read some of those documents. The only document I read that seemed very incriminating was a transcript of a meeting between some Saudis and the Vice President's office." Adrian's face betrayed a look of increased interest as she spoke these words. "That one document was very… revealing, shall we say. And I'm guessing that was what got me into this mess." Jill waited for a response from Adrian.

He finally said: "I can't confirm or deny that, Jill."

"Well, look. All I was trying to do was figure out how the DOE creates renewable energy policy. That's it. I'm not even sure why that document was included in the response. But I can tell you this: I'm not some conspiracy theorist out to get the White House. I'm not some kind of radical. I don't particularly like this president, but I think he's done some good things. He certainly could do better on the energy front. But my point is, I'm just an innocent bystander here. I have no problem forgetting about the transcript entirely. I just want to get out of here! This is *way* over my head."

"I understand, Jill. I can say this. You are right that the transcript was of concern to my agency. We will require that you not mention that document to anyone, ever. If we find out after you leave today that you have discussed this document with anyone else, we will be forced to detain you again. And I can't stress to you how important this is to us." Jill did not like the sound of this at all.

"Understood. I won't discuss the transcript with anyone else, ever." She pondered for a moment, then added: "But my work requires me to discuss energy policy. That's my job, for the most part. Are you saying I can't discuss or use any of the documents I received?"

"We understand your job, Jill. What I am saying is that you need to forget you ever received the documents you received. All of them. You can go about your life and your job in the same way in every other fashion. Just forget you ever got these documents. You won't find any record of them in your office – or in your email. We've taken care of that." Adrian paused for a second, letting his words sink in. "Are we clear?"

"We're clear."

"Once again, I have to stress to you how important this is."

"Understood! Can I get out of here now?"

Adrian left at that point, but returned shortly after with Jill's clothes and the personal items she had on her when she was chloroformed. He stepped outside to allow her to dress herself in her street clothes. Her small purse was part of the package Adrian had brought to her, containing her wallet, her keys, some makeup and various other personal items. Her cell phone was not in the purse. When Adrian reentered the room, Jill asked: "Where's my cell phone?"

"You'll get that when I drop you off." He led Jill down the long hallway to an elevator. Before entering the elevator, Adrian said: "Jill, there's one more inconvenience you'll have to suffer before you leave." Jill groaned. "I've got to put this blindfold on you. As you can imagine, we don't like to reveal the details of our facilities or their location needlessly. You'll have to wear this until we get you back to your car." He held up what looked like a masquerade mask with no eyeholes. Jill allowed Adrian to place the mask on her, wishing only one thing: to end this ordeal. They continued in silence, with Jill concentrating on walking without her own eyes to guide her. Adrian's grip on her elbow, as he guided her, was firm but not forceful.

After what seemed like at least an hour of walking and driving, Adrian finally spoke again: "Okay, Jill, we're here." Jill opened her eyes as Adrian removed the mask. Squinting at the bright light, Jill looked around and recognized Fourth Street in Santa Monica. She was directly outside the parking structure she had parked her car in before going to work to get her running shoes. Adrian handed Jill her cell phone. He said, seemingly sincerely: "Jill, I really am very sorry for this whole ordeal. But I hope you understand it was necessary and that neither I, or my agency, intended you any harm. Good luck with everything. I'm sure I don't need to tell you that you also need to refrain from mentioning your detention to anyone."

"Right," was all Jill felt was necessary as a response. Jill exited the car as Adrian flashed her a small smile. Jill scowled back at him as he drove away. Examining her surroundings in more detail, Jill could tell it was morning, but had no idea what time it was or even what day it was. It was amazing how quickly she had lost track of time while confined in a white cell with no time-tracking devices. As she walked up the pungent stairwell in the parking structure, she turned her cell phone on. She didn't wear a watch, letting her cell phone double as a watch. As her cell phone booted up, the phone chimed, indicating she had a new message. She checked the display to see what time it was. It was eight in the morning. *Well damn! It's time for work.* Just to double check, Jill also checked the day. It was Monday. But Jill was in no mood for work, so she located her car and returned home. She called in sick, claiming a bad cold was slowing her down severely. At home, she turned off her phone's ringer as she fought a strong impulse to talk to someone, anyone, about what had happened to her. Her second impulse – which won the day – was to catch up on some much-needed sleep.

* * *

Jill awoke a few hours later, her stomach rumbling with hunger. Her head finally felt normal and her body was well rested. Remembering that she had received a message, she checked her voicemail. The mechanical voice informed her: "You have three new messages and four saved messages."

The first message was from her mother. "Jill, honey, how are you? I just wanted to call you and let you know that I talked to that hideous uncle of yours, Jonas. He wanted your address so he could send you some information he said you had talked about. I know you don't like him very much, but I thought you wouldn't mind if I gave him your address. Also, I'll be in Santa Monica tomorrow, so please let me know if you can meet me for lunch or coffee. Bye now." *Great! What the hell does Jonas want now? I wish she'd asked me before giving out my address.*

The second message was – lo and behold – from Jonas. "Hi Jill, I have something very important to talk to you about. Let me know if you can meet me somewhere in Santa Monica – soon!" *This is not good!* After her recent ordeal, Jill could only suspect the worst from Jonas. She suspected he was somehow involved in the ordeal with Adrian, though Adrian had never mentioned anyone else. But, she hadn't asked either. Jonas' strange new interest in her work could have been merely coincidence, but, in light of recent events, she was growing more paranoid. And she didn't like the tone in Jonas' voice either.

The third message was from Joe, asking Jill if she had lunch plans.

As she hung up from her voicemail service, her phone rang. She recognized Jonas' number. She hit the button on her phone to silence the ringer. If he was involved in this fiasco, she would definitely not talk to him again. Jill called her mother, hoping she hadn't missed her visit. It still amused Jill that her mother had finally bought a cell phone. Her mother had never been very technologically inclined and had only given in to Jill's pestering to buy a cell phone after Jill convinced her that it was a great safety device as well as highly convenient in other ways. Her mother answered on the first ring. "Jill, you finally call me back. Are you too important now to answer your own mother's phone calls?"

Sue-Mei said this in a teasing tone of voice, but Jill knew Sue-Mei did hate to be kept waiting. "No, Mom. I'm sorry I didn't call back sooner. I've been ... sick. All morning and last night, in fact. I'm feeling a lot better now, so if you want to meet for lunch I can join you somewhere."

"Jill, it's past one now. But let's meet for coffee instead."

"All right. Let's meet at Starbuck's. It's on Montana and Seventh."

"Okay, how long?"

"I can be there in a half hour, if I rush. Are you on your way back home?"

"I was about to head back to Ventura. But I'm not in a great hurry, so don't rush. I'll see you there."

Chapter 16

"Mom! It's so nice to see you!" Sue-Mei was waiting for Jill at a table inside Starbuck's. Jill loved the smell of pungent, well-roasted coffee as she entered the store. A couple of aspiring actors skulked at the corner tables. Anyone in L.A. not working during the day was, in Jill's world, an aspiring actor.

Jill hugged her mother close as her mother said: "You too, sweetie, I'm glad you could join me. Do you want to get some coffee?" Breaking her general rule, Jill ordered a single latte. As she returned to the table where her mother was waiting, Sue-Mei asked: "So what is keeping you so busy that you can't meet your own mother for lunch?"

"Mom, come on, I'm sorry I didn't get your message in time. There's just been… a lot of stuff happening at work." After a pause, Jill added: "The details would really bore you, Mom. Meetings and stuff. About energy policy." She hated lying to her mom, but there didn't seem to be much choice.

"Hmmph. Well, what is going on in your life lately? I feel like we haven't been talking much."

"Not really that much new. I've been working a lot and hanging out with friends. I'm pretty lucky in that I've found some great friends already. Makes up for the fact that most of my friends from Ventura have moved away, you know. And you, Mom?"

"I was just here for the day to do some shopping. I was reading the paper while I was waiting for you and just getting so angry. It's been a year since the war in Iraq and things are only getting worse." *Oh no, two minutes into our conversation and we're already on politics!*

"It is pretty bad. But there are some good things too, right? I mean, didn't they just create a new constitution guaranteeing women's rights and a certain number of seats in the legislature?"

"They just approved an *interim* constitution, drafted by the US-appointed Iraqi Governing Council, that sets flexible *goals* for women's voting rights. And it's hard to see that this achievement in itself makes everything the Colt White House did worthwhile."

"I don't know, Mom, it's tricky. But do we have to talk about this?"

"I would like to talk about this a little, if you don't mind. I'm just so mad. I don't have many friends who understand what I'm talking about. Here's the problem with this country..." Sue-Mei paused to clear her throat, as though she were about to begin orating before a crowd. Many conversations between Jill and Sue-Mei began with "here's the problem with this country..."

Sue-Mei continued: "The problem with this country is democracy itself. It is supposedly a democracy and we still entered into this illegal war with the backing of a majority of Americans. What does this tell us? That democracies can do bad things! And democracy in itself is not the answer."

Jill took a large swig of her latte. If Mom wanted to get political, Jill was going to just have to go political on her ass. "Mom, the whole idea behind democracy is that people get to make their own decisions in life. Live where they want to live. Keep their money to spend as they want. Vote for who they want to vote for. I'll agree that the war in Iraq was entered into for the wrong reasons. But I think we need to focus on the positive things now."

"Jill, darling, you're missing my point. If a powerful democracy like America can do patently bad things – or, at least, as you say, do things without stating the real reasons for doing them – then how can Westerners hold up democracy as some kind of cure-all? If people have their needs met, get to make most of the decisions in their lives, and generally live good healthy lives, does it really matter that they've elected their leaders or not? Have America's elected leaders shown themselves to be clearly better than the unelected leaders in other nations? Democracy is not itself the answer. There has to be more."

"At least in democracies, you can vote out the bastards if they actually reveal themselves to be bastards too often. You can't do that in China, can you?"

"You can only vote out the bastards if people realize they are bastards. In this country, with the media becoming more and more rightwing, most people don't even realize how criminal this administration is. Or how poorly the US is perceived around the world. China is really not that different. Leaders are elected by the National People's Congress, which is accountable to the people, much like parliamentary systems throughout the world. In the US, people think they get to elect their presidents, but when you have two corporate parties basically controlling who the voters get to choose, with little difference between the two candidates in each election, then is it really that different? China hasn't entered into any illegal wars since it took over Tibet, fifty years ago!"

"You've got it all wrong, Mom! Democracy may not be perfect in the US, but it's simply better to have the possibility of voting on our leaders and other things, rather than no possibility at all, like in China and other autocratic nations." Jill was getting flustered. All she really wanted to talk about was what had happened to her over the last twenty-four hours and her mother had to keep on going with the politics all the time. It really became tiresome to Jill. Her mother just didn't seem to get it. Different generations, she guessed. It was like trying to convince her mother that Carson Daly was the best MTV host ever.

Jill pursed her lips and looked at the scone crumbs on the floor. Her mother finally spoke: "Jill, I am happy to see you at least are thinking about these things." Sue-Mei smiled broadly.

"Of course I do, Mom, I'm not an idiot. But can't we talk about normal things once in a while? Like Britney Spears' wedding or, or, the last movie you saw?"

"Britney Spears got married?"

* * *

Jill pulled in to her parking spot at her complex, yawning again as the caffeine began to wear off. Talking with her mom could be exhausting. It was time for another nap. As she turned from her driveway to the street curb, walking to the front door of her apartment, she saw Jonas step out of a car parked on the side of the road. He looked up and saw her looking at him. He yelled: "Jill, I've got to talk to you. Hold on."

The anxiety of Jill's ordeal with Adrian came back immediately. With a gasp, she turned and ran back to her car. She wasn't tired anymore, all of a sudden. If she'd gone to her apartment, he could have broken down the door easily. She fumbled getting her keys out of her purse. "God damn it!"

Frustration building, she found the keyhole and her trusty Corolla started easily. "Thank God!" She pulled back out of her parking spot with a screech of her front tires. She slammed on the brakes, heard Jonas yelling at her. Couldn't hear him. Didn't care. Jill was in no mood to trust her uncle's good intentions.

She stomped on the gas pedal and, with another screech, sped quickly down Sixth Street toward Wilshire. She looked in her rearview mirror. Jonas was getting back in his car. She slowed for the stop sign, scanning visually up both sides of the street as far as she could. She cruised through the stop sign, going about twenty-five miles an hour. Not exactly a "California stop." She was jolted forward violently as her car rolled through the drainage dip in the street, bottoming out. The loud boom and scrape of her chassis hitting the asphalt made Jill wince in empathetic pain for her car. She looked back again. *Shit*! Jonas was not far behind in his car.

Jill arrived at Wilshire Boulevard. The light was red. She stopped, waiting for a break in the traffic so she could drive through the light. Hoping for a break in traffic on Wilshire Boulevard mid-afternoon was like waiting for the Pope to shit in the woods. She held her breath as Jonas pulled up behind her. She was still holding her breath as he screeched to a halt, opened his door and ran to her car.

Jill locked all her doors and gripped the steering wheel so tightly that the veins in her forearms looked as though they were about to separate from her arms. As Jonas made a fist to hit against her window, Jill saw the small break she needed. There was a one car gap in traffic going east – she pulled out into traffic going east, leaving Jonas gesticulating at her as she pulled over one lane to the inside lane. The light was green at Seventh and Wilshire. She turned left sharply and heard screeching tires and angry horns in her wake.

Jill sped down Seventh and risked a peek in her rearview again. No sign of Jonas. She rolled fast through another stop sign, but hit her brakes hard as she saw a car about to strike her. She narrowly missed the car as the other driver swerved. Jill held the steering wheel, breathing hard, sweat beginning to form on her forehead and hands. The driver of the other car hit his horn for a long few seconds as he flipped his middle finger back at Jill. Jill took a deep breath and hit the accelerator again, hard.

She looked back one more time. There was Jonas! She arrived at San Vicente Boulevard. Red light, again. Jonas was gaining on her, but she couldn't even make a right turn this time. There was a lot of traffic, moving very slowly for some reason. Usually San Vicente moved quickly, but not today.

Jonas was half a block away as the light turned green. Jill zipped across San Vicente, all one hundred and ten horses in her car's little engine kicking vigorously. She took a left on Adelaide, thinking she could perhaps lose Jonas by looping around the winding road above the Santa Monica Steps, a famous work out spot. No luck.

As Jill turned the first bend, she saw a large moving truck blocking the narrow road. A car was parked on one side of the road opposite the moving truck. There was no chance even her small car could get between them. "Shit!"

Jill pulled up behind the parked car and jumped out of her Corolla. She ran up the street past the moving truck. She heard a car squeal to a halt and assumed it was Jonas. She approached the first set of steps on the right side of the road. Jill wished she had been wearing her running shoes. But they were still at her office. Instead, she was wearing a pair of flat faux-athletic shoes. Stylish, but not very functional.

She stomped down the first flight of wooden steps, brushing past a woman running up the stairs, headphones on, oblivious to the world.

The woman's sweat wet Jill's arm as she pushed past her. The running woman yelled a protest at Jill's back. Jill reached the first concrete landing and heard fast feet pounding on the wooden steps above her. *Jonas!* "Jill, stop!"

Jill didn't stop. She found new energy from the rush of adrenaline that was prompted by his yelling at her. She seemed to fly down the remaining steps. She took a quick left at the bottom of the steps, heading toward the second flight of steps a couple of hundred feet away. Maybe she could lose him by running up the steps? He didn't look to be in very good shape and he smoked like the proverbial chimney. Jill, on the other hand, ran regularly and ran the steps right here a couple of times a week.

But Jonas was right behind her, she confirmed with a quick look over her shoulder as she approached the second set of steps. Wrong move. Her lace had come undone on her right shoe and she tumbled, hard, as the lace caught under her other foot.

Jill was able to catch much of her fall with her hands and she rolled to absorb much of the rest of her speed.

But she hit her elbow as she rolled, feeling a sharp pain.

Jonas was on top of her.

Not literally, but he was right there – she could smell his cigarette breath.

BOOK IV: DARGAN ON THE RUN

Reaching me, men of great spirit
Do not undergo rebirth,
The ephemeral realm of suffering;
They attain absolute perfection.

Even in Brahma's cosmic realm
Worlds evolve in incessant cycles,
But a man who reaches me
Suffers no rebirth, Arjuna

When they know that a day of Brahma
Stretches over a thousand eons,
And his night ends in a thousand eons,
Men understand day and night.

The Bhagavad Gita: Krishna's Counsel in Time of War,
VIII, 15-17

Chapter 17

"Dargan, come to my office please."

"Sure," Dargan replied and hung up. It was rare that Smith asked to see him in person, so Dargan walked to Smith's office pondering what might be the reason for this request.

"What's up boss?," Dargan asked as he entered Smith's office.

"Dargan, I've got a new project for you. Very important."

"Oh?"

"We at the crusty, but venerable, DOE are joining the information age. We're electronically archiving all of our documents, as time permits. I understand you've been a bit slow lately."

"Uh, yes, I guess." Dargan had been slow through no fault of his own. He had found, within two months of his arrival, that the position for which he had been hired was largely symbolic. There wasn't much interagency coordinating for him to do because the Colt administration's priorities were clearly not focused on renewable energy.

"I need you to oversee the process in our division of making electronic documents from our archived files, beginning with the most recent years and moving backwards."

"All right. Sounds pretty straightforward. Is there a protocol for me to follow?"

"Of course, do we do anything without instructions from on high?" Smith tossed Dargan a memorandum that looked to be about ten pages long. "Good luck and let me know if you hit any snags."

So now I'm a glorified copy clerk. The government is truly wasting taxpayer money on this one. Dargan left Smith's office, fuming inside. He examined the memorandum as he walked back to his office. It had the sexy title of "Departmental Directive re Electronic Archiving Procedures."

Unexpectedly, the grunt work Dargan had been assigned to oversee would be the break he had been hoping for.

* * *

"I'm applying for my Top Secret clearance tomorrow," Dargan had told Annabella shortly after accepting the position at the DoE. His offer from the DoE had been contingent upon obtaining a Top Secret clearance. Dargan was confident that he was sufficiently squeaky clean to pass. He had, after all, been given the offer by Smith, with full knowledge of Dargan's background.

"Oh really? That sounds exciting. What are you going to do if they ask you why you're so fucked up?" Annabella flashed a smile in Dargan's direction from her couch in her apartment where she was lounging in a sheer teddy.

"Funny. I feel pretty confident that won't be one of the questions."

"But seriously, my cream puff, what if they ask you uncomfortable questions like: do you support the Colt administration or are your motives for working at the DOE pure?" The way Annabella rolled the r in "cream" made Dargan want to smother her in kisses.

"I'm assuming that it's not necessary to express fealty to the President. The Constitution yes, the President, I don't think so. We're not that fascistic a state just yet. And my motives are pure, as you know." Dargan grinned back at Annabella.

A few days later, he continued the conversation with Annabella about the questions he had been asked during his Top Secret clearance interviews – under polygraph. "The first question they asked me was: 'Are you a communist?' Can you believe that? In 2003!"

"You said yes, right?"

"You're just so funny, Annabella." The sarcasm practically drooled from his lower lip. "I said 'no,' and their next question was: 'Are you a member of Al Qaeda?'!"

"You said yes, right?" She giggled.

"I'm not even going to respond to that. They asked a bunch more really basic questions.

But here's where it got interesting. They then asked me if I had ever engaged in any un-American activities. I actually had to think about that one for a second, then answered 'no.' I was worried that the polygraph might show this as a lie because I thought to myself: 'many people have accused me of being anti-American because I've criticized decisions made by the White House and the DOE.'"

"Let's hope that healthy self-reflection doesn't disqualify one from serving this great nation."

"Yes, let's hope. But I was worried about that kind of thing before I went in for my polygraph. I mean, I'll admit that I went to work at the DoE without being completely open about my intentions. I told the truth during my interview. Well, for the most part. Well, part of the truth. Certainly not the whole truth. Anyway. I did some research on polygraph machines and found out that it's actually very easy to beat them. This is why polygraph results are not admissible in courts. All you have to do is get really agitated during the calibration process. Sweat a lot, breath really deeply, try to make yourself nervous and get your heart rate up. I practiced a little bit with a friend's jogging heart rate monitor."

Annabella laughed at this: "You really did your research!"

"Just being careful, you know. But, luckily, I didn't have to overtly lie anyway. So now I'll never know if my shrewd counter-polygraph test techniques worked."

"So sad. I'll give you some desert to make up for it."

Dargan looked over at Annabella after this comment. She was looking at him with a mischievous grin, with one hand between her legs and the other beckoning to him.

* * *

Dargan opened the gold-lined pages of the Great Books edition of Aeschylus' plays a week after Annabella loaned it to him. The book gave off the musty odor that all old books acquire. The pages emitted a pleasant crackle as he turned them. The pages were thin, with two columns in small print crammed onto each page. *More bang for your Great Books buck*, he thought to himself. He turned to *Prometheus Bound* and began reading.

MIGHT: Hurry now. Throw the chain around him that the Father may not look upon your tarrying.

HEPHAESTUS: There are the fetters, there: you can see them.

MIGHT: *Put them on his hands: strong, now with the hammer: strike. Nail him to the rock.*

HEPHAESTUS: *It is being done now. I am not idling at my work.*

Dargan scanned the next few lines quickly, until his eyes were stopped again by the vividness of the words.

MIGHT: *Drive the obstinate jaw of the adamantine wedge right through his breast: drive it hard.*

HEPHAESTUS: *Alas, Prometheus, I groan for your sufferings.*

MIGHT: *Are you pitying again? Are you groaning for the enemies of Zeus? Have a care, lest some day you may be pitying yourself.*

HEPHAESTUS: *You see a sight that hurts the eye.*

MIGHT: *I see that rascal getting his deserts. Throw the girth around his sides.*

HEPHAESTUS: *I am forced to do this; do not keep urging me.*

MIGHT: *Yes, I will urge you, and hound you on as well. Get below now, and hoop his legs in strongly.*

HEPHAESTUS: There now, the task is done. It has not taken long.

MIGHT: Hammer the piercing fetters with all your power, for the Overseer of our work is severe.

This is some gnarly stuff!, Dargan thought to himself. He continued reading:

MIGHT: [to Prometheus]*: Now, play the insolent; now, plunder the Gods' privileges and give them to creatures of a day. What drop of your sufferings can mortals spare you? The Gods named you wrongly when they called you Forethought; you yourself need Forethought to extricate yourself from this contrivance.*

[Prometheus is left alone on the rock.]

Dargan read on, learning more about Prometheus' gifts to "creatures of a day":

CHORUS: Did you perhaps go further than you have told us?

PROMETHEUS: I caused mortals to stop foreseeing doom.

CHORUS: What cure did you provide them with against that sickness?

PROMETHEUS: *I placed in them blind hopes.*

CHORUS: *That was a great gift you gave to men.*

PROMETHEUS: *Besides this, I gave them fire.*

CHORUS: *And do creatures of a day now possess bright-faced fire?*

PROMETHEUS: *Yes, and from it they shall learn many crafts.*

Blind hopes? Many crafts? No greater crime than that! The story resonated strongly with Dargan as he finished the short play. He was left dissatisfied, however, as the play ended with no real resolution. He vaguely recalled that it was thought to be one of a trilogy of plays by Aeschylus on Prometheus' sufferings. Out of curiosity, Dargan sat at his computer and jumped online to confirm his vague recollection. Google was truly Dargan's friend.

Dargan read that Prometheus was one of the Titans, the first group of gods to reign over ancient Greece. But he already knew this. Prometheus had sided with the newcomer gods, the Olympians, led by Zeus, to overthrow the Titans. Zeus and Prometheus had not remained in good standing long, as Prometheus came to favor humankind – the "creatures of a day" – over the gods. He also learned that, once bound, Prometheus would suffer as his punishment for his man-loving ways a daily visit by an eagle sent by Zeus to devour Prometheus' liver. Every day, Prometheus' immortal liver grew back, only to be eaten again by the oppressive eagle. *This won't happen to the Dragon. I'll have more forethought than Prometheus. No eagle's going to get my liver.*

Chapter 18

During the electronic archiving process he supervised, Dargan was able to review thousands of pages of documents from various DoE operations, including, most interestingly, documents from the Intelligence Office of the DoE.

The Intelligence Office, Dargan had learned, was one of the fifteen agencies comprising the Intelligence Community. The Intelligence Office was known by the counter-intuitive acronym "IN." He had learned of the IN's existence during his time at the Energy Coalition, but the publicly available information about the agency and its operations was minimal. To refresh his memory, Dargan visited the Intelligence Office's website – surprisingly sparse. He learned that the IN acts as "the Intelligence Community's premier technical intelligence resource in four core areas: nuclear weapons and nonproliferation; energy security; science and technology; and nuclear energy, safety, and waste." The IN's "three part mission" was:

• To provide DoE, other US Government policy-makers, and the Intelligence Community with timely, accurate, high-impact foreign intelligence analyses.
• To ensure that DoE's technical, analytical, and research expertise is made available to the

intelligence, law enforcement, and special operations communities.

• To provide quick-turnaround, specialized technology applications and operational support based on DoE technological expertise to the intelligence, law enforcement, and special operations communities.

As Dargan learned from reviewing the documents he was given to archive electronically, the key mission activity of the IN was protecting energy security. This term, as Dargan would learn, was given a very broad meaning by the IN folks.

Suspecting he may come across some interesting information, Dargan cursorily reviewed many of the documents that arrived at his office as part of the electronic archiving process. What he found was eye-opening. Energy security – ensuring that the nation had adequate supplies of energy for economic growth now and in the foreseeable future – had not been his focus during his years at the Energy Coalition. Rather, he had focused on energy policy from the point of view of environmental sustainability. Dargan's former focus required knowledge of what was feasible regarding renewable energy technologies – pricing, permitting, financing, etc. – but also lobbying efforts to counteract the influence of entrenched fossil fuel and nuclear energy corporations. His had been a losing battle for the most part. The battle was not between David and Goliath. A better metaphor would have been a battle between a fly on David's head and Goliath. The resources brought to bear were that disparate.

Even so, because the public interest – in terms of a sustainable environment and the threat of global warming – so clearly favored renewable energy instead of the fossil fuel status quo, that the policies pushed by the Energy Coalition and other renewable energy advocates did sometimes gain favor among legislators and even the White House.

Importantly, over the last twenty years, a number of trade groups in the renewable energy industry had started playing the Washington power game. Groups like the American Wind Energy Association and the Solar Energy Industries Association learned how to use their limited financial power, combined with wise policy solutions, to influence key legislators. Even so, the victories were far fewer in number than the defeats.

Dargan's interest in renewable energy was piqued even further by his realization of the connection between renewable energy and foreign policy. It was cliché during the debates over the 1991 first Gulf War and the 2003 second Gulf War that these wars were fought for oil. However, no side could prove or disprove their arguments because, as with any large-scale actions, there were many motivations for action and "proof" was not a readily achievable standard. Arguments for or against relied more on compelling narratives and circumstantial evidence. Despite the Colt White House's denials that oil had anything to do with the second Gulf War, it was quite evident to Dargan – and many others – that the war was fought, in significant part, to ensure an adequate supply of cheap oil for American consumers. He just couldn't prove it, and nor could anyone else.

* * *

Shortly after Dargan began at the DoE, he introduced himself to a stranger at lunch in the cafeteria of the DoE building he worked in. Dargan was delighted to learn that the man, sitting at the same table with Dargan, worked for the IN. His new IN colleague, Bill Ramirez, was relatively young, but he knew enough to provide some key insights to Dargan. Bill had been with the IN for three years, joining the agency after obtaining his Ph.D in international environment and resource policy from Tufts University's Fletcher School.

"Seems like you guys are the redheaded step-child of the intelligence community." Dargan smiled as he said this, indicating he wasn't entirely serious.

"Hah! That may be true, but there's a reason for it. We like to keep a very low profile. The CIA, NSA, NSC, FBI, can have the glory. Our mission is just as important, it seems to me."

"Why's that? You provide technical information on energy issues, for the most part, right?" Dargan was being coy. He knew the IN's mandate was much broader than this.

"No! We do a lot more than that. We are the custodians of nuclear energy technology – as a relic of the Manhattan Project and the Atomic Energy Agency, which is now, as I'm sure you know, the Nuclear Regulatory Commission. We also provide a lot of analysis about energy security issues."

"What does that mean? Energy security." Dargan was enjoying playing dumb. It was a new role for him.

Bill furrowed his brow slightly at Dargan's apparent ignorance of this term, but replied: "Energy security is the area of foreign policy that focuses on ensuring we have the energy we need, generally oil. The US imports more than fifty percent of our oil from other nations, and that's projected to grow to seventy percent by 2025. And most of those nations are developing nations. Developing nations are often not very stable. So it's our job to analyze the reliability of our oil supplies and provide technical support for other agencies that... have a more direct role in ensuring our oil supply, shall we say?" Bill smiled mischievously at Dargan as he said this.

Dargan smirked knowingly back at Bill. "Interesting. I feel like I should know more about this, but my focus has been domestic energy policy and, particularly, renewable energy. And I was hired to focus on renewables here at the DoE, too. So can I ask what you guys did, if anything, regarding the Iraq war? I mean, I know there was some discussion of oil as motivating the war, but I know that talk was way overblown. Our leaders couldn't be that cynical, I know. What's your take on this?"

"What do you mean exactly?" Bill looked around the cafeteria as he asked this question. There were no other patrons sitting close enough to hear the conversation.

"Well, you're the energy security experts. So what part did oil play in motivating the war?"

Bill appeared to think carefully before answering. "More than you might think. I can't say much on this, of course. Classified and all that crap. And frankly I can't really say what exactly went through the mind of the President or his advisors when they gave the final approval. No one can. My personal take on it is that terrorism was genuinely a concern on the part of the White House. But I think there was a rare confluence of motivations, including concerns about cheap oil, that made the war seem like a damn good idea to top-level policymakers.

"I'll say this, and leave it at that. The US, with four percent of the world's population, uses twenty-five percent of the world's oil. The Middle East has more than half of the known reserves of economically retrievable oil. That means it can be pumped at prices close to what we see today. Saudi Arabia has control of over twenty-five percent of known reserves. Iraq sits atop another eleven percent of known reserves. This figure could be much larger – as much as thirty percent of world reserves – once Iraq is fully explored. Iraqi oil is *cheap*. And *high quality*. It has some of the shallowest and, therefore, cheapest to recover, oil fields in the world. And US domestic oil production is predicted to drop sharply after 2008. If you believe that these facts weren't part of the policy planning behind the war, then you probably still believe in the tooth fairy."

* * *

"You fuck me so good. So good. You." Annabella was lying on her side gazing at Dargan, sweat beading on her chest, giving a sheen to her shapely breasts.

Dargan lay on his back, staring at the ceiling. The sheets were rumpled. The fan above the bed turned swiftly, but not swiftly enough to keep it cool in the heat of a warm spring day in D.C. Dargan looked at Annabella, looking at him with a little smile on her lips. He looked back up at the ceiling. "Do you have to use the word 'fuck'?"

No immediate response came from Annabella. Then she asked: "What word should I use?"

"I don't know. 'Fuck' just seems so crude."

"Well, I definitely cannot use 'make love.' Should I use 'have sex'? Is that less offensive to you. Or how about 'knock boots' or 'laying pipe'?" Her voice rose as she propped her head up on her hand to more directly address him. Dargan was tempted to chuckle at Annabella's use of the unconventional slang.

"I don't know. I don't like 'have sex' either. It sounds so… clinical. And 'make love,' I don't know either. I mean…"

"I know what you mean, you bastard! You don't love me. Why don't you love me? What the hell is wrong with me?" Her brow furrowed and her eyes narrowed in anger.

"Nothing's wrong with you! I mean, you know we decided to go into this with no strings attached. We talked about that."

"I know what we talked about, you fucker. Things change. I thought you would change over time. I know I've changed. It's been six months now. What's holding you back? Huh? Is it that damn girl in California? Your goody-two-shoes princess?" Annabella sat up and swiveled around so that her legs hung off the side of her bed. Her smooth brown back faced him. Even after their vigorous romp, Dargan still felt the urge to reach out and run his fingers down her back, tracing the contours of her spine and toned muscles.

Dargan noticed the sound of the window-mounted AC unit getting louder.

He finally spoke: "I do still think about Jill. But…"

"But what?" He couldn't be sure, but it sounded like Annabella was crying. He had been going to say that he couldn't be with Annabella even if Jill was not still a factor in his emotional calculus. But he thought better of it.

Instead, he reached out and caressed her side, urging her non-verbally to turn around. He said: "But what's the hurry? Can't we just take it slow and let things develop naturally?"

"Your idea of taking it slow would stretch into decades if you had your way." Annabella cut off the conversation by brushing off his hand, standing and, without looking back, disappearing into the bathroom. As she stood, she knocked a small mirror off her nightstand on to the floor. The razor and tiny crumbs spilled on to the carpet. Annabella appeared not to notice.

She had the most beautiful naked body. Beautiful face. Luscious flowing hair. Intelligent. Funny. But the strong emotion simply wasn't there for Dargan.

* * *

"Dad, did you ever read much about the Prometheus myth?" Dargan and his father, a professor of eastern religions at Columbia University, were having dinner at the Capitol City Brewing Company in the Postal Square Building, northwest of the Capitol. His father had called him the night before to ask if Dargan could meet him while he was in town for the weekend.

"Of course. Not recently, but I'm quite familiar with the story. Not my field, of course. Prometheus, the son of Iapetus, had too much love for mankind. He felt sorry for the struggling mortals and stole fire for them from the gods and tricked Zeus into choosing the bad portions of the sacrifices humans offered up to Zeus. As punishment for these sins, Zeus shackled Prometheus on a rock on a mountain and had an eagle eat out his immortal liver each day. He…"

"Dad, I know the story, I just was asking if you knew about it." His father's penchant for pontification constantly irritated Dargan.

"Oh, well, it is interesting, you know. The Greeks were bloody as all hell. Incest. Eyes torn out. Vendettas. Made for great drama but makes one wonder how on earth people survived during all that turmoil. You've read about Oedipus, of course. But have you read about Agamemnon and that bizarre history? Agamemnon and Clytemnestra, now that's a mouthful..."

"Right, right, right. I just wanted to ask you a question about Hinduism, though, in relation to Prometheus. Remember that Zeus' eagle came each day to eat out Prometheus' liver. I believe the ancient Greeks thought that the liver was the source of blood and bile and was considered the most important organ in the human body. But it seems like the eagle does, in a way, represent time. Each day the eagle comes. Each day the eagle eats out Prometheus' liver. Prometheus is reminded in a very painful way that a new day has arrived – each day."

"Interesting. So what was your question?" Dargan's father grew visibly agitated if he wasn't talking. Dad was still the worst listener known to man.

"Well, I remember reading a long time ago about Hindu cosmology. One of the largest Hindu units of time was the *kalpa*. I remember reading that a *kalpa* is defined as the time it takes an eagle, flying over the Himalayas once every one thousand years with a feather in its talons, to wear down the Himalayas by brushing the feather over the peaks each time it flies."

"Right, right. This is the common definition. A *kalpa* is approximately four billion three hundred and twenty thousand million years. About the same age as the earth. There are four *yugas* in each *kalpa*. In the current *kalpa*, we are in the last *yuga*, the *Kali yuga*, the end times!" Dargan's father grinned broadly and waved his hands as if he were a magician. Ever the entertainer.

"Yes. That's all fine and dandy. But do you think there's any connection between the Hindu eagle and Zeus' eagle? I mean, I'm not positing any literal connection. But maybe some kind of long-term cultural and symbolic connection?"

"I've never thought about it, actually. Don't mind admitting that. That's an interesting one, son. I'll think about it some more."

"Cool. Let me know if you find anything. Enough on that. How's your girlfriend doing?"

"She's fine. Yours?

"Who? Annabella? I don't know if I'd say she's my girlfriend. We... have an understanding."

"Oh really?" Dargan's father's eyes twinkled in a knowing way – a virtual wink wink nudge nudge to the ribs.

"Yeah. She's cool… So I talked to Mom the other day, she said…"

Dad cut Dargan off: "The Greeks were really amazing. As an eastern philosophy type, I often forget how important the Greeks were in shaping much of Western civilization. They began the democratic tradition, extended vastly by nations like the United States, and now being perfected by Western Europe. In light of the interesting times we live in, it's gotten me thinking. Why was Greek democracy so restrictive in terms of who could participate in a meaningful way?"

"I'm not sure what you're getting at. Why don't you just tell me?"

"I'm not being coy. I'm genuinely interested in what you think about this. What I'm trying to get at is that Greek democracy was very limited in terms of who was considered a citizen. Just like it was at the beginning of American democracy. In Greece, it was only free men who could participate as citizens in debates or by holding positions in government. In early America, only white males who owned property could participate. In the US, this has of course changed greatly over time. I literally wouldn't be surprised if, a hundred years down the road, dolphins or chimpanzees are allowed to vote."

Dargan chuckled at this thought. His father continued: "I'm not kidding. And I think that would be a good thing – assuming that dolphins and chimps did in fact display at that time a sufficient level of intelligence to warrant such participation. I also wouldn't be surprised to see the voting age reduced or made more flexible by allowing kids in their teens or even earlier to earn the right to vote by passing a test. Point being that with intelligence and sentience comes the right to have a say in those issues that affect a person. Just like a smart kid gets more respect from her parents, so should smart kids – or even smart animals, assuming they're given the power of speech through technological enhancements or what have you – have a say in how their governments treat them.

"I guess. I guess I haven't really thought about it that much."

"But here's why I brought this up. I think the original Greek democracy and the original American democracy didn't give many people the right to vote or hold office because there was an assumption that people had to be basically on the same playing field in order to have the right to participate in ways that might limit the privileges or rights of others. There was, of course, plenty of bigotry responsible for these decisions too.

"But as more and more people became part of the mainstream economy and demanded access to the levers of democratic power, voting rights in this nation expanded phenomenally. And of course, voting rights are in many ways antecedent to increased economic power – people often vote with their wallet or because of their wallet. And if certain groups don't vote, they're considered outside of the mainstream power structure and will, accordingly, suffer at the hands of that same power structure." This was full-blown pontification, Dad-style, but Dargan found himself interested nonetheless.

Dad continued: "But what I'm seeing lately really worries me. It's becoming more and more clear that economic policies in the US and around the world are accentuating the disparity between rich and poor. Large numbers of people are becoming more and more separated from the power structures of democratic societies through economic forces. People are getting poorer and poorer, even in the US, in relation to the economic elites in most nations in the world today. This isn't sustainable."

"I'm following you. So you're saying that democracy can't really work – at least not for many people – when there's such a disparity between rich and poor?"

"Right."

"And that's a problem because we like to think we live in a vibrant democracy. It is a problem, but I'm not sure how you or I can help make things better."

"Oh, I'm not trying to think up any grand solutions right here. I'm a professor," he winked at Dargan, "I just talk about problems and let more practical people come up with the solutions."

Chapter 19

"Bill, Dargan here, care to join me for lunch today?" Dargan had asked Bill for his card after their first meeting.

"Sure, what time? Where?"

"How about twelve-thirty, at the brewery?"

"Cool, see ya there." Dargan hung up the phone.

Dargan arrived early and found a vacant booth at the back. He hoped to gain more information from Bill, without tipping Bill off to his motivations.

"You know what I don't get, Bill?," Dargan asked shortly after Bill arrived.

"What's that?"

"If we're so vulnerable because of our dependence on other nations for oil, why isn't there more of an effort in the White House or Congress to fix the situation?"

"Well, it depends on how you look at it. First, despite the fact that we get more than half our oil from other nations, we're pretty diversified. We also get a lot of our oil from strong allies. We get the most from Canada, then Mexico. A bunch from Saudi Arabia, then Venezuela, and about one fourth of our imports from all OPEC nations. We also get a shit load from Norway and Russia, who are not OPEC nations. Remember that OPEC only controls about one third of the world's current oil use – but it has control over about sixty percent of known reserves. We also produce almost half of our own oil and have the ability to produce more than that if domestic oil drilling restrictions were relaxed. So even if we lost a major supplier like Saudi Arabia, perhaps due to a coup by Al Qaeda or something, we would see a large increase in oil prices, but it wouldn't bring us to a standstill exactly. Worldwide recession, yes, but worldwide depression, probably not.

"But I would think in today's political climate, there would be a lot more support for ways to make us less dependent on foreign oil. I mean, it's pretty obvious to any remotely impartial observer that we invite some serious problems because of our oil dependency. The fact that we are strong allies with Saudi Arabia – as one example – should make all Americans blush. And if that isn't a relationship based on pure oil politics, I don't know what is."

"Yeah, Saudi Arabia has been a problem for us for a long time. No one likes them. Not the lefties, who see Saudi Arabia as a human rights ogre – and rightly so, I guess, if you care about that sort of thing. And the rightwingers hate the fact that we're so dependent on one nation for much of our oil and the fact that Saudi Arabia, who leads OPEC, controls global oil prices because of their ability to flood the market and reduce prices to knock others out of competition. Or to restrict output drastically to jack up prices if that's what they want to do. And then there's the small matter that fifteen of the nineteen 9/11 hijackers were Saudis... And the Islamists hate the Saudi Arabian royal family for being too friendly to the West and for allowing US forces to be stationed there after the first Gulf War."

"Hmmm."

"So here's the deal. The White House is, in my humble opinion, pretty serious about the whole hydrogen economy thing as a way to wean us off foreign oil."

"Really? I've read some stuff, but it seems to be all fluff at this point. There's no real funding and no real plan of action."

"I'm not so sure. Things are changing, fast. The DoE, with our help, is working on a new hydrogen posture plan, basically a blueprint for developing the hydrogen economy. And they're throwing some real money at the problem. President Colt committed almost two billion dollars over a five year period beginning in 2002."

Dargan couldn't continue his charade of ignorance anymore. "But that's a pittance compared to what the federal government spends to subsidize fossil fuels and nuclear! And from what I've seen so far of the hydrogen economy idea, it would simply replace one foreign dependency with another: natural gas. I mean, here's what I've seen. The administration wants to use natural gas, coal, and nuclear to create hydrogen – from natural gas – for fuel cell cars and fuel cell electricity generators. How does this improve our situation? We just start importing natural gas instead of oil and have basically the same problems as before!"

Bill regarded Dargan curiously for a moment, making Dargan realize he had probably said far more than he should have. He didn't want to arouse suspicion, even though Bill was a low level IN guy. There was no reason to risk Bill talking to Dargan's bosses or to his own bosses about Dargan's interest in the IN or the connections between oil and war. "We'll see, I guess," was all Bill said in response to Dargan's tirade as he cut into his Porter steak that had just arrived.

"Yeah, we will. But I actually wanted to ask you some questions to follow up on our discussion when I first met you in the cafeteria."

"Shoot," Bill said as he chewed his mouthful of steak.

"Are there policy planning documents regarding oil security? That stuff really fascinates me. I want to make sure the loony left isn't right about war for oil and all that."

"Didn't you come from a lefty non-profit before you worked here?"

Dargan realized he may have overplayed his hand. He hadn't mentioned to Bill where he had worked prior to the DoE. This meant that Bill had indeed asked about him. Not good. "Uh, yes, I did. But we were pretty moderate. Effective, you know, not radicals."

"Hmmm. Well, yeah, there are documents, of course. I can't give any to you. Classified, you know. But there was one leaked a while ago, which you may have heard about. It was a report done by the DoE, regarding oil supplies in Iraq. Pretty routine stuff, though. We do that for all oil-producing nations. It just happened to be leaked at a very bad time for the White House. Made it look pretty bad."

* * *

Small fish with large shiny teeth tore into Dargan's flesh as he struggled to break his chains. He was underwater, two monstrous shackles around his wrists, chaining him to a large rock on the seabed. Two even larger shackles restrained his ankles.

He couldn't move his torso, he discovered after trying to push himself off the rock. He looked down and saw a large spike driven through his chest. No blood seeped out of the wound. Instead, the skin seemed to have grown up around the spike as though the spike itself was sprouting from Dargan's bare chest.

He knocked away two fish that had darted in to take a chunk of his skin from his side. His blood seeped away in ever expanding spirals and paisleys. He breathed the water with no discomfort, but tried to avoid inhaling his own blood as it wafted by.

The fish were coming at him faster.

He flailed his arms and legs to keep the fish away. The shackles were so heavy, his arms were growing tired. He knew if he could fend them off for just a bit longer, they'd be gone – for the day.

He frantically tried to keep them away. There were too many!

They bit and bit and burrowed, until one literally wriggled through the growing hole in his side.

Dargan could feel the fish gnawing at his insides.

He screamed, but only water escaped his lips.

Dargan opened his eyes and sucked in a huge gasp of air. He lay in bed, breathing deeply. His sheets were wet with his sweat.

* * *

The IN was housed in a building attached to

Dargan's building – which housed the bulk of the DoE. He approached the entry way to the IN's offices, brandishing his DoE ID card for the security guard seated next to the metal detector at the entryway.

"Whoa whoa whoa. Come over here, chief." The security guard, a white woman with considerable girth and very impressive biceps, stood as she addressed Dargan.

"Sorry, do I have to sign in?"

"You need to do more than that, sport. You need to either work here or have a specific reason or invitation for entering the IN. Which are you?"

"Well, I don't work here…"

"That I know. Never seen you before."

Dargan thought fast. "But I do have an invitation. I'm meeting Bill Ramirez to discuss some issues." He realized he shouldn't have added the purpose for his alleged meeting with Bill – offering more detail than is requested often gives away a lie.

"Really? Well, let's give Mr. Ramirez a call, shall we?"

"Sure." Dargan waited as the guard dialed Ramirez's extension. Dargan waited. And waited. No answer.

"I guess he got confused about your invitation," the guard said with a saccharine sweet smile.

"I guess. That's very… unprofessional. I'll try again later, I guess." Dargan turned to leave.

"Hold it a second. Why don't I leave a message for Mr. Ramirez on your behalf. Not my job normally, but I'll be glad to help out here."

"Not necessary, thanks. I'll just call Bill later." He turned to leave again.

"Hold it right there." Dargan turned, an anxious look on his face. "Please sign in for me. We have to keep a log of all contacts."

"Even for a visit? All right." Dargan filled in his name and work division. As he walked away, he realized he should have filled out a fake name. But maybe the guard would have read his ID card hanging from his neck and seen that it didn't match the name he wrote down. Dargan's first low-level effort at espionage was a resounding failure.

Chapter 20

Dargan located the report Bill had mentioned. It had been leaked in the summer of 2003, shortly after the "major activities" of the Iraq invasion were over. It was a detailed description of known Iraqi oil fields, with projections as to currently retrievable oil and estimates as to their ultimate capacity, given sufficient investment in oil infrastructure and exploration.

But this was not Earth-shattering stuff. It seemed Bill was right. There had to be more. To really make his case, he had to find something watertight. Something that said, in effect: "We went to war with Iraq because of oil. Period." Dargan knew he was extremely unlikely to find anything like this. And it probably wasn't even true. Even if oil was a major motivating factor for the war, there were of course other factors: terrorism; concerns about weapons of mass destruction (completely wrong, as it turned out, though the jury was still out on the charges of outright deception); protecting Israel; and perhaps even a genuine concern about promoting democracy in the region – though this latter goal was highly unlikely to be a real factor when one considered the history of US foreign policy in the Middle East in terms of supporting autocrats.

The US had many allies in the region and not a democracy among them, except for Israel.

The Palestinian Authority was the only Arab government in the region that could lay any claim to democratic governance – but Palestine was not a state and was completely under the thumb of Israel anyway.

Even if oil wasn't the only motivating factor for the war, Dargan had an abiding suspicion that it was the primary factor. There was so much circumstantial evidence – but no direct evidence that he could find!

* * *

"So did you find any connection between the *kalpa* eagle and Zeus' eagle?," Dargan asked his father. Dargan's father had called a couple of weeks after their conversation in D.C.

"No, I didn't. I asked a colleague of mine at Columbia about this and I even did some searching of my own. But no connection, sorry. It's interesting, certainly. But could merely reflect the importance of eagles in many cultures' mythologies. Eagles impressed all human beings who came in touch with them."

"Cool. I was just curious. Thanks for looking into that."

"No problem. How are things with you?"

"So you're going to be in town again, I'm guessing. I don't generally hear from you unless you're planning a visit."

"Dargan, that's not fair. Well, not entirely fair. But you're right, yes, I will be in town again. Next weekend. Are you free to meet for dinner? My girlfriend will be with me this time. Maybe we can arrange a double date with your luscious Annabella."

Dargan wasn't sure he liked his father talking about Annabella this way. "Well, maybe. I'll definitely be around. I'll see what Annabella thinks." Dargan also wasn't sure he wanted to invite Annabella to dinner with his father and his girlfriend. It might give Annabella the wrong impression.

* * *

"Knock knock." Dargan looked up and saw Bill standing in Dargan's office doorway. *I thought I closed the door?*

"Oh, hi Bill. What's shakin'?"

"Nothing much. Just figured I'd drop by and say hello. What are you working on?"

"Nothing that would interest you too much, probably. I've got this lame-ass archiving project that I'm overseeing. They're wheeling DoE documents from the last thirty years up here for me and my crew to archive electronically. Glamorous stuff." Dargan had actually been looking for more incriminating information on the DoE intranet, as a follow up to his reading of the leaked report. He didn't hope to find much information available to him. But he did hope to at least discover who he might talk to.

"I'm sure. You enjoying yourself generally here?"

"You mean working here? Sure."

"Yeah? They keeping you busy? Good work on renewables?"

"Keeping me busy, yes. On renewables, not so much. This archiving project is taking a lot of my time."

"Too bad. Anything new on the energy security stuff? I could tell you were real fired up about that."

Dargan wasn't sure he liked this line of questioning. "Well, I found that leaked report you mentioned. You were right, nothing too juicy." Dargan held up the report that had been lying on his desk.

Dargan's phone rang, saving him temporarily from further conversation about uncomfortable topics. He held up a finger as he checked to see who was calling. It was his boss, Smith. He covered the mouthpiece and said to Bill: "Sorry, I've got to get this." Bill smiled and made a mock salute as he walked away.

"Mr. Smith, I mean, Caleb, what can I help you with?"

"Dargan. Just wanted to check in with you and find out how that archiving project is coming along."

"Just fine, boss. Making progress."

"I hate to ride you, Dargan, but we need that project done ASAP."

"Oh. I didn't know it was that urgent. I'll shift it to top priority, unless I hear otherwise."

"That would be great, Dargan. Thank you."

Dargan resumed his review of the documents that needed to be electronically archived. He was determined to review the bulk of these documents before they were spirited away to the vaults again or made inaccessible to him. Even though he was not required to review the documents in detail as part of his official duties, it was too good an opportunity to pass up. His role was, officially, to act as quality control in terms of making sure that the two people he had been assigned for this task performed their tasks correctly.

Most of the documents were not remotely interesting. But some warranted more than a half-second glance. Dargan opened a cardboard box of documents marked "IN Technology Program." Inside this box were a number of manila folders. He flipped through them quickly, stopping on one marked "Zero Point Energy." He pulled the folder out and placed it on his desk. He started to flip through quickly, as he had done with the vast majority of documents up to this point. His flipping stopped almost immediately, as his eyes were drawn to the descriptions of this technology. He read on, through document after document in the thick manila folder. Two hours after finding the folder, he had skimmed through all the documents in the folder. It was mindboggling. Dargan had a strong feeling that his fishing expedition was over.

Prometheus screwed up by not being far-sighted *enough*. Dargan would make sure that he didn't end up shackled to a rock, with a bird feasting on his liver on a daily basis. It was time – again – to steal fire from the Gods.

* * *

"Dad. Dargan here. Hi. Can we change our plans a bit this weekend? I really need to meet with you one on one, in private."

BOOK V: JARGAN

The highest function of love is that it makes the
loved one a unique and irreplaceable being.

Tom Robbins, *Jitterbug Perfume*

Chapter 21

His speech halting as he fought for breath, Jonas said: "Jill. Jill! Hear me out! I'm not trying to hurt you! I've got something I need to tell you."

Jill had no choice but to listen. "What the fuck do you want?!" She pulled herself to a sitting position facing Jonas, who had stopped ten feet away from her on the sidewalk. Jonas assumed a crouch, down on his haunches, as though he were trying to coax a shy cat to approach him.

"Just calm down, Jill. Jesus. What the hell have I done to make you react like this? I know some strange stuff has been happening to you lately. But I can explain, I think, a heck of a lot of what has been going on." He paused for a breath.

He appeared to be sincere, as best Jill could tell. But she didn't really trust her own judgment anymore. Not since the Adrian fiasco. Still, she had minimal choice in the matter. "Okay, I'm listening." She looked around for people who could come to her aid if he tried anything. No one!

"Can we go somewhere else? We're close to the beach anyway, so let's walk down there." Jonas added after a second: "And there are lots of people there, so you don't have to worry about anything happening."

"Why don't you just tell me now?"

"All right, I guess." He paused, apparently looking at his shoes. Jill looked at Jonas, waiting for him to begin. He finally spoke: "I got a confession to make, Jill. The day after I saw you last, in Oxnard, I was approached by two men as I left my apartment. They wanted to retain my services as a PI." The phrase "retain my services" rolled off Jonas' tongue very awkwardly, as if he had heard it recently in a crime or mystery movie. "I said they could go to my office and discuss, but they insisted on discussing the job right there. They said they knew I was your uncle. I asked them what you had to do with anything and they replied that you were involved in a very sensitive situation involving their company."

Jill interrupted: "What company?"

"That's what I asked. They were coy at first. But then I told them that I wouldn't take them on as a client unless they told me who was paying the bills. They told me they were with Empire Holdings."

"What the hell? This is getting stranger and stranger. That company is a subsidiary of Maxxon Corporation, the huge oil company." Jill had recently conducted an exhaustive examination of Maxxon's corporate structure as part of her nascent campaign against Maxxon. Empire Holdings was an obscure subsidiary that she would never have heard of otherwise.

"Yeah? Well, they told me that you had some very sensitive documents relating to their company. And they needed me to help them get the documents back. I've been really broke, Jill, since I got out of jail. You've gotta know that. Otherwise I would never, even for a second, have considered working for these guys. You may have a poor opinion of me, but I'm not all bad."

"Clearly," Jill replied with sarcasm but also the hint of a smile. Her head was reeling from this new complication to the bizarre events that had befallen her recently. But she was relieved that she could apparently trust Jonas now that he was confessing to her.

"They wanted me to contact you and track down the documents you'd been given recently. They said you got the documents in response to a foya request, whatever that is. I didn't know much about the documents because they wouldn't tell me much. Just that there would be a lot of documents from the Department of Energy. And they said there would be a CD-ROM also. And that's why I showed up last week at the coffee shop. I wanted to check out your workplace and figure out where I could find the documents. How I could get into your office when you weren't there. All that kind of stuff. I'm really sorry, Jill. I can't believe I even considered this. But I did."

"So what changed your mind?" It occurred to Jill that maybe Jonas was still lying to her. If he had gone so far as to feign interest in her work and to stake out her workplace, what else could he do?

"After I checked out your office, I went back home and started hatching a plan to get the documents. Over the weekend, I had a chance to step back and think about what I was doing. And, frankly, to think about the chances of me going back to the slammer. I really am trying to do the right thing nowadays. But it's tough when you gotta make a living! I can only do so many husband track and shoot jobs for jilted wives! But, believe me, Jill, I realize now that I was way wrong in even considering this job. And I realized that you might be in some danger from these guys. They didn't seem all that dangerous themselves, but they were throwing around a lot of dough. Seriously. And with that kind of cash, stakes have a way of getting real high. I thought you would need to know, which is why I was trying to get a hold of you."

Jill didn't reply right away. Instead, she got slowly to her feet, patting herself down to see what was missing and what was bleeding. Her elbow hurt like hell and was scraped, but wasn't bleeding too badly. Hands scratched up a little and her knees were scuffed. Nothing else seemed damaged. She kept a wary eye on Jonas. But her suspicions were rapidly dissipating.

"Honestly, Jonas, I'm not sure whether to believe you or not. But I guess I'm going to have to for now. And it's kind of a moot point anyway. Some stuff went down recently that I can't tell you about, which... well, it makes what you're talking about pretty much irrelevant at this point."

"Really? I guess that's good. Maybe you can tell me sometime what happened?"

"I don't know. I doubt it. But, listen. I knew Maxxon was a bad actor, but I didn't know they would stoop this low. I guess I shouldn't be surprised. They're the biggest corporation in the world. And they didn't get to that position by being good guys. We're about to open a campaign against them at Global Green. But our campaign is going to focus more on bad policies than criminal behavior. Maybe we should do both..."

"I'd be happy to help - discreetly of course - but I'm sure they'll just deny they ever had anything to do with me if you accuse them of this."

"I'm not sure it would be worth our while to focus on what happened to me. There's definitely enough out there that we wouldn't have to go for anything this difficult to prove. They've got a horrible environmental track record and are simply the worst company out there when it comes to concern about the environment and human rights."

They arrived at Jill's car. Jill said: "Jonas, I hope you're telling the truth…"

Jonas replied quickly: "I am, Jill, believe me." She wanted to, but couldn't be sure still.

"Either way, I appreciate what you've told me. I just hope it's all over. This is way more than I bargained for when I took this damn job. I've got to think about what to do, if anything, about Maxxon's involvement in this."

Jill's head started to hurt again as she walked back to her car – thankfully still where she left it and apparently unmolested – and awkwardly said goodbye to Jonas. On the drive home, Jill's anxiety stayed heavy in her stomach as she tried to remember if she had seen Maxxon or any of its subsidiary companies named in any of the documents she'd received. Maxxon had been mentioned many times because they were on many advisory committees at the DOE. And they obviously had a large presence in many things that the DOE did – they were the largest US oil company, after all. But she didn't recall seeing them named in any of the more juicy documents Jill had read. And they definitely weren't included in the transcript of the US-Saudi meeting.

* * *

Jill dragged herself out of bed the next morning with one fervent hope: that it would just be a normal workday. She had slept uneasily, trying to get her mind around what had happened to her – and what she feared might continue to happen. She had been tempted to call Jonas – of all people! – to discuss the Maxxon aspect of this whole mess. At least she could talk to him about one aspect of what was going on without fear, she hoped, of risking the return of Adrian and whoever he worked for. She suspected that Adrian and the Maxxon men were connected somehow, but had nothing to go on to confirm or deny this suspicion other than coincidence. Jonas would normally be her last choice to discuss such serious issues with, but she and he were now connected in a limited way by the strange events that had happened to both of them.

As she brushed her teeth, listening to NPR, she caught the tail end of an update of the ongoing attempt to get Vice President Twainey to reveal who he had met with in forming the National Energy Policy in 2001. Apparently, the parties who had brought the lawsuit – Natural Resources Defense Council, her former employer, and Judicial Watch, a conservative governmental watchdog group – had won their district court case seeking to compel the DOE to release documents relating to the work of Twainey's task force. Senator

Huberson – the Texas senator with strong ties to the energy industry – was interviewed, as an expert on energy issues. Asked to comment on this latest development in the ongoing saga of the Twainey case, she said: "I think this is unfortunate and short-sighted. There is a real need for the executive branch to be able to consult privately with important parties. The President needs to know he is being told the unvarnished truth, and this sometimes requires that what he is told is not made public knowledge."

Jill listened out of habitual interest as she realized that this was probably the very topic that had given rise to her ordeal the last couple of days. Her anxiety came back as she realized how high this went. She alternated between the desire to forget about everything she knew – maybe change the focus of her work? – and to confront the problem head on. She had no desire to get caught up in ongoing intrigue with her own government, but her passion for her work and her innate sense of justice weighed heavily on her. It was one thing to be a desk jockey ferreting out documents and policies from the federal government. It was quite another thing to get caught up in things to such an extent that the feds felt justified in kidnapping her! She spit into her sink, rinsed her mouth out, and attempted to put the issue behind her for the time being.

Jill scooted the few blocks to her office, skipping her morning coffee and paper routine at Elsie's, her favorite pre-work coffee shop. As she walked past the office doorway of Just in Time Travel, a local travel agency on Main Street, she heard a low voice call out her name. She kept walking, but cocked her head to see if she had in fact heard what she thought she had heard. She had: "Jill, right here." She stopped. She knew that voice too well.

Jill turned slowly. Dargan was standing in the recess of the doorway, a baseball cap and sunglasses obscuring his face. "Dargan! What? What are you doing here?"

"Shhh. Come here." Dargan put a finger to his lips and waved his other hand at her, urging her to join him in the doorway. Jill joined Dargan but eyed him warily from a few feet away. Too many weird things were happening to not view this development with suspicion. "Don't I get a hug at least?," Dargan asked and smiled wanly through his scruffy facial hair. With many doubts still lingering, Jill hugged him hard but she was filled with contradictory feelings: confusion, anger; dismay; affection. He smelled bad. And he looked like hell.

"What's going on, Dargan? What are you doing here? And why do you look like such… crap?"

"All in due time, Jill. I don't want to talk very long here. You're probably being followed. I may be too, but I'm not sure. I need you to meet me at the Pacific Sands Motel. It's on…"

"I know where it is. Ocean Avenue between Broadway and Colorado, right? What time shall I meet you?"

"After work. Go through your regular workday and join me after you get off. And don't tell *anyone* that you've seen me or that we're meeting. I can't stress that enough. Okay? Okay?" He spoke very quickly, betraying his agitation. Jill wished she could see his eyes to get a better sense of what was going through his head.

"Okay. I've got a million questions for you. But it's really good to see you!"

"You too, Jill. Go ahead and get to work now, we can't be too careful. All right?"

"All right. I'll… see you later, I guess." Jill managed a smile as she left the doorway. *Dargan! In L.A!* She couldn't help but look both ways as she stepped onto the sidewalk from the doorway. She thought she caught a glimpse of someone turning a corner or ducking into a nook as she looked back the way she had come. But she couldn't be sure.

Chapter 22

Dargan opened the door after confirming through the peephole that the knock he had heard came from Jill's lovely knuckles.

Jill entered and said: "Dargan, you got some splainin' to do."

Dargan smiled despite himself. Jill had always been able to keep him smiling and laughing. She could weave hilarious tales from nothing, chattering on for hours in a way that was completely entertaining and not in the least egotistical. It was what he had loved most about her. But now simply wasn't the time.

"Yes. We've got a lot to talk about." Jill entered, looking awkward after Dargan's less than warm welcome. Dargan wanted so badly to just hug her and kiss her – and to feel her naked body against his again. But he couldn't afford to think about his attraction to her now. And Jill was the one who had blown him off anyway, almost a year ago now. He had no idea if he could ever find the same bond they had before. Jill looked visibly uncomfortable as Dargan stared at her for too long. "It is good to see you, Jill. I've really missed you."

"I've missed you too, Dargan. But this is all way too weird. Please tell me what's going on."

"Definitely. Uh, why don't you sit. Can I get you anything?" Dargan realized he didn't have "anything" to give Jill except water, so he was relieved when Jill replied: "No, I'm good" as she sat on the one chair in the hotel room.

"So what's happening?," Jill asked again as Dargan still hesitated.

"I'm trying to think of where to begin... You know I went to work for the DOE, right?" Dargan sat on the unmade bed across from where Jill was sitting. It occurred briefly to Dargan that he should be embarrassed of his shabby surroundings. But he couldn't let himself be distracted by that kind of thinking either.

"Yeah, I heard that. Few months after I left D.C. I thought it was kind of out of character for you." At least Jill had cared enough to keep track of him a little! He found it hard not to stare at her mouth as she spoke. She had the most beautiful lips, teeth, mouth.

"Right. It was. But I had a good reason for doing it. You know how pissed off I was at the Iraq invasion. Remember how we talked about what we could do to help prevent that kind of thing from happening again?"

"Yes. But I don't remember us coming up with anything very practical. Not at our level of influence."

"Well, I hatched a scheme to infiltrate the DOE in the hopes that I could find information showing definitively that oil was a major motivation for the war. I hoped that if I could find such information, it would prevent other oil-driven wars by educating the public about oil politics and foreign policy. But no such luck. I never found any smoking gun. I mean, I found out a lot of juicy information, but nothing that could rightly be called a smoking gun. Nothing that would *prove* to unreceptive minds the oil/war connection."

"Wait. Wait. I've got to jump in here. I received some documents from the DOE a few weeks ago that included a very incriminating meeting between the Vice President's office and some Saudis. I'm guessing now that you were involved somehow in that. But you're telling me you *didn't* find any smoking gun?" Jill blanched as she said this. As Dargan began responding, Jill cut in: "Oh shit! I'm not supposed to talk to anyone about this!"

"What do you mean? What happened?" He was having trouble focusing already. He didn't need Jill to add to his confusion.

"I don't know. I can't say. I mean… Well, I've already told you the basics."

"Jill, I'm pretty sure we can talk openly here. I don't have any way to know we're not bugged. But I've been very discreet since I've been here. And I'm hoping you weren't followed here. Do you have any reason for being followed?" Dargan stood. He couldn't stay still as his body tried to keep up with his racing mind.

Jill didn't answer his question. "First, tell me if I'm right in thinking you were behind the documents from the DOE being sent to me?"

"You're right on that. I'll tell you the whole story in a minute. But tell me…"

"Damn! It's you who got me involved in this whole mess! If you had any idea what I've been through!" Jill recounted the ordeal of her last two days, including her review of the documents she'd received, her incarceration and the closely related Maxxon side-story, as told to her by her uncle. Dargan listened intently, but cut in frequently to make sure he had all the details right. This was awful. He couldn't believe his actions had caused Jill such troubles. Though in retrospect, it was certainly not too surprising. At least they were together now, even if it was only a temporary reunion.

"Jill, I had no idea it would come to that! I'm so sorry. I've got to admit I feel like I may have got us in over our collective head."

"Ya think? This is way over my head, that I know. Why the hell did you get me involved?"

"I… I… had to find a way to get the documents out of the DOE. And… your FOIA request came in at just the right time. But let me back up."

"Okay."

"Shortly after I began working at the DOE, I was directed by my boss to oversee the electronic archiving of years of DOE records. Including some classified records. I was also responsible for certain FOIA request responses. The ones that had to do with renewable energy. I saw your request come in about a month ago and realized it was my chance to put my plan into action."

"*What* plan?"

"I'm getting there. As part of my archiving job, I gained access to a whole slew of documents. I don't know who was responsible for selecting the documents for me and my team to archive. But there were a lot of them. Not surprising, I guess, for a federal bureaucracy. And we were looking at decades worth of materials. The documents were shipped to my office and adjacent offices when my office filled up. I had the chance to review a lot of the documents and had hoped to review them all initially. But then I got a kick in the ass from my boss to hurry up with the project. It was then that I got my lucky break." Dargan was speaking faster and faster as he continued.

"Okay," Jill chimed in helpfully again.

"You see. Like I said, I never found the smoking gun on that one. I think now that it's probably more accurate to say that oil and energy security issues are the constant backdrop to our foreign policy and that the 9/11 attacks just made it that much easier to act on these constant concerns. But anyway, what I did find is *potentially far more important.*"

Dargan paused for a moment, letting what he had said sink in. When Jill didn't say anything, he continued. "I found that there is a whole division of the Intelligence Office…"

Jill cut him off: "Wait. What's the Intelligence Office?"

"It's normally just called 'the IN.' It's the intelligence branch of the DOE. Normally thought of as being pretty blah. I now know better. One of their main jobs is to ensure national energy security. They apparently take this job *very* seriously."

"So were the guys who picked me up IN people?"

"Probably, but I can't say for sure. From what you told me about what they told you, I'd say so."

"It does make sense."

"Yeah. But here's the more important thing." Jill frowned as he said this. Dargan realized she thought he was downplaying the importance of her ordeal. That wasn't his intention, but he didn't have time to correct every misimpression he gave her. "The IN, as I found out from these documents that just fell into my lap, has been operating a technology suppression program for decades now."

"What does that mean?"

"It means they keep a very vigilant eye on what scientists and inventors and academics are doing in terms of energy technologies. They're on the lookout for technologies that could be used to threaten the US. And, more ominously, what could be used to threaten the power of the large oil companies. This may be hard to believe, but the DOE's IN and Maxxon have been running this suppression program jointly for years. It was begun initially just by the IN. But somehow Maxxon seems to have wormed its way into the process such that it seems to be an equal partner. Maybe a senior partner. I don't know for sure. But I do know that Maxxon is heavily involved."

"That explains it! Now I know why Maxxon was out to get my documents!"

"Exactly. So here's the deal. I found a lot of information on a major suppression effort by the DOE and Maxxon that happened in the last few years. I had all the proof right there in front of me. There has been a lot of discussion in certain circles for years now of what's called Zero Point Energy."

"Zero Point who?"

"Zero Point Energy. ZPE. Zippy. Zippy is a technology that allows us to take energy from the vacuum, essentially. Free energy!" Dargan was pacing on the puke yellow semi-shag carpet and threw his hands in the air as he uttered these words, staring hard at Jill to make his point. Dargan was waiting for Jill to indicate that she realized the importance of what he was talking about. She needed to get this if he was going to make her an ally.

"What? There's no free energy. No free lunch. That's an inviolable principle."

"There is a free lunch! At least there is according to the DOE and Maxxon. And according to many people who write about zippy in various publications and online. There's a lot of theoretical discussion about this out there. But nothing that I came across that was like what I found in the IN documents. Nothing discussing how to actually make an energy generation device based on zippy principles. But the DOE found people who had managed to turn theory into reality. They'd actually created electricity generators based on Zippy principles. More than one. And they dealt with these people in various ways."

"Wait. Wait. Explain how ZPE, Zippy, works, can you?"

"It's been called the ultimate quantum free lunch. The cosmic free lunch! According to quantum physics, the vacuum is constantly producing subatomic particles that blink in and out of existence. It's been theorized that this constant foam of particles blinking in and out correspond to Einstein's cosmological constant, a number that Einstein simply fabricated to make his equations make sense when describing gravitation. It's also been theorized that these virtual particles form the fundamental structure of space. Normally, there's no way to detect these particles, let alone extract energy from them. But under the right conditions and the right apparatus, the particles can be harnessed to produce energy. There are a number of ideas for harnessing this energy, but none has actually panned out publicly. However, there has been at least one invention that produced positive results, and I had the documentation to prove it.

"Way over my head, sounds like. But I had no idea. I've never even heard of ZPE before."

"Believe me, it was the last thing I was expecting to find ferreting through thousands of pages of old DOE documents."

"Speaking of which. I'm confused. You said you didn't find any smoking gun re the oil/war connection. But if the classified meeting transcript wasn't a smoking gun, I don't know what is. I mean, it's open to interpretation, I guess, but don't you think that's pretty powerful proof?"

"Oh, that. That was fake."

"What? I got kidnapped and interrogated and chased *over a fake document*?"

"I doubt it. At least I hope not. No, that was a fake, but there were other documents in your FOIA response. Documents relating to Zippy. I'm pretty sure those posed the real problem for the IN and Maxxon folks."

"Why would you fake a document like that?"

"As a decoy. I figured by the time you had either released that information to the public, which may well be true for all we know, even though I made it up, I would have had time to get the real information out. The info about Zippy. And I made sure that you would see the meeting transcript document before you ever saw the Zippy documents."

"Wait! You're losing me again. Why wouldn't you just spirit the documents out of the DOE building yourself and release them to the press, if that was your plan in the first place?"

"I did have a plan to get the information out without involving anyone else. But I was going to send the documents to you either way, as a backup plan. The problem is, my Plan A didn't work. They changed the passwords on me – long story. The DOE is on lockdown for information transport. They have heavy security precautions against information leaks. Every time you leave any DOE building, you have to go through an extensive search for any kind of documents or electronic storage media. I couldn't figure out how to get the information out that way. And email of course wouldn't work – they check all attachments before they go out. No, after my Plan A failed, the only other way I could think of to do it was through a FOIA response. And yours just happened to come along at about the right time. Truly serendipitous. Or synchronicitous, or whatever. In fact, your request was one of the things that made me realize the time was right to act."

"Why wouldn't you contact me first before you made me a victim of your plans?," Jill asked, with a shade of anger in her voice. She had moved to the edge of her seat and looked up at Dargan with a crease in her brow. She still looked gorgeous. But Dargan knew this one would be hard to explain without giving her the full story.

"I didn't want to risk having the IN men catch wind of my plan. I'm pretty sure I was being tailed and watched even then, which would include tapping my communications. But I'm not totally sure. All I know is that the kitchen was getting real hot. And I had to act."

"So what have you been doing in the weeks since you sent me the documents?"

"It's been less than two weeks actually. I stuck around for a little while, but it became completely clear that I was being tailed. I think the IN men must have been on to me after I sent the

FOIA request. I mean, they must have been able to connect you and me after they found out you were the recipient of the documents. Don't you think?"

"I don't know! I don't know a damn thing about this kind of stuff. This is so far gone from what I'm used to dealing with. You tell me!" Jill was obviously getting exasperated.

"I think they must have made the connection. One thing we know for sure is that they were aware you had been sent the documents. The fact they picked you up is proof of that, at least. What did they tell you about the documents you received?"

Jill thought for a second. "It's strange. I just realized they never mentioned a thing about the contents of the documents themselves. They asked me a bunch of questions, but they never told me exactly what it was I had that was so important. I assumed it was the transcript. But you said that was fake. Did they know that?"

"I don't know. I did a pretty good job on that, I think." Dargan smiled.

"Yes, I'm sure you did. *Jesus!* I can't believe you're actually proud of yourself!" Dargan frowned. He didn't want to upset Jill. Maybe she didn't understand how important what he was doing was. There was still time. Or so he hoped.

Dargan continued after a short pause. "Jill, again, I'm really sorry to get you involved in all of this. But there just didn't seem to be any other way. And, frankly, I'm surprised it worked. What with all their security precautions. It's not like I'm any great espionage expert. There is one thing I did though that might have thrown them off a bit.

"Oh?"

"I encrypted the IN documents re ZPE. And they were only on the CD-ROM you received. No hard copy. That's what I meant when I said I ensured you'd find the decoy before the Zippy documents. Did you see them?"

"No. If I had, I wouldn't have been asking all those questions. Duh."

"Right. I just wanted to make sure. And I would have been surprised if you had seen them. I encrypted them in a subtle way. Not only were they encrypted, but I also added a line to the pdf file that made Adobe, or whatever you were using, stay on a blank screen when you clicked on the document. What I'm trying to say is that if you were browsing through the CD-ROM index, as most people would, and you clicked on the pertinent document, you'd just get a blank screen and an hourglass icon indicating the computer was thinking. To read the document, you'd have to disable my bug and decrypt it."

"Where'd you learn all that stuff?"

"Encrypting documents is not hard. There are a bunch of programs on the market, using various encryption technologies. The one I used wouldn't be hard for an expert to break. But it might have taken a little while for a decrypter to figure out how to disable my stall command. I've dabbled here and there in programming. I am a big geek, as you well know."

"Right." Jill looked down as she appeared to think about what Dargan had told her. She added: "But I'm still not clear on what you've been doing for the last week or so. I mean, you sent those documents out to me a bit less than two weeks ago. Why wouldn't you call me or email me or show up shortly after I got the documents? I'm assuming you wanted to release these documents to the public? What took you so long to get to me?"

"That's a long story, Jill. I'll tell you that part later. What's important now is to figure out how to get those documents back! This whole thing means nothing if we … I, don't get the Zippy documents back." Dargan was pacing again, watching his feet as he walked back and forth in front of Jill. The sound of traffic outside the hotel door became more prominent as the silence continued.

Dargan stopped abruptly and looked at Jill. "You're sure you only made the one copy? And it's gone? You checked?"

"Well, yes. I checked my email and it was indeed gone. And I checked my sent mail folder too. Gone." Silence again. Dargan was at a loss. At the end of his rope. He had hoped somehow that just by seeing Jill again, by being with her, that somehow the shitty situation he found himself in might get better. Some miraculous event might occur that would fix everything. A deep sense of foreboding started rising in Dargan and his eyes welled with tears as the frustration of hitting the end of the road came over him. *What the hell do I do now?*

"Wait." Jill said. Dargan looked at Jill. Her face lit up as she stared at Dargan.

"What?" Dargan asked, afraid to ask for fear of disappointment.

"I just remembered. I made *two* copies of the documents! I made one by sending it to myself via email. But I made a second one on my thumbdrive!" Jill held up her keychain as she said this, showing off her keychain thumbdrive.

Chapter 23

"No way! That's too good to be true!" Dargan leaped in Jill's direction and lifted her into his arms in a tight embrace. Much to Jill's surprise, he planted a strong kiss on her lips. Before she had a chance to reciprocate or push him away – she wasn't sure which she wanted – Dargan pulled away from her. He held her at arm's length, his hands on her upper arms. With his face still close to hers, he continued: "This is great! I knew I could count on you!"

Jill smiled despite herself. "Of course you could. I was just kidding before … not!" It was very rare that Dargan showed such strong emotion. But maybe he'd changed in the year since they stopped talking. She liked his newfound enthusiasm and his elevated mood.

"I don't care if you were kidding or not," Dargan smiled back at her. "I'm just happy we have the documents."

"Actually, you know what. I just realized we have no idea if the documents are really on my thumbdrive. I haven't checked it since I was taken in by the IN. Before we get too excited, we should make sure."

"You're right. Let's check it now." Dargan pulled a small laptop out of his bag. Jill handed him the thumbdrive as Dargan started his computer. It booted quickly and Dargan inserted the thumbdrive into one of the computer's USB ports. Dargan opened his computer's file browser program and clicked on the thumbdrive icon, displaying its contents. He clicked through the folder until he found the file he was looking for. "It's called 'DOEtechprogram.'" He performed a number of quick operations that Jill wasn't able to follow, which brought him to a full-screen display of gobbledygook. "This is the code. Now I've just got to take out my stall command." Dargan scrolled down the screen and highlighted a single line. He hit the delete key, saved the document, and returned to the thumbdrive folder. "Now we've got to decrypt it."

"I feel like we're in a movie," Jill said with a grin. Dargan grinned back at her. She loved his smile, even in his current shaggy and unkempt state. Then he opened up another program. "This is an encryption program. I just need to drag the file into the box." He performed this operation, prompting an hourglass icon to appear on the screen. After a couple of seconds, the icon disappeared and a message popped up: "Decryption complete." Dargan double-clicked on the file. After a few seconds, a large pdf document – 78 pages – appeared on the screen. "Eureka!"

Jill pushed Dargan aside. "All right, let me get a looksee at these damn documents you're so fired up about." As she read through the documents, Jill found her attention equally split between the documents themselves and her feelings prompted by being around Dargan again.

When she had first seen him in the doorway on Main Street, she had immediately felt a twinge of her old feelings for him. And being around him now strengthened that feeling, despite his strange behavior and the highly abnormal circumstances they found themselves in. Despite his obvious qualities – intelligence, compassion, ambition – there had always been something else that attracted her to him. An ineffable quality. Maybe it was simply pheromones, those little keys that seemed to fit the equally small locks in the nose and exerted inordinate influence over the largest decisions about love and affection. But Jill didn't have to stoop to the semi-mystical pheromone explanation to explain her attraction to Dargan. Though it had been almost a year since they had talked, his presence brought back to her all the things about him that she found pleasing. The way he moved. The way he smiled. The way his hair fell. The way he was easily flustered by any sign of her discomfort or disagreement. The whole package.

* * *

Jill knocked on the door of Dargan's hotel room bathroom, turning the door handle and entering as she did so. Dargan had gone to the bathroom as she became immersed in the Zippy documents. She assumed he had been washing his hands because she had heard the toilet flush. "Dargan, I just need to get some tissue to blow …" Dargan looked up, startled. "Oh, sorry," Jill blurted. He was bent over the linoleum sink counter, holding a rolled up bill in his hand. Two lines of yellowish powder were laid out on the counter.

"Don't people knock anymore?" He seemed more embarrassed than angry.

"What are you doing? Is that coke?"

"No, it's not coke. It's… something similar. Honey, I've been under so much pressure, you have no idea. I've had to be completely on top of my game."

Honey? "Well, what is it?" As she asked this question, Dargan bent back down and snorted the first line, plugging his left nostril as he did so.

"It's just meth, Jill. Not a big deal. Just a bump to keep me going and keep me sharp."

"I don't know, Dargan, that's some hard shit, from what I hear."

"That may be the word on the street. But, as they say, everything in moderation." He switched hands and nostrils and snorted the second line. Maybe he wasn't exactly moderating his use lately. But, damn it, he needed it to keep sharp! To stay ahead of the IN men and their Maxxon cronies.

"Stop that! How long have you been doing this?"

"Look, that's not important." He wiped the counter off and returned the bill to his pocket, still rolled. "What's important is that we figure out what to do here." His speech had become faster and his intensity had turned up a notch.

Waving his hand past the bathroom door, Dargan said: "Can we get out of here?"

Frowning, Jill backed out of the bathroom and sat on the bed. "I really don't like this, Dargan. This whole situation. You're obviously not well. You're definitely not the Dargan I knew before. Where did you get that stuff?"

"Oh, I'm the same, Jill, believe me. But listen. I've got to explain some more things to you. And please don't interrupt unless you really need to."

Jill looked away and pursed her lips in disapproval, but said nothing further. She had a strong urge to just leave the situation. At the same time, she was genuinely worried about Dargan, who obviously was *not* his former self. And she was also fascinated by these events – even though she was deathly frightened at the idea of becoming more involved than she already was. Dargan stood in front of her as she sat back in the lone chair in the hotel room, shifting his feet frequently as if he wanted to walk around, but repeatedly stopped himself from doing so.

"Jill, I've told you about Zippy. But I haven't told you what Zippy could mean if it became widespread as an energy source. The implications are staggering. First, power truly too cheap to meter! Mass empowerment in the literal sense. Second, this would close the growing gap between rich and poor, the haves and havenots, the empowered and the disempowered. Zippy would bring democracy to America and the world like it's never been seen before. Think of it!"

Dargan's delivery was rapid-fire and he punctuated his delivery with frequent strokes of his hands, cutting through the air in front of him. This was a new, even more intense Dargan. Jill had suffered through many of his harangues when they had dated. She often enjoyed his monologues. But this was a much more frantic Dargan, amped up on drugs.

Dargan continued, fixing Jill occasionally with an intense stare. "The model for big business for most of the last century and this one has been the vertically integrated oil company. These companies wield tremendous power through their lobbying, their bribes in developing nations, and through their perversion of the scientific process. They even have their own president for Christ's sake! By simultaneously eliminating the power of Big Oil and increasing the power of the average citizen through cutting the shackles of dependency on outside energy sources, we help create true democracy. One person, one vote! Not one dollar, one vote! No more rhetoric about democracy. Action! In just a few years, we would see a society radically transformed for the better. We could lop off the head of corporate power and at the same time radically increase the power of the average citizen. I'm not talking about any half-baked notion of socialist enforced equality. I'm talking about a level playing field. Overnight, we would move to a society ten times more equitable and just than we see today!"

Jill listened intently. Much of what Dargan was saying was old news to her, but some was new. And he delivered these ideas with such conviction and hard-edge clarity that she began to share some of his ardor, despite her misgivings about his out-of-whack mental state.

"But that's not the whole story, Jill. What is life about? Don't answer – just a rhetorical question. Nobody knows. But life *is* about creativity, happiness, family, procreation, spiritual growth. The highest expression of our humanity is through creation of new ideas, new art, new life. The spread of free energy will free humanity from the shackles of work slavery. Who needs to work ten hours a day, eight hours a day, or even six hours a day, when soon there will be machines, using free energy, that take care of all our needs such as food, cleaning, yard work?

"Yes, we'll still need to work a bit to earn money to buy these machines, but soon the machines will be able to make new machines at almost no expense. Because it will all be based on free energy. With free energy and sufficient natural resources, there's no limit to what could be made and what could then free the vast majority of people from wage-slavery. What do we do with all this free time? We create! We make love! We talk! We search for God. We live life. We will have conquered time itself. Kronos will be defeated yet again! With Prometheus' help."

Jill was getting lost. *Who, or what, the hell is Kronos?* "What the hell are you talking…?" But Dargan steamrolled her.

"With free energy comes free time. Don't you see it? Think of what we can collectively achieve when vast numbers of people are freed to focus on science, humanitarian work, spirituality. We could solve the world's problems faster than anyone ever dreamed possible. The world's poor will have food and medicine. New parts of the globe will be made livable because we will have the power to fuel completely self-contained habitats with no regard to energy costs. We will be able to build super-colliders like none existing today to plumb the secrets of the universe. We can explore other planets and send colonists to the Moon and Mars. Can immortality elude us much longer? Kronos will then truly be dead, the Titans overthrown once again! The *Kali yuga* will be defeated! *Kalpa* after *kalpa* will be ours."

Jill sat silently, gazing at Dargan with a puzzled look. She didn't know what to say. Maybe it was best just to let him rant on until the methamphetamine had worn off.

"Don't you see it, Jill? This is about time! By Killing Kronos we become timeless. What is time? Consciousness is time. Consciousness creates time because it is that function of our brains that connects discrete snapshots of the world together. Consciousness creates time! Without consciousness, there is no time. It is only the consciousness of highly complex organisms, like human beings, that brings the universe into being by connecting one moment to the next into a coherent narrative. Don't you see it? By giving time to all of us, I ... Prometheus, is expanding the universal consciousness, the ground of being, *brahman*, the godhead, the Logos, the Tao, whatever you want to call it."

Now Jill was getting more worried. He was making no sense and she really didn't like the way he was talking. Was he losing it? Were the drugs and stress making him a loony tune? Dargan kept going.

"At the same time, too much *self-*consciousness can be oppressive. The Buddha taught that life is necessarily suffering. Self-consciousness is necessarily suffering because we all are born into pain, all must suffer sickness, old age, and, eventually, death. By killing Kronos, we all become mystics! We all have the Buddha inside of us. We can all become timeless!

"This is where it gets tricky. Consciousness creates time and Zippy will kill time. Zippy is the light to help us find Buddha, Krishna, Jesus, to kill time! Kill Kronos!"

Dargan stopped, visibly breathing hard. Jill finally spoke: "Dargan, you've lost me. Some of what you're saying makes sense, but you're really scaring me. I think we should think more about this before we do anything drastic. I think there's a lot more we need to think about."

"I am thinking about it! That's all I have been doing! Check this out." Dargan took a quarter out of his pocket and flipped it to Jill. She caught it and said: "It's a quarter. What's the big deal?"

"Is it tails?"

"Yes."

"What's on the tails side of the quarter?"

"An eagle."

"What does that represent?"

"I don't know. The federal government, I guess."

"Exactly!"

"Do you know why the eagle is on the quarter?"

"Liberty, freedom, all that stuff. It represents the idea of liberty as the guiding principle of our country."

"Right! Well, that's what it's supposed to represent. But that's not the whole story. The eagle on the quarter is the Great Seal of the United States. Zeus' eagle eats out Prometheus' liver every day. Do you know how *painful* that is?"

Before Jill could answer, Dargan went on: "And it's an eagle that measures time in Hindu cosmology. The eagle wears down the Himalayas with a single flight every one thousand years, holding a feather in its talons and rubbing it once over the top of the Himalayas. The eagle creates time! And then there's the eagle on the Great Seal! And who's out to get me, us? The IN! The feds! They're trying to stop us from killing time! The eagle has got to be taken down before it takes us down."

"Whoa, whoa! Dargan, this is crazy talk. Let's just slow down and relax for a bit. Look, I agree with you about Zero Point… Zippy. That's obviously incredibly important if you're right about what you found. But all this other stuff, you're going way too far!" Jill's thoughts of possibly getting back together with Dargan dissipated as she realized that he might genuinely be sick. She'd never seen anything in their year together in D.C. to suggest that he was susceptible to mental illness. But she also would never have believed – until she'd seen it with her own eyes – that he would have become a crystal meth addict! He had showed a tendency toward extreme points of view at times. Even though his record and his professional choices didn't reveal an extremist at work, he had taken some pretty extreme positions in their private conversations.

Whereas she had been generally willing to assume the best intentions of governmental and private actors when it came to energy issues – or political issues more generally – Dargan seemed to always assume the worst and to see conspiracies everywhere. But he didn't call them conspiracies. He called it "institutional analysis," a way of examining institutions and their functioning to determine how outcomes were influenced by the design of the institution itself. Or so he said. To her, it had generally sounded like any other nuts' conspiracy theories. When they were dating, she had found such discussions generally interesting and sometimes mildly irritating. But not serious cause for alarm, as she was feeling now.

Chapter 24

Dargan knew he was making a lot of connections that might strain the credulity of others who were not as knowledgeable about such matters as he was. He just had to figure out how to convince Jill of the truth of what he was saying. People always reacted with resistance and dismay when first learning uncomfortable truths. Gandhi was fond of saying: "First they ignore you, then they laugh at you, then they fight you, then you win." Jill would come to see it his way, he was confident. He just needed to wait for what he had said to sink in and then subtly reinforce it over time. He couldn't be too aggressive or he'd turn her away entirely. He may have overplayed his hand already. But she was still here, strong support for the notion that he hadn't gone too far. Yet. Maybe he should lay off the meth for a bit. But he needed it! If he let his guard or his wits down at all, it could cost him big time.

"I've got to go, Dargan. It's getting late."

"Do you? You're welcome to stay if you like." This was not good. But he had to keep calm and roll with the punches. Subtlety. It wasn't his strong suit, but he needed to try harder.

"I don't think so. I need to do some thinking. And so do you, I think. I'll come back tomorrow, all right?" She spoke in a curt tone of voice that cut right to Dargan's heart.

"Okay, I guess. But can you do me a favor?"

Jill paused. "Sure. Maybe. What?"

"Can you bring me some food? I don't want to go outside unless I absolutely have to."

"Sure. What do you have now? Enough for tomorrow?"

"I've just got some snack food. Enough until lunch or so tomorrow."

"Well, I'll do the same thing I did today, then. I'll work my regular day and then come by after work. All right?"

"Great! Can you also make a paper copy of the Zippy documents at work and bring them tomorrow?"

"Sure." Jill stood to go. "Oh, do you have a number I can call you at?"

"You can just call the hotel. I got rid of my cell phone. Those can be tracked."

Dargan was already standing, as he had been during much of their discussion. He moved toward her to give her a hug goodbye. She stepped back at first, not receptive. Then she apparently changed her mind and gave Dargan a perfunctory hug. Her upper body barely touched his and she bent from the waist to meet him. It was not the full-bodied and wholehearted embrace he'd been yearning for. He had definitely freaked her out, that much was obvious. There was still time.

Chapter 25

Jill arrived at Dargan's hotel room shortly before 6:30 in the evening the next day. She had stopped after work at a local grocery store to get a few things for Dargan. The Twinkies and Doritos diet was not going to cut it. She knocked lightly on the door. She couldn't help looking both ways down the hallway as she did so. She didn't see anyone. The peephole darkened as Dargan looked out. Dargan opened the door with a big smile that Jill couldn't resist returning. "Jill! It's been so long! Good to see you again."

"I got you some stuff." She handed him the brown paper grocery bag she was carrying as she entered the hotel room. She had noticed a hot plate and microwave in his room the day before, so had bought some TV dinners and some eggs and bread for his breakfasts. She had no idea how long he would be holed up in his hotel room. She suspected he didn't either. So she had planned for a couple of days' worth of groceries. "You shaved! Looking good." He had apparently showered too, judging by the lack of B.O. in the air.

"You know. Places to go. People to see."

"Hah! Yeah, your schedule is brutal I'm sure." Jill hoped Dargan wasn't nuts. And she hoped that their current situation could be resolved quickly. Despite her acceptance of how important

Zippy was, she wasn't sure she wanted to get further involved in Dargan's plotting. It was fine and dandy to be an idealist and work hard to change things for the better. But she wasn't sure she was willing to pay as steep a price to satisfy her conscience as Dargan was. Why couldn't he have come back into her life in some normal way? Minus the drama and that whole kidnapping thing.

This time, her second visit, they talked about normal things. Family, friends, small personal dramas. She desperately wanted him to be okay. After an hour or so of "normal" conversation, Jill unconsciously began massaging her arm and shoulder, still smarting from her run in with Jonas. She was sitting in the solitary chair again, while Dargan lounged on the bed in front of her. Dargan, noticing her self-massage, suggested he help her out with her sore spots. He had always been good at giving massages. It was one of the things she had missed most about his time with him. After a moment's hesitation, she said "all right" and joined him on the bed.

She lay face down as he kneaded her shoulder with deft and strong hands. He moved his way down her triceps, probing and soothing. Then he extended the same treatment to her trapezius muscle and her neck, keeping his hands on the outside of her shirt. It felt great. Thankfully, he stopped there. She would have had to stop him if he had tried to go any further, turning an innocent therapeutic massage into something sexual. Instead, he moved away from her and propped himself up on an elbow.

As they lay on the bed together, facing each other, Dargan said: "You know, Jill. We need some kind of insurance policy."

"Exqueeze me?"

"An insurance policy. In case I, or you, or both of us, gets picked up. We need to arrange for someone else to get a copy of the documents and release them to the press on our word – or if they don't hear from us in a given amount of time."

"Oh. Right. Of course. Who do you have in mind?"

"I'm not sure. I was hoping you might know of someone who would be good."

Yet another new twist. Jill considered who of her friends or family she could trust to both agree to such a thing and to actually carry it out if the need arose. She didn't want to get her mother involved. She'd have hours of explaining to do if she asked her mother to hold the documents. Jonas? Definitely not. Rahul? Maybe. He was highly professional and probably wouldn't ask too many questions. Joe? No. He liked Jill too much. She couldn't risk having someone with romantic intentions toward her getting involved. Jamie? That wouldn't be fair to her. She was a new mother with very little background in this situation. Jill already felt guilty, in retrospect, for involving her as much as she had.

"I have a good friend, Rahul, who might help us out."

"Great. Is he reliable?"

"Definitely. He's a lawyer at a well-respected law firm. Highly competent."

"Sounds good so far. Could the IN easily get to him through his association with you? I mean, could they figure out we're using him pretty easily?"

"I don't know. I have no idea if they've been following me still, or how long they were following me before. Wait. Rahul was with me when I first met Adrian on the hiking trail."

"Shit. Anyone else?"

"I don't think so. I've gone through everyone I can think of."

"Hmmm. Well, I guess we'll have to go with him. The fact that he's your friend, and not mine, will be a good way of insulating him from discovery."

"Let's hope." Jill called Rahul the next day and invited him to lunch. He was very interested in her request and pestered her to tell him the whole story. But she couldn't, of course. She told him only that she had some very important information she wanted him to hold. If he didn't hear from her for a week, he was to go to the press – LA Times, CNN, all the big news outlets – and share the information. He agreed to her request, obviously relishing the chance to become involved in a little corporate espionage.

* * *

"You are not going to believe what I got for us!"

"Oh yeah?" Dargan replied as he let her into the hotel room, closing the door behind her quietly. It had been four days since Jill first ran into Dargan on the street. She had dropped by the hotel room every day after work for each of those days. It was almost like a routine had already been created. And Dargan hadn't lapsed into any more solipsistic rants since their first day together. She also hadn't caught him doing any more meth. At least he was being discreet if he was still doing it.

"Check this out." Jill reached into the bag she had set down on the bed, which Dargan or the maid had made. She pulled out two Groucho Marx spectacle sets. Grinning broadly, she placed one spectacle-and-big-nose-with-big-mustache mask on herself. As Dargan laughed hard, she placed the second set on his face. "Your damn nose is almost too big for this thing," she teased. And it was. The Groucho nose barely fit over Dargan's very respectable schnoz.

"Oh this is good," Dargan said as he adjusted the spectacles over his ears. "I wouldn't join any club that would have me as a member!," Dargan said in a clipped, nasal voice. Dargan punctuated his words with theatrical hand movements. Dargan's impression was, as always, just right. Jill collapsed in giggles as Dargan pranced about in a way reminiscent of both Marx and Charlie Chaplin. Regaining control of herself, Jill stood up straight, pushing her chest out, and said: "Mr. Marx, I do believe you are an impostor. I would thank you kindly to decease and resist any further impersonations of yours truly." Dargan chuckled and put up his fists.

"Mr. Marx, I do believe you are the impostor! There's obviously only one way to resolve this dispute. Fisticuffs! Put 'em up!" Dargan moved his hands back and forth, menacingly mocking.

"All right, you asked for it Mr. Marx!" Jill assumed the same stance as Dargan and threw a couple of small jabs in his direction. He bobbed and weaved, ducking her vicious attack.

"You've got to do better than that, Mr. Marx!," Dargan yelled as he ducked under her fists and picked her up with his arms around her thighs. She squealed as he threw her – gently – down on the bed. He pretended to perform an elbow smash, the "professional" wrestling move in which a wrestler leaps off the top rope and lands an elbow on his opponent's brutalized physique. But Dargan made sure that the mattress absorbed his body's weight before his elbow came down on Jill's belly. Jill squealed again, but allowed Dargan's arm to continue to rest over her belly. He looked up at her with a smile, his head at the same level as her breasts. He slowly moved up the bed so that his eyes – framed by empty Groucho rims– were on the same level as hers. Surprising herself, Jill moved toward him and kissed him. Or at least she tried. Instead of her lips landing on his, their large noses bumped with a clack. They laughed. Jill removed her Marx "disguise" and leaned over again to kiss Dargan. Ignoring the coarse bristles of his fake mustache, she savored the feel of his lips on hers. It had been way too long since she shared a kiss with someone she truly cared about.

Jill and Dargan kissed and kissed. There was no hurry. Jill suppressed a giggle as Dargan's mustache tickled her lips and nose. He removed his Groucho getup. They kissed more as Dargan pushed Jill to her back and rolled himself on top of her. She liked the weight of his body on hers. A small moan emanated from deep in the back of her throat. She could feel his penis hard against her thigh. She shifted her thighs and spread her legs slightly apart. He took the hint and shifted himself squarely between her legs. She could feel his penis against her pubic bone and vagina. It had been way too long! His hand was on her side, sliding up inside her shirt. She arched her back against his hand as he caressed her breast from the outside of her bra.

"Your... Your buckle is hurting me." It wasn't really that uncomfortable for her. But her words had the desired effect. Dargan undid his buckle and swiftly pulled his belt off with a theatrical swoop of his arm. She tugged at his shirt with a grin. He obliged and pulled it off over his head. She was happy to see he was still in great shape. Abs packaged like a half dozen eggs in a cardboard wrapper. Shoulder muscles rippling. He reached down and undid the top button of her pants. "Heyyyy," Jill said softly as she put her arms over her head, suggesting a young child needing help undressing. Dargan smiled and pulled her shirt over her head. He took a moment to admire her semi-naked body before leaning down to kiss her again. As he did so, he reached under her back and deftly, with one hand, unfastened her bra clasp. She helped him by removing the unhooked bra from her shoulders.

Dargan lay down next to her and pulled her onto her side as he kissed her. Jill loved the feel of her breasts against his naked chest, losing herself in his lips, his tongue, his skin. "Oh my god, you feel good," she murmured to him. He replied with a low "mmmm." She heard the noise of her pants coming unzipped as Dargan broke away from her lips. He pushed her gently to her back and positioned himself between her legs again. He took her pants by the thighs and pulled. Jill lifted her butt, allowing her jeans to slide off. Her panties started to come off with her jeans, but she stopped them with one hand from sliding very far. Dargan pulled her hand away and whisked her jeans and panties off in one fell swoop. Naked before him for the first time in more than a year, Jill remembered fully the pleasure of her time with him in D.C. The conversation, the laughter, the climbing, the friendship, the sex. They made love slowly. As Jill came, her tears welled, finally overflowing. She didn't know if they were tears of joy or sorrow.

* * *

In the four days since they were reunited, neither Jill nor Dargan had seen anything suspicious. Hence the Groucho masks. "So these are our disguises?," Dargan had asked after their lovemaking.

"Yup. They're so over the top the bad guys will have no idea."

"You may well be right. I'm willing to risk it." They had agreed that it was reasonable to go out in public. The risk seemed minimal at this point. Surely they would have located Dargan by now if it was their intention to take him into custody?

At times, Jill feared that Dargan was completely off his rocker and that he had imagined the threat from the IN. If so, the only danger she had to worry about was from Dargan and her renewed feelings for him. But then the very real memory of her IN incarceration came back to her. And she truly wanted to believe that Dargan was not sick. They had discussed the possibility that he had been a victim of identity theft. This would have explained his inactive ATM and credit cards. And his inability to log in to his email accounts. But it still didn't explain her incarceration or the Maxxon agents paying Jonas to retrieve the documents from Jill's office.

They had dressed leisurely. They were in no hurry, but Dargan had gently pressed Jill to get ready. "Hold your horses, Dargan! I'm just enjoying relaxing with you." Jill smiled at him.

He smiled back and gently beat her with a pillow, saying: "I am holding my horses! But I really want to get some fresh air with you. C'mon, ya laggard!" Smiling, she brushed the pillow away and got out of bed. "That's better," he said, as he watched her slowly get dressed. She made a show of it for him. She picked up one of her socks and mockingly moved it back and forth between her legs as she wiggled her hips. Dargan laughed as she camped it up even more.

They finally got ready to go out shortly after eleven PM. Jill was back in her rather plain outfit: medium tight long-sleeve yellow T with her favorite pair of jeans and some low pumps. Dargan was also in jeans, but wore a button down shirt, untucked, with non-descript leather shoes. And of course they both wore their Groucho Marx masks. Giggling at each other, they left the hotel room. For Dargan, this was his first time going outside in five days. They had no particular plan, but wandered in the direction of the Santa Monica Pier. "It's amazing how quickly I missed not being around people," Dargan said as they strolled.

"I bet. People are highly addictive." They held hands as they walked, taking in the sights along Ocean Avenue.

They suppressed giggles as they walked past other people with a straight face. As people approached them, they smiled and some laughed aloud. Dargan and Jill approached the Pier and Dargan suggested they check out the festivities. "It's somehow fitting, don't you think?" The Pier was a perpetual carnival, with fair rides, restaurants and amusement booths. A ferris wheel graced the middle of the pier, a sight visible from miles around.

As they crossed the street, Jill saw, in the corner of her eye, a swift movement, suggesting a person in a hurry. She turned and saw a large man in a suit approaching fast from the direction they had come. Another muscular man approached them, walking very deliberately, along the other side of Ocean Avenue. Even though there were a moderate number of pedestrians there, these two men stuck out like the proverbial sore thumb, largely because of the speed and purposefulness with which they moved. "Dargan," Jill said, pointing toward the man across the street. They stopped in the middle of the crosswalk. The red hand of the walk signal flashed insistently. They turned and saw the other man approaching equally deliberately. Dargan tugged on Jill's hand.

"Let's go." He started running, pulling Jill with him. The man across the street starting jogging in their direction. He was about a hundred feet away. Jill and Dargan crossed under the Santa Monica Pier sign and started running full speed. Dargan let go of Jill's hand. Jill looked back and saw the two men, now together, running after them. She couldn't believe this was happening! After all this. She prayed that they weren't IN men. Maybe they were tax collectors or something. Better IRS men than IN men! She heard a voice: "Stop! Stop or we'll shoot." Not IRS men, apparently.

Jill looked back up the hill, hoping she wouldn't trip over herself. She saw the two men at the top of the hill brandishing guns. Dargan looked back at Jill: "Don't stop! They won't shoot when there are people around!" Jill had no time to think. Instead, she just ran and found herself almost out of control as she and Dargan headed down the very steep grade of the road leading to the pier itself.

"Stop! This is your last chance!" Jill and Dargan kept on going. They couldn't have stopped if they'd tried, it was so steep. Strangely, there were no people on the sidewalks of the steep grade.

Dargan was about ten feet in front of her when Jill saw a hole appear in the back of his shirt as his right shoulder jerked forward.

Then she heard the loud crack of a gun shot.

Dargan fell, rolling forward over his right shoulder.

Jill screamed and tried to slow herself down. She succeeded and stopped a few paces after Dargan, at the bottom of the steep hill.

She turned and saw the IN men running from the top of the hill. Dargan had pulled himself to one knee and looked dazed as he struggled to get to his feet.

The front of his shirt blazed with crimson blood. The Groucho mask was hanging from one ear.

"Oh my God, Dargan! Stop! Stop! This isn't worth it!"

"No, I can't let them catch me, us. C'mon." Amazingly, Dargan heaved himself to his feet and started running at a slow pace again. Jill ran beside him and offered her shoulder for support. He didn't take it.

"Dargan! This way," Jill said as she saw the steps leading down to the bike trail approaching on the right side. Dargan veered toward the steps as Jill led the way. They stumbled down the steps with the IN men about two hundred feet away. The stairwell was small, but they were able to muddle through fairly quickly.

Jill dragged Dargan's hand, his ailing body following, toward the bike path that ran under the pier. Maybe they could find a hiding place under the pier, Jill thought. There were a number of pilings on either side of the bike path. At night, they were not lit at all. A perfect hiding place in a very imperfect situation.

Jill led Dargan into the darkness on the right side of the bike path. She went back as far as she could, stumbling in the darkness. There was some illumination from the lights lining the pier and the ambient light of the city and carnival rides above. They trudged through the sand, trying to put as much distance between them and the entrance to the bike path. Dargan fell to his knees, got up again, and then fell again. He fell to his back and lay in the dim light, wheezing. Blood covered his lips.

"Dargan, you're going to be all right!" *This couldn't be happening!* She didn't know where to begin, blood seemed to be leaking from his nose, his mouth, his eyes, his chest, dripping down his shirt onto the cold sand. She needed to get a hold of herself. She was a take-charge kind of person! But that part of her seemed to have oozed away with what seemed like all of Dargan's blood. *Pull yourself together!*

As Dargan ranted to her about his crazy stuff, she tried to assess the extent of the damage. She ripped his shirt open. There was a clean exit wound on his right pectoral. At least they hadn't been using hollow-nosed bullets. Very humane... Jill could see small lights at the north end of the bike path, where they had entered the tunnel. She assumed the lights were the IN men's flashlights. She didn't have much time. She had no idea whether the IN men would help Dargan or try to finish him off. She had to do what she could to stanch the bleeding now.

The blood was flowing down his chest into his chest "cup." Pooling there. Tears streamed down Jill's cheeks, making it hard for her to see what she was doing. She needed to find something to plug the bleeding. She ripped her left shirt sleeve off at the shoulder. It was a much softer fabric than Dargan's shirt and would make a better plug for his wound. She leaned over Dargan to insert the small wad of fabric. Her tears fell onto his chest as she did so, mingling with his blood. Dargan, delirious, leaned up weakly to see what she was doing.

Jill heard the IN men getting closer. She saw a flashlight beam pass over them – and then return to pierce Jill's back with its light. They were caught. As abruptly as Dargan had come back into her life, he would now be taken away from her again.

<u>Chapter 26</u>

Dargan opened his eyes to a brightly lit antiseptic room. His eyes ached as they adjusted to the bright light. His body ached even more. He looked around the room. There wasn't much there, but it looked like a hospital room. He was lying on a single bed, the upper part of which was angled slightly upward.

There was a wooden chair to the right of his bed and a cabinet and sink along the right side of the wall. There was a door in the center of the wall to Dargan's left. There were no windows. What looked like a camera or some other surveillance device stared at him from one corner of the ceiling.

The last few hours of his life came back to Dargan with full force. What had happened to him? Where was Jill? He looked down at his bandaged right shoulder and chest. His right arm was in a sling. Dargan realized he must have been shot. At the time, it felt like he had been punched by a giant fist. His memory of what happened after that was very fuzzy. He remembered lying on the cold ground, looking up at Jill. She had been crying and he had been trying to explain to her why Zippy was so important.

Dargan slowly sat up, his head throbbing. He stood, wobbly, and shuffled his way to the door. Walking ten feet was incredibly difficult. Dargan felt like his head was about to burst. And he had almost no energy. He tried the door handle. The door wouldn't open. He banged weakly on the door, twice, and yelled: "hey! Anyone there?" No answer. There was an electronic card reader next to the door. Dargan assumed that it was necessary to swipe a card to open the door, even from the inside. He and Jill must have been picked up by the IN, Dargan realized. He was being held by the IN in some pseudo-hospital.

He felt unimaginably weary. He needed a bump. Badly. He looked around the room, in the cabinets and under the bed, for his things. No luck. No clothes. No meth. *Fuck!* Where was Jill? He laid back down on the bed and examined his hospital room/cell. His head hurt badly and he couldn't think straight. There had to be some way out. He closed his eyes to think better about his unfortunate situation.

* * *

"You awake? How you doin' there, Mr. Brennan?" Dargan opened his eyes – slowly this time. He must have fallen asleep again. His eyes adjusted quickly to the light and he saw a kindly looking middle-aged man leaning over him.

"I … feel like crap." His mouth barely worked. The words came out as though he were a two year old just learning to talk.

"We'll get you back in tip-top shape in no time. You just relax. You're out of the woods already. Strong as an ox. Not many people could take a bullet like that and be as in good shape as you are. But it did miss all your vital organs. You're lucky."

"Yeah. Good. I guess." The throbbing in his head got louder. "Who are you? Where am I?"

"I'm Doctor Jones. You're in a DOD high security facility. I don't know what you did, Mr. Brennan, but that's not my business. My only business is to make sure you get well. And looks like you're well on your way."

"DOD? Oh, Defense. How do I get out of here?" Stupid question, he realized. The doctor, if he was indeed just a doctor, would have no idea how Dargan could leave.

"Like I said, that's not my department. You just need to lie back and relax for a while. I'm sure everything else will work out fine once you're well." The doctor left, making sure that Dargan was lying in his bed as he opened the door. Dargan couldn't have done anything to try and escape even if he had tried. He lay back again and closed his eyes. The throbbing receded as he drifted off again.

* * *

He was shaken awake again as someone shook his shoulder gently. "Mr. Brennan? Mr. Brennan? Can you hear me?"

Dargan opened his eyes slowly, anticipating the bright lights this time. "Who are you?" Dargan made out two figures on the left side of his bed. One was of a thirty-something man with chiseled features and short dark hair. The man was the one who had spoken to him. The other was a woman, also likely in her thirties, with long blonde hair tucked behind her head. Carnie! Dargan recognized her as the woman who had interviewed him with Smith, his boss at the DOE. Since he began working there, he had barely seen her and spoken to her over the phone on only one or two occasions.

"Mr. Brennan. We're hear to ask you some questions. Are you able to talk with us?"

"Who are you?"

"We're with the IN, Dargan. You know what that is, don't you?"

"Yeah, sorta." So he had been right! Small comfort now that he was apparently incarcerated for who knew how long. He had not guessed that Carnie was IN, though. He couldn't imagine why she had been working as an IN agent in the DOE unit headed by Smith.

"We need to ask you some questions about the documents you sent to Ms. Boyd. Are you strong enough to talk with us?"

"Do I have a choice?"

"Certainly. We don't have to talk now, if you're not up to it. But we will talk eventually." There was a hint of menace in the man's voice.

"Give me five minutes and I'll be ready."

"Okay. We'll be back in five minutes to escort you to the interview room."

* * *

Ten minutes later, Dargan was seated at a small table in another brightly lit, windowless room. The male IN agent handcuffed Dargan's left hand to the table, which was bolted to the ground. His head still hurt, but not quite as much. He wondered how bad the withdrawal symptoms would get. He'd only been doing meth on a regular basis for the last few weeks. He'd borrowed some from Annabella while he was finishing his preparations at the DOE. And when he'd finally flown the coop for California, he stole the rest of her stash. She'd get over it. He hoped that only a month's regular usage would not lead to any severe withdrawal pains, like he'd heard about with heroin and other highly addictive drugs. But right now, he just felt like he couldn't think straight and the craving was getting worse.

"Mr. Brennan. May I call you Dargan?"

"I guess." The man with short dark hair was seated across the table from Dargan. Carnie was at his side, a sour expression on her lips. On the table in front of Dargan was a small tape recorder. The man leaned forward and hit the record button as he spoke. Other than the table, the chairs, and the tape recorder, the room was almost bare. A few extra chairs were stacked in one corner. And a small cabinet graced the wall across from the door.

"Great. I'm Agent Grant. This is Agent Carnie. I believe you've met."

"Yes, we've met. No polygraph machine?"

"No," Carnie replied, surprising Dargan.

"How do you know I'm telling the truth?"

"At this point, we don't think we have to worry about that. The jig is up, Dargan. And it's time for you to come clean." Carnie delivered her words with cool precision, cold enough to turn steam into ice. "We know it was you who sent the documents to Ms. Boyd. As I'm sure you know, we detained Ms. Boyd and … impressed upon her the need to make sure the public did not get wind of the documents at issue. As far as you're concerned, we need to know what you have and what you plan to do with it."

Dargan couldn't know what they knew. They could deduce that he didn't have the documents any more, since he hadn't gone public yet. But they had no way of *knowing* if he had them and simply had not yet decided to go public – which was the truth of the matter.

"We know you have the documents, Dargan," the man added. *Oops!* They must have been listening in on Dargan and Jill at the hotel. But then again, Dargan realized, there may be numerous ways in which the IN had learned of Dargan's plans; espionage techniques that he knew nothing about. It wasn't like any energy policy issue that he might have dealt with during the normal course of his work. On work issues – and most life issues for that matter – Dargan made a point of gathering all the information he could find in order to paint the biggest possible picture of his "subject." Once his mind was comfortably around the big picture ideas, he felt comfortable delving in great detail into smaller scenes comprising the big picture. When it came to intelligence issues with the DOE, or any other governmental agency, he simply didn't have the big picture yet. Especially now, with his head in a thick fog.

"We do have the documents. You may have obtained the documents at my hotel room by now. But we have an insurance policy. If anything happens to us, the documents will be released. If we're not heard from in a certain amount of time, the documents will be released. You know. Standard insurance policy."

Grant spoke, flashing a warm smile at Dargan: "We understand. And we're not here to harm you or to try and intimidate you. We're here to persuade you that you don't want to release those documents."

"Right." Dargan smiled back. "Ain't gonna happen. Don't even waste your breath." Dargan was serious. He knew what had to be done. He had only hesitated up till now in releasing the documents because he wanted to have an excuse to be with Jill and because he wasn't sure yet how to best release the news. He wanted to make the maximum impact. And he wasn't sure the major corporate news outlets would be particularly friendly to the widespread release of hard news and technical information about Zippy. They would surely know how threatening it was to their interests.

The discussion continued for some time. Grant and Carnie tried various tactics. "It's your duty, Dargan, as an American, to give the documents you stole back to us. You don't understand how dangerous the documents you have are." Dargan stonewalled and repeated his assertion that he would not be swayed. After an hour or so of back and forth, the agents seemed to have reached the end of their arguments. Dargan was exhausted and just wanted to sleep.

"All right. This is not productive anymore," Grant stood. "Let's get you back to your room."

* * *

A few hours later, after a short nap, Dargan found himself back in the "interview room." Same routine: empty room, left arm cuffed to the table leg, Agents Grant and Carnie interrogating him. Carnie began with the same line: "Dargan, you've got to realize how important it is that you turn over the documents. I hope you realize that we can't let you go until you do." Everyone in the room knew this was an empty threat. Dargan's insurance policy, Rahul, would release the documents if he didn't hear from Jill and Dargan within a week. Dargan didn't bother repeating his assertions from their previous tete-a-tete. He just sat in his chair and attempted to keep his face as blank as possible. Carnie, seeing the futility of her efforts, stopped talking. She reached into a pocket in her suit jacket and pulled out Dargan's baggie of meth. She set it on the table as Dargan's eyes lit up.

"Oh, so you like that, do you?," Carnie asked. Dargan tried to maintain his impassivity, but found himself glaring with suppressed anger.

"We thought you might. Never ceases to amaze me how smart people get hooked on crazy shit like crystal meth. You want some of this? Got a little headache perhaps?" Carnie smiled a wicked grin. Grant looked on with no reaction.

Dargan remained silent, but he wanted a bump. Badly. He couldn't give in, though. "What do you want?," he asked. Maybe they'd give him a little bit if he told them something. Anything. Just not the important things.

"You know what we want, Dargan. Your insurance policy. We have the documents you and Jill were in possession of before we picked you up. We need your insurance policy."

"What do you want to know?"

"Don't play games, Dargan. We need to know his or her name. Where we can find him or her. How soon the policy will kick in if the person doesn't hear from you."

"I can tell you how long you have." This would not matter. If the IN held Dargan and Jill for a week or more, the documents would be released. And that would be fine with Dargan. He hadn't yet decided how he was going to release the documents. But if the release happened through a process he had set in motion, but through which he had no direct involvement at this point, it made no difference to him.

"That would be a start. How about a line for telling us how long we have?"

"Deal." Dargan could already feel the rush of energy through his body. Pavlov's crack addict indeed. Carnie opened the baggie and poured a few crumbs onto the table.

"Can you give me a credit card?" Grant handed her a credit card from his wallet and watched, with a bemused expression, as Carnie cut the crumbs into powder and arranged them in a neat line in the middle of the table. Dargan moved up on his chair. He wanted it badly. But he didn't want to look that anxious. He didn't want to give them too much power over him. Just one line and he'd be fine. He wouldn't tell them anything else.

"Do you have a dollar bill, Agent Grant?" Grant handed Carnie a five dollar bill, which Carnie competently rolled into a tight cylinder. "All right, Dargan, lean over here and take a sniff."

Dargan stood and leaned over the table. "Are you going to hold the bill and plug my nostril?"

"Yes." As Dargan leaned, Carnie moved the rolled up bill toward his nose. Before he could snort the sweet powder, he felt a sharp push on the top of his head. He fell back into his chair.

"You think I'd let you have it that easily, Dargan? You think I'm stupid? Now tell us how long till your little insurance policy kicks in."

Dargan fumed. "Why you fucking b…"

"Don't go calling me names now. Remember whose house you're in. Be a big boy, now. Tell me how long."

Dargan considered leaping forward and licking the powder up. It wouldn't work as well if he ate it. But he'd get some of the same effect. But he'd reveal himself as a complete marionette to his own cravings if he did so. For the sake of his own pride and to avoid revealing how much he wanted a bump, he remained seated and meditated on suppressing the craving.

"C'mon, Dargan. I'll keep my word. Just tell me how long and I'll let you have your line."

It wouldn't matter either way, Dargan reminded himself. Either he and Jill worked out something with the IN in less than a week's time, in which case the insurance policy wouldn't matter. Or they would not reach any kind of agreement during the next week, causing the insurance policy to kick in. It wouldn't make any difference if he told them how long they had. "A week," he blurted out. He didn't bother mentioning that it would actually be only a maximum of five days until Rahul released the information because Jill had set up the insurance policy at least two days earlier. Dargan had no way of knowing how long he had been held by the IN, but suspected it had been no longer than a day or two.

"Really? A week. Very good. Ok, lean in."

Cautiously, Dargan leaned in again. This time, Carnie followed through. She clumsily held the bill in Dargan's right nostril and held another finger over his left. "Okay, ready?," Dargan asked before he inhaled.

"Ready. Do your thing," Carnie replied. Dargan sniffed, moving his nose rapidly down the line. Surprisingly, Carnie was able to follow the line with the bill she held. Dargan leaned back, sniffing sharply a few times to make sure the powder got all the way in. *God that feels good!* Finally, his head was clear again. He could think. And he resolved that he wouldn't tell them another damn thing. Getting one little bump made him realize he had the strength to kick his bad habit if he needed to.

"All right. Now you're yourself again. Let's talk turkey. Another line for cooperation. Who is your insurance policy?"

Dargan just sat and stared. He wouldn't tell them another damn thing. He didn't need to anymore.

"Who is your insurance policy?"

Stare.

"Dargan, you know you can have more if you cooperate."

"You screwed up, Carnie. You're not going to get another thing out of me."

"We'll see about that. Just wait till your craving comes back." But her expression belied her words. Dargan could tell she realized she had lost this hand.

Dargan was escorted back to his cell.

The IN agents didn't wave the meth in his face again.

Chapter 27

Jill saw Dargan shuffle through the door and felt a tremendous sense of relief. He was heavily bandaged and his right arm was in a sling. He looked like hell. But he was alive! "Dargan!," she cried out as he entered.

He looked up at her and gave her a big smile. "Jill! I've missed you." He sounded good, even though he looked bad. His skin was much paler than it had been. His cheeks were sunken and the lines in his face looked heavier than normal. Despite his smile in her direction, Jill could tell he was suffering.

"Me too. Are *you* all right?"

"I'm doing all right. Shoulder's okay. They said I got lucky. Bullet missed most everything important."

Carnie stood as Adrian prompted Dargan to sit in the chair next to Jill, on her right side. "All right, let's stop the lovefest, you guys will have time to catch up later." Carnie maintained her habitual slightly sour expression as she spoke. She cuffed Dargan's right hand around the leg of the table closest to Dargan.

Jill had been brought to the interview room a few minutes earlier. She had to suffer the indignity of soft cuffs yet again. She had been guarded by Agent Carnie until Adrian arrived, Dargan in tow. It had been strange seeing Adrian again. Almost as strange as seeing Dargan again earlier that week. She felt some embarrassment now when considering that she had found Adrian attractive.

They had tried many times to prompt her to reveal who their insurance policy was. They'd tried the nice guy approach. And the hardball approach – they'd threatened to keep her indefinitely if she didn't tell them. They had also tried to wear her down through repeated questioning by different people rotating through the interview room, asking the same questions over and over. She had resisted their efforts. Thankfully, they had not attempted more drastic techniques. It was America still, after all. There were laws.

Jill was still confused by a lot of things surrounding Dargan. But she knew that she loved him and that ZPE was incredibly important. She wasn't about to say or do anything without at least consulting Dargan first.

Adrian sat in one of the chairs across from Jill and Dargan. Carnie remained standing and said: "We've got to wait for two more people, so hold tight."

Dargan leaned in Jill's direction and whispered: "How are you? You look all right."

"I am all right. Just a little scared," Jill whispered back. Carnie and Adrian saw their exchange but didn't intervene again. Jill was scared, but not as scared as she would have been had she not previously been in this very situation. There was a major difference, however, this time around: Dargan hadn't been with her and she hadn't seen anyone shot prior to her first appearance with the IN! She knew now that the IN agents had the capacity to kill. Or the intent, at the very least. She was relieved by Carnie's statement that she and Dargan would have time to catch up later. So there would be no summary execution... Despite the stories she'd heard and despite the crazy political climate they were living through since the 9/11 attacks, it was still a highly advanced nation they lived in with strong civil rights protections. Or was it?

The door opened again and a man and a woman walked in. Adrian and Carnie stood as a show of respect.

"Ms. Boyd, Mr. Brennan, this is Deputy Director Chu and, as I'm sure you know, Senator Huberson," Adrian introduced the newcomers. *Huberson! I should have known she was involved somehow!* Dargan nodded his head at the newcomers, betraying no surprise that Huberson was involved.

Director Chu spoke first. He sat on the end of the table closest to Jill, exuding an avuncular glow. Not avuncular like Jonas. Avuncular like uncles were supposed to be: warm, respectable, kindly. "Like Agent Grant just said, I'm the DOE Deputy Director, for Intelligence. Senator Huberson has a long-standing interest in energy issues and our nation's energy security." He paused and then continued. "Now, we're not here to browbeat you. I apologize if our people have been … less than friendly. We're here to persuade you. I understand what's happened." As Chu spoke, he looked back and forth from Jill to Dargan, alternating eye contact with both. In addition to his avuncular glow, he exuded an aura of competence. A man who got things done. Not a man to be messed with. Someone you should trust because he knows what's best for you. Jill didn't like him.

"We understand you, uh, came across certain documents and that you now hope to make those documents public. I have no doubt your intentions are the best. But you must understand we can't allow that to happen." He paused, waiting for either Dargan or Jill to speak. Jill glanced at Dargan. He just looked back at Chu with a reptilian stare. He looked like he was suffering, despite his earlier assertion that he was fine.

"You've told us about your insurance policy. We hope you understand that we will find that person and … take care of him." Jill looked at

Dargan. She hadn't considered the possibility of the IN tracking down Rahul! It was obvious now that she thought of it. But how would they know about Rahul? They obviously hadn't been tailing her the whole time since Dargan had contacted her. If they had, they wouldn't have let her give Rahul the documents. Would they?

"You have no idea who that person is. You'll never find him," Dargan responded, surprising Jill.

"Really? We're halfway there already. You've just let us know it's a man." Chu smiled at Dargan condescendingly. Dargan looked away, obviously disgusted with himself. "You think you're good at this kind of thing? Do you?" Chu stared pointedly at Dargan, waiting for an answer.

"I got this far, didn't I?"

"Hah! You know how you got this far? You were helped. You really think you could have done what you did without help from someone else? You obviously have a few things to learn."

"What are you talking about?," Dargan asked.

"You didn't know? Interesting. You really did think we were that incompetent. No, Dargan, you had help. Your boss, Agent Carnie's alleged boss," Chu winked at Carnie, "had been plotting against us for some time. He helped you. He was the one who arranged for you to coordinate the electronic archiving process. He was the one who arranged for you to receive the IN documents. Why do you think IN documents were included in that project? That's right. Caleb Smith. And how do you think you were able to send out classified documents as part of a FOIA response? That's right, Smith approved your response. He's been dealt with, trust me. Thanks to Agent Carnie's good work, we found out his plans. And yours."

Jill was dumbfounded. And Dargan looked like he felt the same way. But he responded: "You're obviously not as good as you think you are, either. If you were, I wouldn't have gotten this far, would I? Despite your spying on your own agency," Dargan sneered in Carnie's direction, "you couldn't stop me in time."

"True, Dargan, true." Chu tilted his head to the side, conceding Dargan's reasonable point. Chu was reasonableness embodied, or so he hoped to project, Jill realized – along with a healthy dose of intimidation. "But here we are. And we are in a quandary. You both have resisted telling us who your insurance policy is despite our best efforts. We are constrained by certain rules – luckily for you. Unluckily for us. We have a job to do. And that job is incredibly important. I don't think you, Dargan, or you, Jill, appreciate that."

Huberson, silent during this exchange, spoke finally: "Let me jump in here, Director. I think I can give some perspective." Huberson had been standing against the wall to Jill's left. She stepped forward as she spoke. "You, Mr. Brennan, and you, Ms. Boyd, are both professionals. I'm sure you know much more than the average person about US energy policy. But I'm not sure you realize the enormity of what we're dealing with. You know that the US currently imports more than half of all our oil needs. This will grow sharply in the coming decades. And international forces hostile to the US will probably gain in strength before they become weaker. This indeed puts us on a very precarious footing, making the need for energy independence very real. But we have to gain energy independence in the right way. It has to be evolutionary, not revolutionary." Huberson paused to assess the impact her words were having on Jill and Dargan. Jill thought she was sounding fairly rational so far. She glanced at Dargan, glaring with his stone face at Huberson, as he had been glaring at Chu. The senator continued. "If we allowed ZPE to be released, do you have any idea of the events that would follow?"

Dargan couldn't restrain himself any longer, apparently, as he said: "How about energy independence, as just one event that would be unleashed? How about no more wars fought for short-sighted energy needs?" Dargan's disdain was apparent.

"Maybe so, Dargan. You know I respect you. I found you to be a highly intelligent, sincere and hard-working advocate on the Hill, Dargan, even if your policy recommendations were … impractical, to say the least." Jill glanced at Dargan in surprise. Dargan hadn't mentioned that he'd lobbied Huberson. Dargan returned her look with an almost imperceptible rise of his eyebrows.

Huberson continued. "But let's think this through. Maybe we *could* quickly achieve energy independence – if this technology could be commercialized on a sufficient scale. But if it were, think of what it would do to our economy. Do you know how many people Maxxon alone employs?" She paused for a second, but neither Dargan nor Jill chimed in. "They employ more than sixty thousand people in the US alone. Twenty-five thousand in my state. And more than a hundred thousand throughout the world. We know how devastating ZPE would be to Maxxon's core business model, believe me.

"But this isn't just about my reelection, or corporate profits, or corporate greed, as you would call it. This is about jobs. Livelihoods. Continued US leadership in the world. Think about all the other employees in the oil industry. And the electrical industry, for that matter. If ZPE were commercialized on a large scale, with personal free energy generators in everyone's cars and house, there would be no more utilities, no more power stations. Massive job losses! Massive drops in the stock market!" Huberson had become very animated. She had a great speaking voice and style and she used these attributes for all they were worth.

Much of what she was saying was probably accurate, Jill conceded to herself. But she could think of numerous rebuttals, as she was sure Dargan could. Jill did not speak, however. She was still too bewildered by recent events, and too unsure of her own views on the larger implications of ZPE at this time. She had found the best way of dealing with the IN's efforts to get her to reveal the identity of their insurance policy had been silence. So she continued this policy. Dargan also kept silent for now.

"And that's not all. Think of what a drastic cutback in oil demand would do to every oil-exporting nation. Forget Venezuela. Forget Russia. Think of the Middle East alone. Every economy in that region except Israel would collapse overnight. Unrest and revolution everywhere! Wars breaking out as different power centers fight with one another for the last remaining treasure as the river of oil dollars becomes a stream and then suddenly dries up. You think the Middle East is a tinderbox now? It would become a bonfire overnight and may well lead to widespread war throughout the world. You think Islamist terrorism is a problem now? It would become epidemic if these nations collapsed. Don't you see?"

Huberson stopped. She and the IN agents waited for a reaction from Jill or Dargan. Jill had to admit to herself that these were all valid points. Some of them were issues that had occurred to her when Dargan had first told Jill about Zippy.

Dargan finally spoke: "This is all bullshit. First, you lack any credibility at all. Maxxon is one of your biggest contributors! And the oil industry as a whole is your single biggest contributor. Everyone knows you're in the pocket of Maxxon and other oil companies. Second, there are ways to phase in ZPE technology to avoid the problems you're talking about. You're taking every worst case scenario and treating it as fact. You're highlighting only the negative possibilities and ignoring the tremendous benefits that would flow from Zippy."

Huberson opened her mouth to respond, but Jill surprised herself by cutting Huberson off before she was able to speak: "I don't know, Dargan. I think she's made some valid points." She hadn't planned on speaking, it simply came out. She had also surprised Dargan, she could tell by the expression on his face as he turned to look at her. Huberson, sensing a good turn of events, stood to leave. "We'll give you a chance to talk, alone," she said, as she ushered the IN agents to leave the room with her.

* * *

"Oh my god, Dargan, it's good to see you," Jill blurted out the moment the door closed.

"You too, Sweetie," Dargan smiled at her. "Keep in mind we're being taped, of course." He motioned with his eyes at the corner of the room where a small camera stared at them. Dargan quickly lapsed into the previous conversation. "But Jill, what do you mean 'valid points'? It's all bullshit! Can't you see that?"

"I don't think so, Dargan. I mean, I agree with you that Zippy would be an amazing benefit to us, to everyone. But I also see the risks that Huberson raised. She's probably right on some of her points. The fact is, we really don't know what would happen if this technology got out. If it's truly free energy, then it could be used to create all sorts of things, including weapons. And it would almost certainly bring down all oil companies practically overnight. That was one of the first benefits you told me about!

"That's definitely possible. But it'd be a good thing if they're gone!"

"I agree it would be a good thing in some ways. But how can it be a good thing if hundreds of thousands, millions, of people become unemployed? If the US economy contracts by half or something drastic like that? And I think Huberson's probably right about the effect in the Middle East, don't you? If oil is quickly replaced as an energy source, what would those nations do? They are practically one-industry nations. I just think we need to think long and hard about this before we do anything drastic."

"No, no, no! I can't believe you're buying Huberson's crap! All the problems she talked about are surmountable. I can't believe you're actually considering not releasing Zippy to the world. I need your support on this, Jill. In many ways. And we need to show a unified position on this. The fact that they're watching and listening to us right now, showing an un-unified position, is not good."

"Dargan, I want to support you in every way possible, you must know that. But I just couldn't live with myself if even a quarter of the problems Huberson predicted came true. Yes, there would be great benefits, but I don't think we have to baptize the world with fire. I think we can do it in a better way."

"Well how then? What else can we do?"

Jill thought for a few seconds.

"How about making Huberson support a strong renewable energy program. Maybe a

Marshall Plan for renewable energy? You know, massive investment in renewable energy instead of in traditional fossil fuel subsidies." Jill waited for a reaction from Dargan. He looked away as he pondered.

"Well, there are plans like that already being talked about. You know, things like the Apollo Alliance – using the Apollo space program as a model for a massive national effort to increase energy efficiency, renewable energy and get us off foreign oil."

"Right! And create huge numbers of jobs at the same time! I've heard of the Apollo Alliance." They were silent for a few moments. It looked like Dargan was actually considering what Jill had proposed. Dargan finally spoke again.

"I'm still not sure, Jill. And we have no way of knowing if Huberson would go for it. It would be such a departure from her previous policies, it might be hard to explain to her constituents." A knock came at the door. As Jill and Dargan craned their heads to see who was knocking, Adrian's head appeared from behind the door.

"Had enough time?"

Dargan responded: "I guess. For now."

"All right, I'll get the Senator and the rest of the crew."

Once the door closed again, Dargan said to Jill: "We've got a lot to think about. Why don't we suggest that we're willing to compromise, but need to think about it some more. Suggest a delay until tomorrow."

"All right." The look on his face brought Jill even further down emotionally. He looked like a father who had just lost his only child.

Huberson, Chu, Adrian and Carnie reentered the room. Dargan requested more time to think about what had been discussed and to think about various options. It was apparent that they had been listening to Jill and Adrian as they did not protest Dargan's request. Jill had a good feeling about her suggestion. It seemed like it might actually be workable. It would be a tragedy for Zippy to be kept from humankind. But sometimes it was best to leave things unexplored. Like Pandora's box.

Chapter 28

The low hum of electricity and air ducts was the only sound Dargan could hear as he lay on his cot. He didn't feel good at all. His body hurt no matter what position he lay in. During the excitement and anxiety of the interrogations/negotiations with Huberson and the IN agents, he had been temporarily distracted from his pain. Now it was back in full force. What's more, his head was also consumed with a dull pain. His resolve to give up his meth habit was still strong. But that didn't mean his craving had magically disappeared.

It was hard to think and if there was ever a time that he needed to do some good thinking, it was now. Jill's agreement was imperative. If she disagreed with his plans to release Zippy to the world, he would have no way of stopping her from disclosing their insurance policy. She had said she agreed with him about Zippy's importance – this much was true – but her apparent buy-in to at least some of Huberson's arguments had him tremendously worried. He was impressed and reassured that she had not given them the insurance policy information thus far. She was as strong as he had always suspected her of being. Thinking about this, he felt a pang of guilt at his own moment of weakness in giving the IN agents even the little information he had. But that was old news and it wasn't productive to dwell on it now. He had to get Jill alone again.

He lay on his back staring at the ceiling, waiting, waiting, for things to fall into place in his mind.

After some time, Dargan heard a click and saw the handle of his cell door turn. The door opened and Agent Grant appeared. "Dargan, I just wanted to check with you and see what we can do to help reach some kind of resolution here. I hope you realize we're not the bad guys. We're just doing our job. A very important job, especially in these crazy times. Sounds like Jill is starting to get on board with us. What do you say?" Grant's tone was meant to indicate one youngish cool guy talking to another youngish cool guy. He didn't know, obviously, that Dargan had never been particularly cool – and hadn't cared to be. Grant's tone only increased Dargan's resentment of his current situation. But he also realized that he needed to be as collected and rational as possible.

"I need to talk to Jill again, in private. That means no tapes, no video. Private."

"Hmmm. I'll see what I can do. I'll be back in a jiffy." Grant left the room. As Dargan waited, he realized that Grant had been awfully relaxed about security. He very likely carried a concealed gun. And there was no doubt that Dargan's sorry state made him seem less of a threat. Dargan hadn't seriously thought about any kind of heroic actions – largely because of his injuries and because the problems he really cared about didn't seem likely to be solved through any kind of violence on his part. He returned to pondering what to say to Jill if he was allowed to talk to her again, one on one. Things were not falling into place, as they normally would if his head was in its usual state. *Think, Dargan, think!*

The door opened again and Carnie entered. Dargan didn't offer a greeting. He was relieved to see Jill follow Carnie into the room.

"Mr. Brennan. You and Ms. Boyd will have an hour to discuss things."

"Great." As Carnie turned to leave again, Dargan added: "What about the camera?" Carnie offered a thin-lipped smile, moved the sole chair in the room next to the camera, stepped up on it and jiggled the camera out of its socket.

"One hour," Carnie repeated as she swiped her key card. The door closed behind her.

Jill walked to the side of Dargan's bed and hugged him as he lay there. He groaned as she squeezed his right shoulder; Jill immediately pulled back: "Oh! Sorry! Shit! Are they giving you any painkillers?"

"It's okay, hun, I'll survive." His eyes welled with tears from the pain. Jill, either in empathy to his pain or from her own anguish, started to cry. She took his left hand and sat on the bed with him, tears slowly trickled down her cheeks. They sat silently for a few minutes, enjoying being alone together again, even in the horrible circumstances they found themselves in. Dargan gently squeezed Jill's hand and gazed at her, hoping she would feel his tremendous joy at being with her again. No need to say it explicitly. A few wisps of her beautiful hair fell over her face. "Honey, can you let your hair down for a minute? You know I love to see your hair down."

Smiling wanly, Jill pulled the tie out of her hair and let her hair fall over her shoulders. Jill's hair was naturally wavy, but she usually straightened it or wore it in a pony tail. Dargan had always preferred her wavy look, but Jill had generally ignored his preference when they were dating in D.C. It seemed that the grass was always greener when it came to women and their hair. Dargan ran his hand through her hair. He couldn't help himself. She looked so beautiful and sad. "I love you more than I can say, Jill. You know that, don't you?" Jill mouthed a silent "yes" as her tears fell. Dargan felt good for the first time since he had woken in his cell/hospital room.

Jill eventually broke the silence. "Dargan. What are we going to do? We're seriously in a bind."

"I don't know, Jill. I really don't want to give up on Zippy. It's the answer to so many of humanity's problems. How can we agree to let that be kept hidden?"

"I know how potentially important Zippy is. But I really just want to get my life back. Our life back. I want to be with you. We just need to figure out how to put this behind us. Can't we compromise like we talked about?"

Dargan didn't answer immediately. After a long pause, he responded: "Jill, you've got to realize that much of what Huberson said really is bullshit."

Jill cut in: "You don't know that Dargan! We can't know that. Maybe there are ways to phase Zippy in that would avoid some of the drastic consequences Huberson talked about. But the major benefits you talked about would require that *she* be right for those benefits to actually happen! Like the end of the oil companies. If Zippy became widespread enough to cause their demise, then massive unemployment would necessarily result. You can't have it both ways!"

Dargan was silent again. She was probably right. But he couldn't admit that or he'd lose any chance of convincing her to stick with their original plan. Many different ways of responding to her words flashed through his mind, but he couldn't decide how to actually verbalize what he was thinking. He just couldn't think straight. It was incredibly frustrating for him because he was normally super fluent and articulate. Ideas rolled off his tongue at a mile a minute. Not now.

"Jill..."

She cut in again: "Seriously, Dargan. You're being too extreme. It's always been your problem. You're a purist and you dig your heels in when you can't convince people of your position. We don't live in a perfect world. We can't be purists all the time. We could achieve so much if we get Huberson to agree to the renewable energy Apollo project idea. Other legislators would be persuaded much more quickly by her than any Ted Kennedy type because she's been so far to the right on energy issues. You know, Nixon to China and all that. Isn't that enough for you, for us?"

Again, Dargan paused for a long time before responding. "Do you know why I sent you the FOIA documents?"

"Huh? You told me already. Because you couldn't figure out any other way to get them out and my FOIA request happened to come along at the right time."

"That's not entirely true. I had another way of getting the documents out. My Plan A. I could have made it work if I wanted to. But I sent the documents to you because I wanted to be with you again." This wasn't the whole truth. Dargan had flubbed his Plan A. And sending the documents to Jill was definitely the best Plan B he had. But he probably could have figured out some other way of doing it.

"What?… Well, if that's the case, then all the more reason to compromise! I *want to be with you again*. And I just don't see us returning to any kind of normal life if we go ahead and release Zippy. I really think the Apollo project compromise is the best solution."

They lapsed into silence. What Jill said made some sense, but it devalued the importance of Zippy drastically. As much as Dargan wanted to put this whole thing behind him and just be with Jill, he was incredibly reticent to simply let Zippy go. Could he let Zippy go? Jill looked at Dargan, waiting for a response. Eventually, Dargan spoke again. "All right. Let's do it. Let's propose a compromise. And we keep Zippy secret *if and only if* Huberson agrees to champion the Apollo Alliance project or something like it."

Jill broke into a large smile and leaned over to hug Dargan again. She stopped when he raised a warning hand. Instead, she kissed him and said: "Really? Awesome! We might actually be able to put all this behind us before too long!"

"Maybe." Dargan smiled wistfully. They continued to talk about the broad outlines of an actual legislative package that could be fashioned for Huberson: who might write it, how ambitious it could be, who they could count on in Congress to support such a plan.

The door opened again and Carnie reappeared. Jill spoke first: "All right, we're ready to see Senator Huberson and the others again. Carnie nodded her assent. Dargan swiveled his body to allow him to place his feet on the floor. As he stepped off the bed, he purposefully stumbled, prompting Jill and Carnie to rush to prop him up before he fell. As Carnie placed her hand on Dargan's side to steady him, he stepped behind her and looped his left arm around her neck. He squeezed hard. "Okay, you bitch, do you have the meth on you? *Do you*?" Carnie tried to respond, but only gagged, as Jill watched in shocked horror. Dargan loosened his grip ever so slightly. She croaked out a "yes."

"*Where*?"

"In ... my ... left pocket."

"Jill, reach in her left pocket and get the plastic bag in there, quick. Carnie, if you try anything, I'll snap your fucking neck."

Jill looked bewildered, not sure what to do. "Now, Jill!"

Chapter 29

Jill was momentarily paralyzed. *This is crazy.* After Dargan barked at her a second time, Jill jumped into action. She had to do something before Carnie was strangled to death. Jill reached into Carnie's left jacket pocket. She pulled out the small baggie, containing about a teaspoon of the rough powder. Dargan barked at her: "Now, open it and give me some of that."

"What? What do you mean?"

"Pour some of it into my mouth. I don't have time to cut it. C'mon. *Do it!*"

Carnie's face was getting blue. Hadn't they just agreed on an arrangement that would have created a satisfactory outcome for all parties? Feeling nauseous, Jill opened the baggy and attempted to pour a little of the meth into Dargan's mouth. She fumbled and the entire contents of the bag slid into Dargan's waiting maw. He swallowed it without bothering to chew. She could tell the difference in him immediately. His eyes widened and he stood up straighter. Jill had no idea what that amount of the drug would do to a person like Dargan. She hoped neither did he.

Dargan finished swallowing. "Oh, that's good." His body quivered. "Okay. Now we're going to get out of here, using Carnie as a hostage. They don't know yet what's happened here because they don't have their eyes. I'm assuming that the camera was also their ears, but we can't be sure. Either way, we have to act because they'll notice Carnie's absence very quickly, I'm sure.

"What the hell are you doing, Dargan? I thought we had it all worked out!," Jill asked, frustration evident in her voice.

"Jill, I'm sorry, but Zippy is just too important. There's no way we can just let it return to the memory hole, never to see the light. Zippy will transform humanity – for the better. Yes, there will be some short-term negatives. But these will be far outweighed by the positives. You'll see, Jill. But look, we don't have time to argue. I'm going to use Carnie as a shield to get us out of here. You've got to stick as close as possible. But look out for her arms and feet in case she tries anything. I'm going to keep her borderline passed out."

"Dargan, this is a bad idea!"

"*Shut up!* I'm not going to argue this one. Now come on."

Dargan, obviously much stronger now, moved toward the door. Jill, I need you to help me again. Take out her key card and open the door – slowly."

Jill didn't move. She shook her head slowly back and forth. She didn't know what she could do to stop Dargan from hurting himself, Carnie, or her. But she knew this was not the right thing to be doing.

"Come on, Jill, grab her key card!"

Jill still didn't move. Dargan exclaimed: "Fuck! I'll do it myself." He shook off his sling as Jill watched, mouth agape, and took Carnie's keycard from her belt, where it was attached by a retractable cord. As he used his right arm, his eyes narrowed with pain, and his breaths came more quickly. It had been less than two days since he was shot. Even the meth couldn't cure that problem, though it could give him the strength to ignore the pain temporarily.

Dargan swiped the keycard through the card detector and the lock clicked open. "C'mon Jill!" Jill followed, unsure of what else to do. Dargan awkwardly swiveled Carnie, who looked extremely uncomfortable but still conscious, around and opened the door with his right hand. He kicked it all the way open with his foot and swiveled Carnie around again so that she could be forced to walk through the door first. Jill followed closely behind.

"All right, no one here still. Good luck so far. Carnie, which way to get out?" Jill could see Dargan loosen his grip slightly. Carnie didn't speak. Instead she gestured to the right. "Good girl. Just remember to cooperate and no one gets hurt."

It was strange for Jill to see and hear Dargan acting so aggressively. She hadn't known it was in him. Then again, maybe she had. She had tried to forget about his chilling tale of his teenage act of self-defense – leading to a homicide. She had only ever seen the gentle Dargan and that was all she wanted to see.

"Dargan, there's a camera," Jill said after spying a small camera-like device twenty feet to the right of the door they had just left.

"Shit, that means they're on to us, if they're watching." They walked as fast as they could – which wasn't fast – down the hall. Dargan kneed Carnie in the butt to encourage her to go faster. The end of the hallway was about a hundred feet away. They arrived quickly. Before Dargan could ask Carnie again, she pointed to the left. "You better not be leading us astray, Carnie," Dargan whispered in her ear with clenched teeth. But as Jill turned the corner, it looked like Carnie was pointing them in the right direction so far.

There was an elevator fifty feet down the hallway to their left. Still no IN agents or anyone else. "Hit the button," Dargan commanded Carnie. She did so, pressing the down elevator button. The elevator dinged at them immediately. Apparently Carnie had taken the elevator earlier. Or someone else had. The trio entered the elevator and Dargan swung Carnie around again so that she faced the doors.

"Which floor?" There was no conveniently marked number with a star next to it, indicating the main floor. Carnie reached out a finger to touch the button. Dargan let her move close enough to reach the button. But instead of pressing one of the floor number buttons, she pressed the red emergency button. "You bitch!" Carnie gagged as Dargan throttled her again.

"Dargan! Don't! You'll kill her!"

"She'd deserve it!"

"No she wouldn't! Loosen up, *now!*" Dargan relented and loosened his grip again. Jill exhaled in relief. She couldn't handle someone's death on her conscience. She felt guilty when she killed a fly, let alone a human being. The braying of the alarms was loud around the elevator. If the IN agents hadn't figured out yet that Carnie had been abducted, they surely knew now.

"Jill, push the button for floor one. That's as good a guess as any. We just have to hope that they haven't figured out yet what's happened" Jill hit the button, not knowing what else to do at this point. The elevator moved slowly. They had been on the fifth floor in the unknown building. Jill moved closer to Dargan and Carnie as the elevator came to a stop. "Brace yourself, Jill. They'll probably be here. Just stay behind me." The doors opened.

As expected, the lobby was not empty. There were a number of people fanned out around the elevator, guns pointed at Dargan, Carnie and Jill. There were four men, dressed in dark suits, Adrian among them, facing them with guns drawn. Two of the mean leaned against the wall to the left of the elevator and two against a bannister that defined the mezzanine overlooking a large lobby. A stairway curved down to the lobby to the right of the elevator. Adrian called out: "Dargan, let Agent Carnie go, *now!*"

Dargan spoke to Jill *sotto voce*: "Jill, stay behind me. We're moving."

Then he directed his voice at Adrian: "Sorry. Ain't gonna happen just yet. Now you listen to me. We're getting out of here now. Carnie won't be hurt if you guys just relax. I don't want to hurt her. And I'm sure you don't want to hurt her either. But I will if you so much as move a muscle. I'll snap her neck in a heartbeat. So we're going to move very slowly at the same time as you all back up. We're going to go down the stairs to my right. Understood?" Without waiting for a response, Dargan kneed Carnie again and began shuffling forward. Jill followed close behind.

Seeing that they were temporarily outmaneuvered, Adrian waved to the other agents to fall back. The agents kept their weapons trained on Dargan, but they crept backwards as Dargan and company moved forward. The stairway down began about ten feet from the right side of the elevator, so Jill couldn't see the lobby immediately. A second before they had moved forward enough to turn onto the stairs, she heard a commotion below. Loud footsteps, metallic clacking, and whispered commands. It sounded to Jill like they had even more company.

Adrian yelled out: "You're screwed, Dargan. We just got our backup. There's no way you can get out of here. Give up now before it gets ugly. Believe me, we don't want to harm you. We just need to make some kind of deal on the documents and then you and Jill can return to your normal lives. Be smart, Dargan." Dargan stopped, forcing Jill to stop also.

Jill couldn't keep quiet any longer. "Dargan. Please! Please listen to him. Let's just cut the deal we talked about and get out of here. This isn't worth it! *Please!*"

Dargan didn't respond. He appeared deep in thought. He turned to look at her. Jill's hopes went up as she met Dargan's eyes. In the same instant, Carnie twisted sharply in Dargan's arm and elbowed him in his right shoulder. Dargan cried out and released his hold on Carnie's neck. Carnie pulled away and ran in the direction of her fellow agents. Dargan recovered in an instant and ran after her. Jill watched, aghast.

Dargan was five feet behind Carnie. He closed in on her quickly because of his long legs. He reached out to grab her pony tail, but Carnie dove forward, eluding his grasp.

As Carnie's body disappeared from Jill's view, she saw, in the space now no longer blocked from view by Carnie's body, Adrian, gun outstretched, pointing right at Dargan. Adrian's face mixed fear and duty in equal parts.

"*No!*," Jill cried out. Too late.

The gun bucked before she heard the noise. Dargan's body jerked upward. Then again. And again.

He staggered against the railing to the right. Jill moved forward to aid him, oblivious to the danger to her.

Dargan turned his head in her direction.

He looked confused. Sad. Apologetic.

His hand, covered in blood, slipped on the bannister as he attempted to support himself.

His torso fell against the bannister as his hand slipped.

He fell over the railing and disappeared from view.

Jill reached the place at the bannister he had been. She looked down. About twenty feet below, Dargan's broken body lay sprawled on the lobby floor. IN agents fanned around him, looking unsure of what to do. Beneath Dargan's body and beneath the feet of the IN agents, Jill recognized the splayed eagle of the Great Seal.

Frantic, Jill turned and scrambled down the stairs as fast as humanly possible. She pushed her way past the IN agents surrounding Dargan. They saw that she carried no weapons and let her through. Dargan was staring up at the ceiling, sucking in quick shallow breaths.

Again, Jill kneeled over his bleeding body. Again, she sought to find where his wounds were. This time, there were too many. His head was bleeding profusely from where it had struck the floor. "Dargan. Why didn't you listen to me? Why?"

"Jill," Dargan said in the tiniest whisper. Jill leaned close to listen. "Jill, I always … felt like … I was going to die young. I never told you that."

"No. No you didn't, Dargan."

"I also … didn't tell you … that I never … wanted to live a normal life."

"No. No you didn't."

"I'm hung, Jill.

"You're Prometheus, Dargan. You can't die." She also spoke in a whisper, wishing to believe her own words.

"I guess… Prometheus … wasn't immortal … after all."

She paused, waiting for him to speak again. He didn't. His eyes closed. "Dargan, my Dragon. You know I love you," Jill whispered in his ear. An almost imperceptible smile appeared on his lips. His labored breathing stopped.

Epilogue

Jill stared out the window at the still-green hills passing by at seventy miles an hour. She was in Rahul's BMW. He was driving them to Santa Barbara. It had been a week since Dargan died. She still couldn't believe he had come and gone so fast. It seemed a cruel joke that the universe, or God, or whatever, had played on her.

Jill hadn't been back at work yet. She'd been lying in bed most of the day each day. Her mother had visited. Rahul had visited. Joe had visited. Even Jonas had visited. Rahul had suggested a day trip to Santa Barbara. It was all she could do to drag herself out of bed and walk to his car. They hadn't exchanged more than twenty words the whole trip. Rahul had tried to coax her into conversation. She hadn't given in. It seemed pointless to talk. The last important words she had spoken were still with her.

Shortly after Dargan breathed his last breath, Jill was back in the white interview room at the unnamed DOD building. Jill found her clarity finally. "I want you to become a born-again environmentalist, Senator. You are going to announce to the world that you have finally seen the light and that it is now imperative that the US engage in a massive public works program to get us off foreign oil. Become completely energy independent. And soon. Do you understand?"

Huberson had just stared at Jill. Jill continued: "I can't *prove* you're a part of this energy technology suppression program. And I can't prove your political decisions have been dictated by any connections to Maxxon or other energy industry types. And I can't even prove that we go to war for oil. But I do know this. If Zippy is released, Maxxon is done and so are most of your other big financial contributors. Game over for them. Game over for you. So you had better make this your cause, Senator. You're a dyed in the wool greenie, as of today."

The palm-studded hills of Santa Barbara appeared on the right side of the freeway. A sign passed: "SANTA BARBARA NEXT 12 EXITS."

Afterword

The Apollo Alliance is a real project. It is a large coalition of labor, business, and non-profit organizations, that hopes to convince Americans that the need for energy independence is worthy of a new Apollo-type mission to wean us from fossil fuels. You can learn more about it at www.bluegreenalliance.org.